Farm Fresh and Fatal

by

Judy Hogan

Mainly Murder Press, LLC
PO Box 290586
Wethersfield, CT 06129-0586
www.mainlymurderpress.com

Mainly Murder Press

Copy Editor: Paula Knudson
Executive Editor: Judith K. Ivie
Cover Designer: Karen A. Phillips

Copyright © 2013 by Judy Hogan
Paperback ISBN 978-0-9895804-0-3
Ebook ISBN 978-0-9895804-1-0

Published in the United States of America

Mainly Murder Press
PO Box 290586
Wethersfield, CT 06129-0586
www.MainlyMurderPress.com

Dedication

For Donna

~

Acknowledgments

I thank Sharon Ewing for the title and for hosting me at four Malice Domestic conventions. I have learned so much from Sisters in Crime, their subgroup the Guppies, and especially from the subgroup Guppy Press Quest. The Malice conventions have also helped, especially Luci Zahray, the "Poison Lady," who was my back-up for the poisons mentioned in this book.

I thank the Chatham County farmers who were always supportive at the Pittsboro Farmers Market when I sold bread and vegetables there. So many people have helped me be a better farmer and a better mystery writer. I'm very grateful to you all.

One

Monday Morning, April 1. A fight broke out during the second market, but the opening day of the first farmers' market in Riverdell went relatively smoothly. The third market was when the murder occurred.

Penny and Kenneth were searching madly for snails in the lettuce when Nora Fisher, their new market's manager, drove her yellow pickup in and parked near their garage apartment. "You go talk to her," Kenneth said. "I'll keep checking the romaine. The red lettuce was the hardest. All those curlicues." He was moving slowly on hands and knees down the rows they'd cultivated with the rototiller only the night before.

When Penny caught up with her, Nora was out of her truck and standing at the chain link fence that kept their neighbor Leroy's chickens in the orchard. "These White Rocks yours, too, doll?" Nora wore faded blue bib overalls over a man's white shirt rolled up at the sleeves. Her closely cropped curly brown hair gleamed in the sun.

"Hi, Nora. Welcome to Greenscape. The chickens are Leroy's, but he's part of our operation. He has to work today. Mostly he has them like this, out in the orchard, to pick bugs and fertilize the peaches and apples."

"How exactly does it all work? Andy lives next door?"

"Yes, he got us started when he became Shagbark's first sustainable ag agent about three years ago." She pointed to where she and Kenneth had been working. "Our vegetable garden takes up most of his and Jan's backyard."

"Who's the guy working in the lettuce?"

"My husband Kenneth."

"Who else works?" Her questions were pointed, sharp, and her voice harsh, no nonsense. This was more like an interrogation than Penny had expected, but then she hadn't known quite what to expect when they joined the market. At their first meeting the farmers in the new Riverdell Farmers' Market had decided to hold up the highest possible standards, which was fine. If only the snails wouldn't count against them.

"We all work. The whole neighborhood works. Andy, his wife Jan, their eight-year-old twins, Leroy, when he's home evenings and weekends, and Kate and Belle in the big house." Penny pointed behind them. "That is, when they can. They have big job commitments. Leroy and I will do the market."

"Let's have a look at your lettuce. Organically grown, you said on your application, but not yet certified?"

"That's right. We don't think we'll focus on being organically certified but more on sustainability–organically grown, selling locally."

"No trouble with pests?"

There was something so fierce about Nora. She didn't beat around the bush. Should Penny confess their new snail and slug problem? When they'd discovered slimy critters the night before, they'd been frantic to get rid of them before the inspection the next morning. They had decided not to bother Andy yet. Leroy had said to put down salt, and they had, but the snails appeared to be alive and well this morning. They were hand-picking them off and cutting back the ruined leaves to give to the chickens, who were delighted with this unexpected feast.

Penny sighed. She was too much of a truth-teller to deny their new problem. She didn't know a week of rain could bring out so many slugs and snails. She'd been so happy that these spring crops were getting such a good watering. Might as well be out front with Nora, who was definitely an out-front person. "Actually, we've had pretty good luck managing our pests until last night, when we started finding snails. Kenneth is picking them off right now."

Nora laughed. "Nasty little buggers. Have you tried diatomaceous earth? Another trick is saucers of beer. They love beer, makes 'em drunk as lords, and then they die. Hey, this is beautiful lettuce."

"Kenneth, this is Nora. She says to put out saucers of beer." Kenneth rose, all nearly six feet of him, brushing back his dark hair with streaks of grey with the back of his hand. "Sorry not to shake your hand, Nora, but mine are grubby."

"Pleased to meetcha, Kenneth. Try beer on these buggers. Are you a farmer here, too, in this neighbor commune?"

Kenneth looked startled. "I help Penny and Leroy, Andy and his family. We all take our turns. We've been eating out of this garden and orchard and getting eggs from Leroy's chickens for years, and when we're here, of course we help out."

"Where else would you be? Ah, but you're a Brit, right?"

"Welsh, and Penny and I spend part of the year in Wales. Normally we'd be there for the winter, go about September, back in March …"

"This year we'll do the market." Penny cut him off and caught his eye. "We'll go to Wales when the market finishes." Why was he bringing up their old pattern of September-March in Wales now during this inspection?

"Thanksgiving is when we close the market," said Nora, "right before. Let's see. You have romaine, red leaf and buttercrunch. Is that right?" She didn't pause for an answer. "Carrots, onions and radishes look good. Those peas along the fence, too."

Penny hadn't been sure exactly what they were being inspected for, and Nora's abrupt manner didn't encourage questions, but she hadn't so far seemed disapproving. They had to grow their own vegetables according to the rules of the market they'd adopted at that meeting they'd attended, and bring only high quality produce. She knew that much, but was there more to it? Nora was like a drill sergeant. Other people didn't normally make her nervous, but Nora seemed unnecessarily stern.

"You guys seem to know what you're doing. Good weed control." She watched as Kenneth walked over to feed the chickens the snails and damaged lettuce.

"We keep learning. It's a sharp learning curve," said Penny, wishing Nora would ease up some.

"You're lucky to have Andy close by to help. This sustainable ag stuff is hard, even harder in a greenhouse like mine is. The house does keep birds out of the fruit, but I can get a disease like that." She snapped her fingers. "Then everything's decimated overnight. A week like last week with all that rain? I hold my breath we don't get downy mildew, and then we need sun like mad to ripen things early. Greenhouse farming is tough, but I'm a sucker for anything hard to do."

This made Penny smile. "Actually, I am, too. Three years ago I wouldn't have imagined I'd be a farmer or, for that matter, do it on top of teaching English at St. Francis, which I began about a year ago."

"Oh, you mean that black college in Raleigh?"

"Yes. Sammie Hargrave, who's doing cut flowers, is my colleague there. We've been egging each other on so we'd have things ready for the first market. A challenge," Penny laughed.

"Sammie a friend of yours?" Nora turned away to walk back to her truck. They passed Kenneth, who waved. She would see Nora off, and he'd be back picking snails, bless him.

"I shouldn't say anything." Nora's normally loud voice dropped. "But Sammie's cut flowers turned out to be controversial for the board. I was afraid they weren't going to accept her into the market."

Penny stopped and stared at Nora. "Why not? She grows beautiful flowers and has for most of her life."

Nora continued in a low voice. "Don't get me wrong, doll. I think she's a great addition to our new market. People like to buy flowers for special dinners and stuff. The big markets in Carrboro and Raleigh welcome cut flower vendors. Sanford doesn't allow them, but so what? It's nothing to do with her being black. It's that she's not really a farmer. She's a backyard gardener." Nora did at least look abashed at what she was saying.

"So are we," Penny said. Nora started walking again, but Penny stayed where she was. It had to be racist. Either that or incredibly stupid. "Wait, Nora. Don't walk off. This is very important to me. What's the difference between Greenscape's backyard farming, or call it gardening, and Sammie's backyard full of flowers?"

Nora shook her head. "I shouldn't have said anything, doll. She's approved, okay, but two board members voted against her. I won't name names, but they're both creeps. Forget it. She'll be great. She looks like a tough cookie. That's what it takes sometimes."

"That's not the point, Nora. This sounds like subtle or not so subtle racism to me."

"No. It's just your kitchen variety politics. I hate it, but it'll blow over. Don't worry about it. Forget I said anything. God, don't tell her about this." Nora pulled open the driver's door of her yellow pickup. "I gotta go. See you Wednesday."

"But Nora, I can't forget this. She's my good friend. It's plain wrong."

Nora, however, had decided to leave. She smiled and started her engine. Apparently she was in a hurry, or she was embarrassed. Or what?

"Later, doll. Don't worry." Nora waved and drove off.

Penny thought, she said she'd see us Wednesday. Did that mean they were approved? The snails hadn't ruined it? But Sammie, her dear, dear friend. What would she do about that?

"You're determined to stay until Thanksgiving then?" Kenneth asked. He was preparing open-faced egg sandwiches topped with their green onions and mozzarella cheese, which he'd slip into the toaster oven long enough to melt the cheese.

Penny looked up from patting the lettuce dry. They had rescued some that was mostly okay, no snail holes that couldn't be torn out and discarded.

"Not determined, but I thought we would do the market the whole season, Leroy and I. Why? It will give us a little extra money."

"Thanksgiving until mid-January gives us only about six weeks in Wales."

"Is that okay with you?" She thought they had already discussed this, but maybe he hadn't realized how far into the fall the market would still be open.

He didn't answer but opened the door of the toaster oven and slipped in their sandwiches on a piece of aluminum foil.

"Kenneth?"

"Mmm?"

"Is six weeks enough for you?"

"I'm just worried you'll overwork, love. You've got the teaching for another six weeks and the market, too. Why is all this falling on you? Couldn't some of the others take a shot at the market? It shouldn't be only you and Leroy, should it?"

"I thought we'd already talked this over, and you were okay with everything." Penny set down on the table the bowl of salad with their onions and radishes on top of the lettuce and a garlic and malt vinegar dressing poured over it. She looked at him, but he was watching the sandwiches to be sure the cheese melted but didn't burn.

"Kenneth?"

"Mmm?"

"Salad's ready."

"The sandwiches are coming up, too." He carried over the toaster tray and slid one onto each of their plates.

Penny's stomach muscles tightened, but she sat down and took a deep breath. He would talk to her when he was ready.

He sat down and took her hand. "Good to sit down, isn't it, love? Look what a feast we have before us. A lot of work, but such good wholesome food." He smiled at her, and she squeezed his hand. "Yes, and we have earned this lunch. Kenneth, are you okay? You act like something's bothering you."

"I'm fine. I'm just worried about you, love. Remember the long, leisurely days we have on Gower? How will you get your writing done with so many other things pressing on you? The market takes a lot of time. Couldn't Andy take a turn at it? It's his yard. He takes time off for other things."

Penny wondered why all this was hitting now. Had the snails set it off and the extra work they'd put in, or was it Nora's visit? She was rather fierce. Or maybe he had thought they'd leave in September as they used to. Slowly she said, "Andy told us that since he's an agent, it's better if he doesn't sell, too. He's there to advise and help us, and he puts in time here, but he wants the farmers to run the market."

Kenneth nodded. He helped himself to salad.

"Did we get all the snails off?"

He grinned at her. "Yes. I gave each leaf careful attention and patted them all dry. No snails in the salad." Then he looked serious again. "What about Belle or Kate? Couldn't they take an afternoon off and maybe trade off weeks?"

"They've asked to put in money, for seeds and to buy vegetables, because their jobs have such long hours. Belle's P.R. work is never done, she says, and when she gets home she's no good for anything but supper and bed. Often she's not even here until after dark. Kate works long hours, too, and their work laps over to weekends. But Kenneth, Leroy and I are happy doing it. You have your part-time work at the Sheriff's Department and Feed and Seed. I'll be extra busy, true, for six more weeks, and then I'll be a lot freer. I did promise the others I'd do the whole season."

Kenneth set his sandwich down and nodded. "I know. You love doing this, don't you?"

"Yes. But if you're not happy?"

"I'm fine."

Did she believe him? He was smiling. She wanted him to be okay. She did not want to do this if he was unhappy, but what about Sammie? Should she say anything to her? She hated this. What would she want Sammie to do if their roles were reversed? She'd want to know so as not to fall into some trap. No one wants to know someone is being vicious behind her back, but better to know than not to know. She'd call her. Nora hadn't wanted her to, but Nora hadn't impressed her as the wisest person on earth.

Two

Wednesday Afternoon, April 3. First Market. Penny held
their improvised cash box in her lap, a cylindrical mint chocolate
chip ice cream container, her left hand steadying the large
cardboard box of eggs as Leroy Hassel, beads of rainwater
emphasizing his skinhead look, drove his work van around the
last curve and drew up at the gate to the high chain link fence
beside the squat brick building of the Agriculture Extension
Service in Riverdell. Through her window, cracked enough to let
in air but keep rain out, she could hear the drum roll of the rain
as it beat on the new red tin roof of their shelter. Was it beating
out a welcome or a warning? Now where had that thought come
from? The posts that separated the individual stalls were
varnished a bright red and should have been cheery. They would
have reflected the sun, had there been any.

"Locked," said Leroy, "and it's two-thirty. We worked so
hard to be on time. I hope we don't have to sit here long. Where
is everybody?"

Penny glanced in her side mirror. "Here comes Andy."
Shagbark's Sustainable Ag agent's new green Toyota pickup had
rolled to a stop just behind them. It was the first time Penny had
seen the new shelter since Andy finished getting it built in time
for their first market. She'd heard his blow-by-blow accounts of
how he had fought for the funds to build it.

She could hear Andy Style's voice now: "It's ridiculous not
to have a market with a good shelter when the county is full of
farmers."

Now, in his blue slicker, Andy hopped down from his
pickup, unlocked and pushed back half of the double gate,

anchoring it with cement blocks, and waved them through. Leroy rolled down his window. "Where do we park?"

"Pick a stall. You're first. Then back up to it. I hate that it's raining–watch out for the mud—but a lot of farmers plan to be here, rain or shine, and I've made sure this first one is well-advertised, so hopefully we'll have customers. Welcome, guys." He grinned, pushed his wet red hair out of his eyes and ran back to his pickup.

Leroy pulled forward and stopped. "Where do you think, Penny?"

"Maybe the middle and opposite that second gate?" Leroy eased the van halfway down the hundred-foot shelter and backed it into position.

Penny pulled up the hood of her very old red plastic rain jacket, mended with duct tape. Hugging the ice cream money box, she stepped down, avoiding the worst puddles. There was no way to avoid the squishy red mud as she walked under the shelter. Leroy was already pulling out from the back of the van their table and two folding chairs. Andy had followed them down and helped set up the table.

As she unpacked them Penny reveled in the beautiful red leaf, romaine, and butter crunch lettuces, their roots in water, their leaves curly and crisp. They had rescued most of them from the snails, and they did look good. She'd never believed she could grow beautiful lettuce. The red, white and purple globes of the just pulled radishes, their leaves looking good enough to eat, made her feel like she was a farmer, after all. She had planted the lettuce and radishes, pulled snails off the lettuce twice a day since they found the problem, weeded them faithfully, and made sure they had enough water. As she reached for the crate of lively green onions, their dark green stalks stiff and their white bulbs aglow with vitality, another farmer in a large red truck pulled in. Ragged burlap that looked like it had done service for at least twenty years hung over its bed.

"That will be George Gardiner," Andy said. "He does plants. I'll go greet him. If you need anything, holler. I'll check in with you later."

"We're fine," Penny said. "When you have a chance, come back and tell us what you think of our display."

"Impressive so far." Andy smiled.

"You taught us all we know." Penny laughed and turned back to arranging their three kinds of lettuce. She was especially proud of the romaine, which she'd never grown before. She made sure they had enough ice in the trays around their roots to stay fresh. She must be a farmer if she was selling lettuce at a farmers' market. When had it begun? Andy and Jan had been in school at State while their babies were little. The twins were eight now. They were five when Andy pulled them all together, the children, too, and persuaded them to help plant and care for the big garden in his backyard.

A heavyset man with a greying beard, mustache and buzz cut, wearing a clear plastic rain poncho over his overalls and a straw hat covered in grey plastic, walked up. "Howdy. I'm George Gardiner, Plants and Flowers. Specialties, Shade and Wild. I've got some lovely hostas and some columbine in orange and purple today."

"Hi, George. I'm Penny Weaver, and this is Leroy Hassel." Leroy turned from hanging their Greenscape sign on the wire running between the posts, nodded and went back to the van for the chalkboard with prices. With newcomers Leroy usually said very little.

"Gorgeous lettuce," commented George, his hands in his pockets, watching as Leroy hung the chalk board from the wire. "Organic lettuce for $2.50. Not bad. Some folks charge $3.00, and it's not even organic. Maybe we can trade later. Customers don't show well when it rains. It's so frustrating when you have a lot of leftovers. I hate rainy markets."

"Then you've been in markets before?" asked Penny.

"Sorry? I'm deaf in my left ear." He turned his right ear toward Penny. When she'd repeated her question, he said, "Yeah, Sanford market. Saturday morning. It's good that Riverdell has one now. Uh oh, here comes Giles. Natch, he'll grab the other front spot. Sibyl won't like that one little bit. I'd better warn him."

"It's first come, first served, right?" Penny watched as a huge new black pickup backed into the other spot at the front.

"Eh?"

Penny shouted: "First come, first served, right?"

"That won't make no nevermind to Sibyl." George took off with long strides as if anxious to get back to his truck.

Penny couldn't worry about Sibyl, whoever she was. Too much to do.

"I hope the wind doesn't change directions and blow the rain in from this side," said Penny. "Not a very promising start for our new market. Will you be warm enough, Leroy?"

"It's April, Penny. A little rain won't hurt me." Leroy wore his usual cut-off jeans, tee shirt and flip-flops. Once they were set up, he'd hung his rain jacket on a hook to dry. How could he stand it? Penny had worn jeans and three layers, including a down vest and her plastic raincoat, and left both on. She was barely warm enough.

She and Leroy had just sat down behind their table, when a large blue, moderately worn pickup, pulled in beside them. A muscular man emerged. He wasn't wearing rain gear. About Penny's height, a blond crew cut, freckles and a lip scar. Had he once had a harelip? "This spot taken?" he asked.

"It is now," said Leroy.

"We open at four?"

"Four to six. I'm Penny Weaver, and this is Leroy Hassel. We do Greenscape, and you're … ?"

"Herman Hicks. Shagbark Organic Vegetables. You new?"

"First market," said Penny. "Our neighborhood has been growing vegetables about three years, and Leroy, you've had chickens about nine years, right?"

"Since Sampson Pine made formaldehyde famous around here. You been at the Sanford market? You look familiar. I think I bought eggplant from you last year."

Herman nodded. "I'll have that later. My first time here. So we just take whatever spot we want?"

"First come, first served." Didn't these farmers know the rules?

"Suits me." Herman pulled down his truck's tailgate and began hauling out his table. Leroy jumped up to help.

Herman looked to be in his thirties, his blond crew cut beaded with rain. His face had a blank look. He was strong, had his table lifted out and set up before Leroy could do anything, so Leroy lifted out some of his crates, and they started talking. Penny heard Leroy ask him "What's a Paleo-Conservative?"

When they opened the broccoli crate, Penny had to get up and look. It looked so rain fresh, the tiny florets were at the perfect moment, just before the yellow flowers opened. She loved broccoli, especially fresh picked. "Great broccoli, Herman. How much?"

"Two dollars for two big stalks. I picked this morning."

"Will you save me some? My husband Kenneth and I love broccoli."

"You can buy it now. Farmers can buy before the market opens, at least in Sanford."

Penny turned to go back to the van for her purse, but Leroy said, "I'll get it, some for me and Seb, too." He pulled out a ten-dollar bill. "Three bunches. One for you, Penny, one for Andy and them, and one for Seb and me." Penny took the plastic bag from Herman and put it in the back of the van.

Herman was saying, "A Paleo-Conservative is just a conservative in the best sense, not one of these Neo-Cons you hear about these days like George W. I don't trust government much. You wouldn't either if you knew what's really coming down."

Penny avoided conversations in which people had a political axe to grind unless, of course, she agreed with them. She looked at her watch. Nearly three-thirty. Only four farmers here? Then she saw a big, old-fashioned, brown station wagon lumber down the drive to the shelter and bounce through the gates, both open wide now. Behind it was a small green van. Herman walked out into the main part of the shelter where the clay, with the fine gravel spread over it, was relatively dry. "That will be our baker Sybil and then the cheese lady Rosalind. Their Gum Springs Goat Farm is next to mine on Gum Springs Road."

Aha, thought Penny, the Sibyl has arrived. Would George's prediction come true? Would she fuss over not getting a front spot?

She watched as a short, thin woma, with short curly grey hair, walking stiffly with a slight limp, stepped down from the driver's seat, having stopped near where the man in the big black pickup was unloading vegetables. She saw him turn to Sibyl but couldn't hear what he was saying. He was tall, too, over six feet but stoop-shouldered and lean. He shook his head. Sibyl said more loudly, "I always have this spot in Sanford."

"This ain't Sanford." He shrugged and went back to arranging his vegetables.

Sibyl climbed back in her big station wagon and pulled into the shelter, turning right so that she was next to George. A young, slender woman with long blonde hair climbed down from the passenger seat and pulled open the back of the station wagon. Andy went over to greet them. The younger woman smiled up at him as he welcomed them, but Sibyl ignored him and kept hauling out her boxes and unloading breads and some small packages wrapped in waxed paper, cookies maybe?

Penny thought: I could do baked goods. But at the moment she had her hands full teaching at St. Francis College three mornings a week for another month, and then finals. It was challenging enough to do the market Wednesday afternoon. Fortunately, Kenneth, Andy and his wife Jan, even their twins helped, and Leroy took Wednesdays off from his carpentry work to pick and clean the vegetables in the morning, then do the market with Penny in the afternoon. She had high hopes that this market venture would bring in extra income during the time she and Kenneth spent in the U.S., and she could eventually quit her teaching job and focus more on her poetry.

Herman and Leroy walked over and stood in front of their table. "Sibyl looks mad to me," Herman said, "but Giles is stubborn. His vegetables are genetically modified, did you know? That's like poison. Plus, it's wrong. Nothing in the Bible about changing the genetic codes of Creation."

Penny didn't know exactly how they modified the genetic code these days. She'd read that they were trying to arrive at crops that would feed more of the world's hungry people, but Andy had told her it was scary. Very little research had been done as to the effects of this food on human beings.

"What are genetically modified vegetables like?" asked Penny, hoping to get him off his political soapbox. It didn't work.

"Go have a look. Just don't eat them. Actually, I'd advise staying as far away from them as you can. Who knows? They may be contagious." He laughed, but if he thought his joke was funny to others, it was clear he himself wasn't amused. "I saw his greenhouse tomatoes at Sanford. He says they're better three weeks after they're picked. What does that tell you?"

"That they'll ship well?" said Penny.

"They bounce when you drop them," said Herman. He smirked at her. "My tomatoes don't bounce."

Leroy laughed. "Ours don't either. You could use ours to throw at politicians. Splat."

Herman grinned. "Giles's would probably kill the politician. They're as hard as baseballs."

They all turned to look when Sibyl shouted, "First come, first served is wrong. I sell hot bread. How am I supposed to have hot bread and get here early enough to get a good place?"

Andy leaned toward Sibyl. "All the places are good." The young woman with Sibyl left their table and strolled toward Penny.

"That's Abbie coming toward us," said Herman, "Sibyl's daughter. Sibyl's a good woman, and we all buy her cookies, cake, and things. Wait till you see her jelly display. She has about fifty different kinds of jelly and jam."

As she walked up to their table, Abbie smiled, revealing dimples in both cheeks, and the amusement in her blue eyes suggested she'd left her mother so she wouldn't laugh at her. "Hi, I'm Abbie. Your lettuce is beautiful. Maybe trade later? We've got brownies, slices of apple and pecan pie, hot bread, but the bread'll probably be gone by five."

"I'm Penny, and this is Leroy. He has fresh brown eggs, too. Two-fifty a dozen." Penny noticed that both Leroy and Herman were staring at Abbie with a male appreciation that could be awe but was probably lust. The young woman was too attractive for her own good. She still had her red rain slicker on but had pushed back the hood. Her long blonde hair fell straight down her back, and her eyes were lively with intelligence. She was very aware of the effect she was having on the men. No doubt she smiled to be sure the dimples showed. She looked so young and fresh, as if life was such good fun and had yet to disappoint her. As far as Penny could tell, she was totally unfazed by her mother, who was still yelling at Andy.

"Your mom's pretty mad, huh?" Herman nodded in the direction of Sibyl's discourse on the market's injustice, and Abbie flashed her dimples. "Mama likes the spot George has. She'll get over it. I'd best get back, help her stack the jellies. Good to meet you, Penny and Leroy." She walked away, her slim hips swinging with a barely concealed sensuality. Herman and Leroy stared, mesmerized, after her.

Several more vehicles were pulling in. Oh, here came Sammie. Her black pickup was behind an old yellow Toyota pickup. That would be Nora, who quickly swung out wide and backed up on the right side of Penny. Sammie drove through and pulled in directly across from them. Penny had ridden with Sammie or her husband many times in that truck, often to solve crimes that Derek Hargrave, as Shagbark Sheriff's Department Detective, was investigating. Sammie was a serious asset to the market, all the more reason to be upset that she'd proved controversial. She hadn't yet reached Sammie to tell her what was happening behind the scenes. Maybe she'd have a chance today. She was the only person of color so far that Penny had seen among the vendors, and she was bringing such amazing cut flower bouquets. Plus, she was company in this new venture for Penny. She didn't want Sammie to get discouraged and pull out. They could help each other when they had problems and generally compare notes. She would go over in a minute, but she wanted to see who else was arriving.

The healthy-looking woman with an elaborate blonde braid piled on top of her head, in the small green van, had already pulled in across from Herman and was setting out her goat cheese. "Gum Springs Goat Farm," her banner read. It was quarter to four, and suddenly the farmers were piling in. Next to Penny, Nora, her curls kinky in the damp weather, was wearing a yellow rain jacket that matched her truck. She had slammed the driver's door, ignored Penny and hurried down to where Sibyl was still yelling at Andy. What was her last name? Oh, yes, Fisher. Would she be as fierce with Sibyl as she had been when she'd done their inspection? At the moment she was angry, judging by the loud, harsh sound of her voice, which was much more penetrating than Sibyl's.

"What the hell you doing, Sibyl? First come, first served. Market's about to open. Get ready for your customers, and stop yelling at Andy. This is our first day, remember? I'm not going to let you screw it up."

Sibyl turned away, silent and stiff, and with gnarled hands began stacking her jellies of many colors–red, orange, green, yellow, purple, even blue. Raspberry, peach, mint, apple, grape, blueberry? No sun to shine through them, but they did look beautiful. Why she needed to bring fifty jars and stack them in a vulnerable pyramid, Penny didn't know. It looked tedious and time consuming. It was an attention-getter, she supposed. Anything to get people to stop at your table.

At five minutes to four, it began happening fast. Having subdued Sibyl, Nora had set about plugging in a large coffee urn on one of her tables and setting out a box of assorted tea bags, a jar of instant coffee, creamer and sugar. Then her own vegetables, various unusual greens such as arugula, which Penny had seen in the seed catalog, several kinds of herb transplants, greenhouse tomatoes and cukes. She was obviously busy, so Penny waited to say hello. Sammie waved to her once she'd hopped out of Derek's pickup. Penny went over to help her set up. "They're beautiful, Sammie!"

"Thanks. I hope to hell people come and buy them. This rain stinks, even if April showers do bring May flowers." As usual Sammie looked like a flower herself. Her dusky skin set off her red rain hat and jacket and bright yellow sweater with a red tulip embroidered on it. Yellow loop earrings dangled from her ears, and she wore shiny new yellow boots.

"You look just like your tulips," said Penny. "That should help sell them."

"That's the idea as long as we get people. Oh, Nora's opening the customer gate. Must be time. Are you nervous?"

"A little. You?"

"Very much. Selling flowers should be a piece of cake after knocking student heads together to persuade them to write decent essays, and I'm not talking impressive or astute, but flowers? I've been sweating this for days. I only learned Monday that I was approved. Fortunately, the flowers aren't nervous." She grinned.

Penny called, "See you soon," and scurried back across the broad aisle people would walk down to peruse the displays and shop. She had just reached their table when she heard a bell ringing behind her and turned to see Nora brandishing a cow bell. "Market's open, everybody. Welcome to the very first day of the very first Riverdell Farmers' Market." Her voice was strong and happy. She said hello to everyone before returning to her table, where she told them to help themselves to tea or coffee.

A line of customers had been waiting for the gate to open and now streamed in. There were about fifteen people, elderly, couples, women on their own, even a whole family including mother, dad, a baby in a stroller and a toddler. Penny smiled at them all and watched as they moved out to browse the tables. Their lettuce and Leroy's eggs stopped quite a few, and they were both busy for about ten minutes filling orders and collecting money. More people came in, both by the small gate and through the big gates where their vehicles had entered. By 4:30 p.m. Penny estimated forty people had been through, and they were still arriving a few at a time. She could see that Sammie was selling some of her tulips, and the goat cheese was popular. Herman sold out his broccoli and had only a few cabbages left. Sybil always had a crowd at her table, and Penny saw people walking around eating her cookies. Nora was the only one other than Giles with greenhouse tomatoes, and she had a steady stream of customers, too.

On the other side of Herman a young, good-looking farmer had pulled in minutes before Nora rang the bell. It wasn't until 4:45 p.m. that things slowed enough that she and Leroy could take turns browsing the other vendors' wares. Leroy urged her to go have a look, find out if the Gum Springs cheese lady would trade cheese for eggs and see what Sibyl had. Maybe he could get a treat for Seb by trading eggs. But first she wanted to talk to Sammie.

"You selling pretty well?" she asked. Sammie still had a half-dozen beautiful bouquets of yellow and red tulips, some of the red ones with white stripes, beautifully arranged in slender glass vases.

"Not bad for Day One. I could have done better with more lead time. I waited to get a cooler until I knew I'd be in the market."

"Any idea why it took them so long to approve you?"

"Because I'm black?"

"Sammie, I hate to say this, but I think that may be it. From what Nora said some of them wanted to argue that you were only a backyard operation, not a farm. That's crazy, because we're as backyard as you are. There must be more to it, but Nora, who made me promise not to tell you, seemed to think the ones making trouble were creeps."

Even though Sammie was tough and had more common sense than most people Penny knew, she could tell that what she'd said had hit her between the eyes. She was staring at her flowers as if to draw strength from her tulips, which could only be called jubilant. It was a new century, but subtle forms of racism didn't go away, and oh, how she didn't want Sammie to suffer, even if she was strong and resilient.

Sammie looked up at her after a minute, smiled grimly and said, "Fact of life, Penny. Ugh. But there are always some creeps. I never get used to it, but I am not going to let it get me down. So there. Thank God they didn't block me. Then I would have had to sic Derek on them."

"You're pretty dangerous yourself," Penny said, wanting to remind her of her many strengths and revive her sense of humor.

"Oh, you mean the karate?"

"I bet they didn't know about that."

"Probably not. Uh oh, here's a potential customer. Hold on, Penny. Yes, may I interest you in some fresh tulips?"

Penny waved to Sammie and wandered past Herman and his cabbages. Next to him was the young farmer's display of a leafy green with red, yellow, orange and pink stalks. And another curly, very dark green one. Both were the most beautiful greens she'd ever seen, perfect in their vitality as was the young man, slim but strong looking, wavy blond hair combed back, smiling happily at her as though he was thoroughly enjoying himself. He looked as alive as his greens. When she looked up, he was smiling. "I picked them two hours ago," he said.

"Hi, I'm Penny Weaver. We're Greenscape on the other side of Herman."

At Herman's name he smiled and nodded. "I'm Mark Judd, ma'am. Happy to meet you. You ever try chard?" He pointed to the rainbow array of stalks he had rubber-banded together.

"Chard? So that's what it is. No, I never have."

"Aren't you selling eggs? If you have any left, I'd be happy to trade chard if I don't sell it all. This one is curly kale. All organically grown, though I'm not certified yet. Working on it."

"I'd love to trade. Your onions are impressive, too. They look like they might jump up on the table and run away."

Mark laughed, obviously pleased.

"Everything's beautiful, Mark. We have onions, but these are amazing, and your carrots. I'll see you later. I'm going to look around and then relieve Leroy so he can browse."

At that moment Abbie came up. If Mark had looked happy before, now his happiness shone out of him. It was as if he couldn't stand still, as if he wanted to grab Abbie and hug her. He couldn't stop smiling.

"Hi, Mark. I love your chard. Want to trade later for cookies or apple pie?" Penny glanced back at them as she turned to walk over to the Gum Springs Goat Cheese table. They were both laughing that laugh that means two people thoroughly enjoy each other, can't get enough of each other, with that sensual, helpless quality running under the laughter they can't seem to control. Those two were powerfully attracted, if she was any judge.

She'd heard of Gum Springs Goat Farm for years and eaten their cheese often, but she'd never met Rosalind Mann. Their cheese won prizes, and she'd read articles about Rosalind and her husband Rex in their local paper.

As she got to Rosalind's table, the rain suddenly began to thrum hard on the tin roof, and it was blowing from the west, the side Rosalind was on. Rosalind reached under the table and pulled out two large blue umbrellas and used them to protect her cheese display as she slipped back into her rain jacket and hood. Then she smiled with real interest in her eyes at Penny. "Nasty rain. Can I help you choose a cheese? Our special today is raspberry flavored."

"Hi, I'm Penny Weaver, and you're Rosalind, I'm guessing. I've loved your cheese for years, and I'm very happy to meet the cheese-maker finally. Leroy and I are doing Greenscape over there. He wondered if you might be up for trading later, maybe eggs for cheese?"

"Of course." Rosalind smiled. "I've heard of you, too, Penny Weaver. You helped get safe storage at the Shagbark nuclear plant and got that Sampson Pine factory to get rid of its high levels of formaldehyde pollution. Then there was Rick Clegg's election. I know who you are. We're fans of Rick's. Welcome to the Riverdell Farmers' Market. I'm so happy we finally have one here. Not even the rain can dismay me today."

"Thanks, it's a new venture for our neighborhood, though Andy, who lives next door, has gotten us off to a good start. Rick and Cathy are good friends. They're away right now for some months while he does research in France. Their boys are like my own kids. I miss them all."

"I bet you do. Why don't you sample some of these cheeses and see which ones you like?" Rosalind was obviously younger than Penny, maybe by ten years. Mid-fifties? She had the vitality that went with hard, outdoor work, but she looked worn and tired, too. Unflappable but not indefatigable.

By the time Penny moved on, she saw it was after five. Very few customers had stayed when the rain began to pound down. Fortunately, it was coming down straight now, but thunder rattled in the distance, and they still had an hour to go. She wanted to check out Sibyl's table and then get back and relieve Leroy.

Sibyl's hot bread was gone. She was removing the sign when Penny walked up, but there were plenty of goodies left. Woven baskets held small packages of brownies, chocolate chip cookies, oatmeal and raisin cookies, sections of apple, pecan and cherry pie. "Very tempting," Penny said, and Sibyl smiled.

"I love pecan pie, so I'll take two of those. I'm Penny, by the way, doing Greenscape with Leroy." She pointed. "Next to Nora. He wanted to know if you'd be up for a trade, eggs maybe? We have lettuces, onions and radishes, too. He has his little boy Seb coming for supper tomorrow and would love to treat him." She handed Sibyl a $5 bill and took the pie sections.

Sibyl sounded calm, nonchalant, but she kept glancing down to where Mark and Abbie were still talking. "Oh, sure, we can trade. Anyway, at the end of the market, I usually give away my leftover baked goods to the other farmers. They don't freeze that well." She shifted the baskets a little and removed the one that held the pecan pie. Penny wondered how she managed with such arthritic hands. "If you want to get rid of your lettuce or eggs, even better. I'm happy to get them. I use a lot of eggs, and I don't try to do lettuce any more, though I have a lot of fruit bushes and trees for the jam and herbs for my own cooking. I don't bring much to market any more but baked goods, jams and jellies. I make more money that way."

The way Sibyl beamed at her, you'd never know she could go on a warpath as she had only an hour earlier. Queen of the Baked Goods, thought Penny. No harm in that. She hadn't seen any competitors for Sibyl, so she was the only baker. "Thanks, Sibyl, I'll tell Leroy." As she turned away Sibyl said, "Oh, you're down there near Mark, aren't you? My daughter Abbie is schmoozing with him. Could you ask her to come back? I'll be packing up soon."

Penny nodded and walked over to say hi to George, but he was engaged with a customer over a purple columbine plant. She caught his eye, waved and went over to look at Giles's dreaded genetically modified tomatoes. Even though it was chilly, and Penny was glad for all her layers, Giles was red-faced and sweating, and his skin looked blotchy. His overalls and plaid flannel shirt apparently made him hot, as he mopped his forehead and stuck his none-too-clean handkerchief back in his hip pocket before saying politely, "Interested in some tomatoes, ma'am? I have collards and cabbages, too."

Penny picked up a tomato. It was red but it did feel hard. "Not vine ripened?"

"Greenhouse, but take it home, put it in a paper bag for three weeks, and it will be perfect for eating. These are amazing tomatoes. They outproduce and outlast all the other varieties."

"What are they called? I'm Penny Weaver, by the way. Leroy and I do eggs and vegetables."

"They don't have a name, just a number, and I've got it at home. He pulled a card off a small stack on his table. "Here's my card. Call me, and I'll look it up. Need some collards today?"

"Do the collards have a number, too?"

"Yes."

"I'll pass. Thanks, though. See you around."

At that point a tall, lanky, middle-aged man, bald with a red face and red mustache, strode up to Giles's table. "Giles, my man. How's business?"

"Not so great, Kent. Rain. Some folks early but not many now."

"Yeah, rain keeps 'em away. Your birds okay?"

"Oh, yeah. Another week, and they'll be ready for processing."

Penny moved away, though curious who the new man was. Kent? A farmer who'd started late and had no crops yet? Not the usual customer, she thought, the way he was talking shop with Giles.

After she had delivered her message to Abbie, who looked so happy chatting with Mark, she told Leroy the good news about the trades. It was about ten minutes later when she noticed the bald man deep in conversation with Abbie in the middle of the aisle while Sibyl doggedly packed up her jellies, one after the other. Abbie was so entranced by whatever Kent was saying that her mother wasn't getting much help.

Three

Wednesday evening, April 3. It was after seven when Penny and Leroy arrived back at #7 Whitfield Mill Road and unloaded. The rain had slowed to a drizzle. Leroy departed for his basement apartment next door to prepare for Seb, his three-year-old son and Penny's grandson. Her daughter Sarah was bringing him for Penny to keep during the day Thursday, and then Leroy would have him overnight. She knew Leroy looked forward to his time with Seb. Sarah had never wanted to be married to Leroy, which Penny understood. He was a genuine loner and maybe couldn't take on that kind of partnership, but with their farming efforts, it was easy for her and Leroy to work together.

She waved him off, knowing he was happy, and a genuinely happy Leroy was rarer still. She wished he could know the ongoing contentment and ease of the deep emotional partnership she experienced with Kenneth that had been a long time coming. They'd been in their mid-fifties when they met, and then the attraction had been electric and all-consuming. The current was steady now but always there.

Once she'd changed into dry clothes Penny joined Kenneth in the kitchen of their garage apartment to finish getting the supper together. She cleaned and stripped the tough outer skin from the broccoli stalks while he started the omelet to which he would add some of the creamy chevre cheese from Rosalind. While the broccoli steamed, Penny made toast and a pot of Earl Grey tea. She set out the slices of pecan pie. High tea. Perfect.

"You're pleased with your first day?" Kenneth asked as he lifted the edges of the omelet to let the liquid center run out so it would cook faster.

"I'm exhausted now, but given the rain and the cold and its being our first time, yes. We sold most of the lettuce, some onions and radishes, and Leroy sold about six dozen of his eggs. Then we traded for some cheese, and Leroy got some pie. Oh, did you see the beautiful chard I brought home? Also a trade for eggs. I've never eaten it, but it's almost too beautiful to cook."

The toast popped up, and Penny reached for the butter dish.

Kenneth put a lid on the omelet and turned down the heat. "You liked some of the other farmers?"

"Yes. A few were pretty strange, but mostly they were welcoming and friendly."

"You sound cautious, love. Who wasn't friendly?" A worry note had come into his voice. His brown eyes looked anxious. How to reassure him?

Penny set the toast on the table and watched Kenneth flip the omelet on its side and lift it out. She never got tired of watching him, of having him present, not across the ocean as they had lived before, and for a few years after, their marriage. He was the home she was always eager to return to. Now he leaned his strong body back against the kitchen counter, still holding the spatula in his right hand.

"Not so much unfriendly as strange, love. They were all nice enough to Leroy and me, but I am worried about Sammie. Nora says there were two farmers on the board who didn't want her to be in the market. They made some excuse about her being a backyard gardener, not a real farmer, but Sammie and I are sure it's racism."

Kenneth didn't say anything. When they were settled and the broccoli was steaming in its bowl between them and melting the pat of butter Penny had put on it, she said, "It's so good to sit down. Whew."

"But Sammie came and sold her flowers okay? Was she worried about it? Have you any idea which farmers were against her? Who's actually on the board?" Kenneth persisted.

"I don't know, Kenneth. I think Rosalind is and Nora. I'll have to ask. At the meeting we had it wasn't clear to me. None of them were obviously hostile to us or to Sammie. Still, it's there, a hidden problem and a nasty one."

"Give me the rundown on the various farmers then."

Penny told him about Giles of the genetically modified seeds, Herman who was a Paleo-Conservative and didn't believe in government or hybrid vegetables, and especially distrusted genetically modified seeds. Sibyl Kidd, the amazing and popular baker, and her fuss over not getting the spot she wanted.

By the time she'd recounted all her observations, and Kenneth had said Herman sounded like he could be a racist with his Paleo-Conservative views, someone knocked. Kenneth opened the door to Nora in her yellow rain jacket, her brown hair damp and a mass of unruly curls. "Come in, come in," he said. "I remember you came to check out our farm, but I forget your name now."

"It's Nora," said Penny. "Please join us. We were just going to eat some of Sibyl's pecan pie. We have plenty to share. Cup of tea?"

Nora shrugged out of her dripping rain jacket and held it up. Kenneth took it. "I'll just hang this in the bath. Please sit, Nora. Penny will pour you a cuppa. Tell us how you think the first market went."

When Penny had divided the pie and poured everyone tea, Nora said, "I was going to ask you. How did it seem to you? I got there late. Blasted truck, I had to get my battery jumped, so I didn't have time to check in with you all. How were your sales?"

"Not bad. We had hoped for a little more. We brought home about thirty-five dollars. The lettuce and eggs sold best. We traded, too, so it was okay. The rain didn't help, of course."

"Yeah, the rain that we all so need, but it's the pits during the market. My sales were down, too, compared to my usual at Sanford."

"You're kidding? I saw people lined up for your tomatoes. You must sell a lot on a good day."

"Right much. Were you there when Sibyl first got her panties in a twist?"

Penny laughed. "Oh, yes, Leroy and I were the first ones there, and George warned us that Sibyl was going to be upset when Giles took her favorite spot."

"The bitch. This is a new market. We're not Sanford. We voted on first come, first served at our last meeting, which she didn't bother to come to, and then she throws a hissy on our first day. I could have docked her."

Penny glanced at Kenneth to see how he was reacting. If she was reading him right, he was singularly unimpressed with Nora. "Sybil said something about having to come later so her bread would still be hot."

"That's bullshit. She just likes to be Queen of the Mountain and have everybody else kowtow to her every whim."

"Andy was patient with her, but she'd been yelling at him probably ten minutes before you got there."

"Andy's a godsend, but you have to be tough with her. If I hadn't been late, I could have shut her up earlier."

"She does make a good pie," Penny said. Kenneth nodded. They'd all eaten every crumb of the pie. Did Nora realize she was going overboard? Perhaps. She seemed to become aware that all her listeners weren't sympathetic and calmed down. Sibyl's sales had certainly looked good to Penny. Her baked goods were obviously popular and sold well. She'd been envious. "Sibyl was selling well, it looked like."

"Oh, she sells well, wherever she has her table. She's just a controlling bitch, and I've had it up to here with her. I have to work with her on the board, see. She's the secretary." Nora hit her hand flat against her neck.

Penny saw an opening. "Who else is on the board, Nora?"

"I am, and then Rosalind is President. Sibyl's secretary. George is treasurer, and Herman and Giles are the other two.

Herman's weird but a nice guy. George isn't bad, but Giles and
Sibyl both can be total pains-in-the-neck."

Penny wondered if Giles and Sibyl were the two whom Nora
had called creeps and who didn't want Sammie in the market.
She would observe them, see how they acted around Sammie.
Giles and his genetically modified vegetables didn't seem very
popular with any of the farmers, but Sibyl was one they
appreciated, and she seemed to get away with her tantrums
despite Nora's scathing remarks to her.

Kenneth got up suddenly, gathered up their plates and went
to turn on the kettle. He was clearly uncomfortable with the drift
of the conversation. Penny changed the subject. People had their
weaknesses and strengths, for sure. In any organization, as she
well knew, there were difficult people, but she had found that
they didn't inhibit getting good things accomplished if you went
about it the right way. They were usually cowards at heart and
switched sides rapidly once they saw no benefit to opposing
what the rest wanted and could be carried out, with or without
them. True, clearly Sibyl had the weakness of wanting one
particular spot, but the woman knew how to make a rich,
custardy pecan pie with a light-as-a-feather crust.

"What about the man Kent, who came by around five?
Who's he? Another farmer? He didn't act like your usual
customer."

"Oh, he's the ag agent for poultry. Talk about shitty people.
He's one, too, and I don't see why he has to hang around our
market. Andy could get someone else to take pictures."

"He's going to take pictures? That's a good idea."

"Oh, it's a dandy idea, but he'll just use it as an excuse to
chase all the women."

Kenneth had poured water on fresh tea leaves and set the pot
with the cozy over it back on the table. "Can't the women
manage him, tell him to shove off if they don't like him?"

He sounds more and more like an American, thought Penny,
but it has been eleven years since we became lovers and he first

came to the U.S. He had adapted very well, really. She loved Wales and his home in Gower, but somehow they'd ended up in North Carolina more and more, even though they used to do half the year in each country.

"Sure, they can tell him to get lost," said Nora sarcastically. "That wasn't hard for me, even if he was an ag agent. But the young ones? They're more vulnerable, probably intimidated, because he's a big county agent, which suits Kent fine. I saw he'd snagged Abbie today."

"Abbie?" asked Kenneth.

"Sibyl's daughter," Penny explained. "The pecan pie lady. Abbie was there helping her mother."

"What are you worried that this man Kent might do," asked Kenneth, "take her virginity? How old is she?" Penny knew Kenneth hated it when a man's behavior was stereotyped and dismissed.

"Abbie's about twenty-five, but she still lives at home. She's naive. Plus, he's a bastard."

"So you want to protect her," pressed Kenneth.

Nora stared at Kenneth. She obviously didn't like being challenged. Another Queen of the Mountain?

"Abbie does seem innocent," said Penny, "but maybe a word to the wise is all she needs?"

"Complex there. See, her mother likes Kent, and Abbie's father died when Abbie was little. He committed suicide. I've watched Abbie at the Sanford market. She's drawn to older men."

"She seemed to be enjoying talking to Mark Judd before Kent got there, and Mark is her age, I'd guess." Penny glanced at Kenneth, who was nodding. "Anyway, Nora, isn't it her problem? She didn't look in any danger when I saw them chatting."

"Oh, he can be very flattering. He took me in for a while, and I'm the suspicious type. Abbie's a sweet girl, especially when she's away from her bitchy mother. I'd just hate for her to get hurt. He's one of these men who are so very seductive even though they hate women, and as soon as they win the game and get them in bed, they treat them like shit. His wife left him, and now he preys on younger women. He's not choosy. Any woman who will listen to him is in danger, as far as I'm concerned." Nora stood. "I'd best mosey on. I want to ask Andy a few things. I'm glad you all are vendors. Your sales should pick up gradually. It takes a while sometimes."

Kenneth retrieved her raincoat, which Nora shrugged into. "Maybe the sun will shine next week," Penny said. She was thinking that the sooner the behind-the-scenes racism was shown to be ridiculous, the better. They stood at the door and watched Nora skip her way down the steps. The rain had finally stopped, and the wind had cleared away the clouds to reveal the moon sliver sailing in the night sky.

At breakfast the next morning, before Kenneth left for the hardware store Feed and Seed where he worked when he wasn't needed by the Sheriff's Department, over their second cup of coffee, Penny said, "You didn't like Nora much, did you?"

"Not much, no. I don't like her squashing people like that, calling them 'bitch' and 'bastard.' She's too quick to condemn. She doesn't look at the whole picture. Then she's quite fierce. She scares me."

"You?" Penny set down her coffee cup so she wouldn't spill it. "A confident, reasonable man who can charm the socks off a snake? Nora scares *you*?" Penny laughed.

"Women can be scary, you know," he said so seriously that she wasn't sure he was joking. This didn't sound like Kenneth.

"So can men," she said cautiously.

"Ah, but you women read our feelings, and we have nowhere to hide."

"Why is that scary?" She looked at him over her cup.

Then he smiled. "Being loved is scary. You never figured that out? I thought you were so wise."

"I think I'm discovering a whole new side of you, Kenneth, and it's been, what, eleven years almost since you stirred me up so much I couldn't think?"

He reached for her and kissed her gently, then with a more deliberate passion. If the sound of a small fist banging on their door hadn't interrupted, the kiss might have led to other things, even though they both knew he was due at work in half an hour and Sarah was bringing Seb over for the day, his daycare center being closed for spring break.

"Seb," Kenneth said and gave her one last gentle kiss. The pounding continued until Kenneth opened the door and ushered in their three-year-old grandson, who carried a small blue dump truck under his arm.

"Gampa, me bring truck. Gamma, kiss Seb." Penny stooped down and hugged him, then picked him up and smiled at Sarah, dressed to the nines in a frilly blouse and dark skirt, her blonde hair swept up on her head. She was loaded down with his small duffle bag of clothes, a favorite bear and several more trucks.

"Thanks, Mom. Here's his clothes and a few more toys. I want you to meet someone." As she said this, a tall, thin man slouched slowly into the room as if he wished he were shorter and somewhere else entirely. He was only a little taller than Kenneth, but he was apparently very self-conscious about his height.

"This is Henry Sutton, Mom. We're dating now. Henry, this is my mom and her husband, Kenneth Morgan."

"Pleased to meet you, Henry," Kenneth said immediately and strode over to shake hands. Was he relieved to know Sarah had another boyfriend after the disaster Brian, the last one, had been? But was this one any better? Penny wished the new young man would stand up straight. She wondered if he could. Perhaps the slouch was permanent by this time? He wasn't a spring chicken, maybe thirty-five? More? Of course, unbelievably, Sarah was nearly thirty.

"Henry's a musician, Mom. He plays the guitar in coffee shops and bars and stuff. He has a gig tonight. That's why Leroy's keeping Seb. He'll get him about five and give him supper."

"Daddy," said Seb and wiggled to get down. He walked over to Sarah and tugged at her skirt. "Daddy?"

"Not now, Sebbie. Grandma will take care of you now, and Daddy will give you supper when he gets home from work. You can play with your truck now."

"Okay." Seb nodded his blond head with its hair that stood straight up, then walked into the living area and began running his truck along the edge of the coffee table.

"Do you have time to sit down?" Penny asked. "Coffee? Oh, and I have some lettuce, onions and radishes for you, left from yesterday's market."

"Thanks, Mom."

"You all farmers?" asked Henry, looking interested for the first time as Penny pulled a bag of vegetables out of the refrigerator.

"We have a big garden, an orchard and a pasture full of chickens. Seb's dad does the chickens."

"When's the market?"

"Wednesday afternoon from four to six in downtown Riverdell next to the ag building."

"That's cool. Sarah, let's go next week."

She turned to him, smiling. "Oh, sorry, I have to work till five, but I could get there about five-thirty, if you want to walk over and meet there."

"You have time for coffee now?" Penny lifted the coffee pot.

"No, Mom, we can't stay." Penny set the pot down. "I have to get to work. Henry's dropping me off, and then he has to go by the restaurant to make sure everything's set up for tonight."

Penny had been watching Henry. He stayed slouched, even when he was talking. He was very pale, like he never got out in the sun. His dark blonde hair was cut short, and he had dark bushy eyebrows, which didn't belong on his ascetic face. Sarah was lending him her car? Was he also living with her? Penny wasn't sure why, but there was something about him that felt insincere, too casual, even indifferent to other people despite his seeming enthusiasm for the market. Seb completely ignored him, as if he didn't exist, and Henry ignored Seb. She hoped Sarah, in her eagerness to construct a nuclear family, hadn't made another major mistake.

"You'll have to come back when we can have a natter," Kenneth said.

Henry looked at Sarah, clearly puzzled.

"A natter means a chat. Kenneth is Welsh," Penny explained.

"Okay, yeah, man. That'd be real cool. Later then," and he followed Sarah out the door.

"Bye, Mom."

"Good to meet you, Henry." She said the words, but she didn't mean them. He was so fake.

"I'd better get a move on, too, love. I've only got ten minutes to get to work."

She put her arms around him. "Later, man," she whispered. He laughed, squeezed her tight, and went out the door.

At about seven that evening as they were doing the washing up, as Kenneth called it, he brought up the subject of Henry.

"You didn't like him, love, did you?"

Penny set a pile of plates in the dishes cupboard. "Who?"

"Sarah's new bloke."

"Henry," she said. "Right. He's okay, but I don't trust him."

"A musician? He can't be all bad, can he? Besides, we hardly know him. Sarah likes him. He was interested in your market."

"Apparently, yes."

"You don't have to live with him."

"Hopefully not."

"Give her a chance, Penny."

"Do you think she could tell I was less than enthralled?"

"Maybe, but I read you so easily. I can see what you're thinking before most people do."

"I know." Then she grinned. "Now that's scary."

"What, love?"

"The way you read me when I don't think I've revealed anything."

"It's called 'getting to know you, getting to know all about you,'" he sang.

She flipped her towel at him.

"But seriously, don't you want her to find a good bloke she can settle down with and be happy, her and Seb?"

"Of course, but there's absolutely no way Henry would ever make her happy."

She probably shouldn't have said that. How would she know what would work for Sarah? But she thought she could size up people who wouldn't work, couldn't possibly. The first one, the husband Ed, hadn't, though it had taken Sarah several years to declare an end to his tyranny. Then there had been Brian, who hadn't wanted Seb to see Leroy, his father. Now Henry.

"You're certain, love? You feel certain that you know what Sarah needs?" Kenneth let the dishwater out and began carefully wiping off the stove and kitchen counters. When Penny had rinsed and stacked the last dishes, he wiped down the double sink.

"Not certain about what will work for her and Seb, of course, but I have a gut reaction to someone like Henry, who feels so totally fake. It makes me suspicious. Is he hanging around Sarah so he can use her car, sleep in her bed, eat what she cooks?"

"People who love each other do those things, Penny."

"You think I'm overreacting?"

He squeezed out the sponge and left it near the detergent bottle by the sink. "A bit. Give her a chance, Penny. Finding the right person does take some trial and error. You and I took a while. Sarah's what? Twenty-nine?"

"She'll be thirty in the summer."

"And we were?"

"Mid-fifties. Okay, I get it, but he seems so utterly fake, so totally useless."

"That's quite harsh, love. Couldn't you reserve judgment for a few weeks?"

"Yes. But normally you see through fake people, too. Why are you defending Henry so hard?"

She followed him into the living room and sat down by the lamp table where she'd left the essays she needed to read for the next morning.

Kenneth took the arm chair opposite, by the window. It was getting dark. "Soon it will still be light after we have our tea."

"I know. So what else is on your mind, Kenneth? I read you pretty well, too."

At first he didn't say anything. He stared out the window, which had a view into their orchard. "Peach blossoms are lovely," he said. "Will we get everything through frost?"

"Hopefully," said Penny. Something must really be bugging him. She waited. He stared out the window a few minutes longer. Penny was about to pick up the essay on top of her pile when he said, "It's Sarah more than anything. I want her to be happy, her and Seb. I worry about her when we're in Wales, and I know you must, too. She may be nearly thirty, but she's still not settled the way I know you want her to be, and the way I want her to be."

"Right."

"Penny, we've been here now a whole year plus a few months, and we'll have to be here until you finish teaching, and now until the farmer's market finishes in November. We won't have been to Wales for almost two years."

"Now you're admitting that this does, in fact, bother you? I wondered."

"I miss Gower. I like it here, but I get homesick–*hiraith*? Remember I taught you that word a long time ago. I've been feeling this great yearning for home lately."

Even though she should have guessed he was unhappy, his words hit Penny like a punch in the solar plexus. Good, loving Kenneth was unhappy and wanted time in Wales again. Two years ago they would have been in Wales October through March, but she'd taught at the college both spring and fall, when they were short a teacher, and then they had stayed over Christmas break and been housesitters for her chairman, Oscar Farrell. After that, Andy had asked them to take over the lead role in their big neighborhood garden, and seeds had been ordered and planted, and now there was the farmers' market. Kenneth had seemed fine with it all, but he hadn't been. She'd been too busy to pick up on his *hiraith*. She hadn't been tuned in to him as she should have been.

Her feelings swirled, mainly guilt, then sadness. It would be hard now to pick up and leave for the six months they used to give Wales. She was hired to teach January through May and was so connected now to Seb, to her students at the college, to Oscar and Sammie, her colleagues there, and now the new farming and marketing commitment. A web of connections. She hated it when there was no easy answer, only pain any way she looked at it for her or for Kenneth. Why did life have to be so hard sometimes?

"I'm sorry, Kenneth. I didn't know you were feeling bad. I got caught up in the teaching and now the garden and the market."

"I know, and you're happy, Penny. I love being here, too, and having time with Seb and my occasional work with the Sheriff's Department, but I am homesick. I can't seem to help it. I want to walk along the cliffs on Gower and natter with my friends there. I miss my sister and her family. If Sarah could be happier and more settled, don't you think you'd feel more like getting back to our regular time in Wales? I know you love Wales, too. Isn't it Sarah most of all that keeps you tied here?"

She'd never thought about it quite like that. Was it Sarah that made her reluctant to pick up her roots again like they'd done for most of their eleven years together? Or had she simply forgotten Kenneth's feelings and assumed that if she wanted to stay longer in the U.S., he'd want that, too? Her life felt so full and satisfying. It shocked her to think that maybe his didn't.

A chasm opened in front of her where she had assumed solid ground. She couldn't lose him. He was part of her, wasn't he? Only right now he was miles away. She glanced at her watch and over at her papers. She still had three hours' work ahead of her. They needed to talk. That was clear, even though she dreaded it. She knew marriages had to grow. No matter how much you loved someone, things never stayed the same, but after guilt it was fear she felt. She couldn't lose Kenneth, her mainstay. It was scary to be standing where she was now, looking down into an enormous chasm just as if there'd been an earthquake and the earth had split open.

She sighed. "Kenneth, I'm so sorry. I didn't know. We'll figure this out." She sounded superficial to herself, gliding too quickly over the pain he must have felt a long time before he said anything. He had tried to avoid bringing it up. She had asked him if he was okay with staying until Thanksgiving, and he'd said he was. But now?

"I know you have themes to mark. Go ahead, Penny. We can talk later." His smile wasn't like Kenneth. He needed her now but knew she was too distracted by her papers to be able to give him her full attention. If he'd been angry, it would have been easier. What scared her was his sadness that had lain heavily on his spirit, and she hadn't noticed or tried to find out his feelings. At least she hadn't tried hard enough.

Four

Wednesday afternoon, April 10, second market. Because Andy was out of town for a conference, he'd given Penny a key so she and Leroy could open the market on the next market day, April 10. They had the first of their carrots to take this time and some spinach, as well as the lettuce, onions, radishes and eggs. The sun was shining. The sky was a brilliant, cloudless blue, and by 2:30 p.m. it was up to seventy-six degrees.

"This should be a good market," Penny said to Leroy as he stopped his van before the gate. Penny hopped down and went to unlock it and push it open. As she put the second cement block in place to hold it open, she saw Giles Dunn's big black pickup pulling in behind Leroy's van, and behind him came George Gardiner in his red truck with the tattered burlap to protect his shade plants from the sun.

"Uh oh," she said as she climbed back in. "Week two, and Sybil will not be happy. I hope Nora makes it early. Without Andy or Nora, Sybil may explode like a firecracker, and I'll have to deal with it."

"If anyone could calm her down, you could, Penny," offered Leroy as he backed up into the spot they'd had the week before.

"Thanks for your belief in me, but I hope I don't have to try. Oh, here's Sammie. I'll give her the job." She laughed. But what if Sybil was one of the racists?

"She'll use her karate chop?" Leroy grinned as he opened his door.

"I'm not sure karate chops work at the Farmers' Market," she said. "I wish they did."

They set to work unloading and arranging their produce and eggs, and Penny forgot the problem of Sibyl and the spot to which she was partial.

She'd gone over to help Sammie unload and arrange her iris bouquets in vases when she heard Leroy mutter, "Poultry agent on the horizon." When Leroy had learned there was an agent specifically for poultry, he'd asked him to visit his chickens, which Kent had done only the day before. When he left, Penny told Leroy what Nora had said about Kent. Leroy had found Kent helpful, but he respected Nora and believed her views on Kent entirely, when Penny told him that Kent was apparently not reliable where women were concerned. Was Leroy now warning them?

Penny looked up and saw the lanky form of Kent in shirt sleeves headed their way with a camera on a strap around his neck, his bald head pink and shiny. She didn't think she was in any danger, but who knew? She walked back to their table.

"Are you Penny Weaver? Part of Hassel's operation, Greenscape? Is that right?"

"We're together," Leroy interjected. "A bunch of us who are neighbors do it. Andy and his family are in it, too, and Penny's husband Kenneth."

Penny was amused that he stressed the word *husband*. Leroy was acting protective. She didn't see this bald man as much threat to her marriage. He had no sex appeal that she could pick up. The real threat was how she and Kenneth were going to resolve their differences about how much time to spend here and in Wales. She didn't want to pull out of the market, but maybe she should. In any event she didn't have time to worry about that problem right now.

"I wanted to get photos of the farmers today. You want me to take yours here behind your table?" As he talked he was backing up and adjusting his lens, which was focused on Penny standing behind their table.

She sat down in the chair next to Leroy's and said, "Sure, this is fine."

Sammie, in her purple, blue and yellow ankle-length dress, was making faces at Penny as she smiled for Kent's shot.

"You're next, Sammie," she said without moving her head. "Sammie Hargrave behind you has cut flowers. You'd better do her next. She's very photogenic today."

Sammie crossed her eyes and wiggled her ears, turned around and went back to arranging her iris bouquets.

Kent turned, but he didn't go toward Sammie. That was strange, after she'd encouraged him to do her next. Just then the large station wagon that could only be Sibyl's pulled to a stop between George's plants and Giles's display of baseball hard tomatoes, collards that could have been mistaken for elephant ears, and purple and white turnip globes that would make good spinning tops. Kent headed that way.

Penny hoped she didn't get pulled into a new fight over who had what space. Where was Nora? She looked at her watch and saw that it was 3:10 p.m. Why hadn't Andy given the key to Nora? Why didn't she arrive with the first farmers? Did she make a habit of being late? Penny decided to sit tight and see if the principals would settle this themselves.

Then she heard Sibyl yell, "Every week? You can't be a gentleman once in awhile?" George answered, "First come, first served, Sibyl. I was here when the gate opened." George had walked over to her car. Sibyl was standing a few feet away from it.

Kent walked up to Sibyl. "What's the problem?" he demanded authoritatively. Sibyl went into a long monologue while George went back behind his table and fussed with his plants.

Abbie got out of the passenger side of the station wagon and walked down to Penny's table. "I told Mama she'd best take another place, but she's stubborn sometimes." Abbie didn't look worried. She turned to watch Herman back in next to Penny and

Leroy. "Does he give you the creeps?" she asked quietly, nodding toward Herman.

"He's very committed to organic vegetables," Penny said. "A bit over the top with his conservative politics."

"Too right." Abbie smiled, dimples blooming in her cheeks. "Paleo-Conservative." She giggled, her eyes shining. "If I were buying healthy vegetables, I'd buy from Mark, but Mama's been buying from Herman for years and Nora's greenhouse tomatoes."

"We had some great broccoli from Herman last week." Penny hoped the stall contestants would settle and be peaceful, but Kent hadn't struck her as diplomatic. Sibyl's voice was rising again. "It's not fair. If he wants fair, let him take turns. He had it last week. I should have his or Giles's place this week."

To distract them both from Sibyl's argument Penny said, "But Mark had beautiful chard, and that was delicious. All his vegetables were beautiful. I wanted to eat them on the spot."

Herman had been opening his tailgate when Sibyl's voice rose. He abandoned what he was doing and walked fast down to the front of the market. Kent was now arguing with George and pointing in Penny's direction.

Abbie said, "There goes the creep. I'd better go back to Mama."

"Why creep?" asked Penny.

"Oh, he hangs around me all the time. Mama's nice to him, but I wish he'd leave me alone." She ran toward Sibyl's station wagon. Sibyl was back in it, reversing, and now George was yelling at Kent, "Damn bitch. Why can't she obey the market rules like the rest of us? You ain't helpin', Mr. Kent Berryman." He was glowering at Kent, who turned and moved over to talk to Giles, ignoring George.

Then George said, "Hell," and began putting plants back in his truck. He turned when Herman approached and made sure he knew, too, what was coming down. Penny wondered if she should interfere. She was so new to all this market stuff and didn't have a role really. She wasn't on the board, but it was board members who were fighting. She had no authority that she could see to interfere. Still.

"Shall we send Sammie down?" asked Leroy. Sammie, hearing her name, walked over to watch with them. "That Sibyl is a pistol," she said.

"Not the only one," said Penny. "Should we do anything? Nora could probably settle it, but she's late."

"Let them fight it out," said Sammie. "What happened to our photographer?"

"He's down there, adding fuel to the fire of another fight over Sibyl's place. You think I should do anything?"

Leroy said, "We couldn't stop them anyway."

"Is this childish or what?" asked Sammie. "Sibyl and George must both be in their fifties or even sixties. You'd think they'd act like grownups." Penny couldn't disagree.

Now George, half packed up, walked over to Giles. "Why don't you have to move?"

"I got here first, buddy."

"I got here second. Mr. Berryman ain't our market manager, ain't even our ag agent. Where the hell is Nora when we need her?"

Kent then took George's arm, which George flung off. "Don't you dare touch me. You ain't my bossman. You ain't shit here."

At which point Giles walked over and said to George, "Just pack up and leave, buddy. The customers will be here. If you disagree, talk to Nora when she gets here. Kent's just tryin' to help."

"He's not helping," said Herman, who'd been standing close to George. "He's messing everything up, and you're not helping either, Mr. Genetically Modified."

"Maybe I better go up there," said Penny. "It's getting worse." She walked toward the contestants.

As she did she saw Giles raise his fists as though to take on Herman. George started laughing and turned away. But instead of punching Herman, Giles shoved George from behind, yelling, "Pack up, plant man, and move your ass out of the way."

Penny didn't know what she could do. The voice of reason didn't go down well when people were this angry, but she could try. George gave Giles a murderous look and went back to packing up his thirty or so plants, folding up his table. Penny stopped about six feet away from Herman, who said to Giles, "You wanna fight? I'll fight you."

Giles turned. He was at least six inches taller than Herman and even more muscular. "Better go unload your organic veggies, Hicks." He said *organic* like it was a dirty word. Herman looked around as if to say, "Can't anybody stop this jerk?" Then he saw Penny, who said mildly and, she hoped, effectively, "Hadn't we better get set up and ready for the customers? It's almost four." Herman stared at her and then turned away. He looked furious as he was striding back to his truck, his head down. Penny looked at Giles, who shrugged and went back behind his table. "You best stay out of it, too," he said. "Fight's over before it got going anyhow."

George was loading his truck and getting ready to move it. Minutes later he drove his truck over and parked next to Penny on the other side. Then he began patiently unloading his plants one at a time. Most were too large to do two at a time.

"I'm sorry you had to move," said Penny. "I wish Nora were here. Is she often late?"

"Eh?"

"Is Nora usually late?" she asked loudly.

"She's always late," said George sourly, "but we voted. I don't get it. Why is Sibyl so stubborn? She's wrong, plain wrong, and then Berryman jumps in. What business is it of his?"

"It's nearly four." This time Penny spoke loudly. "Surely Nora will turn up soon. She does seem to know how to settle disputes. I had no idea farmers were so passionate about their spots."

George looked up after placing a large, fully leafed out hosta plant just so. It looked like a small, joyful green and white striped tree. "I tell you one thing. People shove me around, don't follow the rules? I'm outa here."

"Here comes Nora now," said Penny. "Talk it over with her. Don't pull out. We'd miss your beautiful plants."

"Eh?"

"Nora's coming."

"Hurray," said George sarcastically.

Nora pulled up on the other side of George, hopped out and walked over to his table. "You're in the market manager's spot, dear," she said lightly. Not, Penny thought, the wisest way to start the conversation, given what had just happened to George.

"It's mine now, Nora. Where were you when we needed you?" He lifted out another plant to place in front of his table. Penny could see that he didn't have the space he needed for arranging all his plants, not like he did with the corner space at the front of the market. She walked over to give support to George, who had been so summarily thrown out of his spot by Sibyl and Kent.

"Hi, Penny. What do you mean, George, 'when we needed you'? What happened?"

George shrugged. "Penny will tell you. I have to get my plants set out. Market opens in five minutes, Nora. Where were you when the fight broke out?"

"What fight?" But George turned away.

"Penny, what's going on? Are you okay?"

"I'm fine, Nora." She explained that Kent had told Sibyl she could have George's spot, flying in the face of the rules.

"Well, damn." Nora turned and walked fast toward Sibyl's table, where Kent was helping her unload her baked goods and Abbie was stacking jellies in a pyramid.

Nora had a carrying voice, so Penny could hear her up-front challenge to Kent. "I have a bone to pick with you, Mr. Berryman. I'm the manager for the Riverdell Market. We have rules, in case you hadn't been informed."

Everyone stopped what they were doing except George, patiently sliding his plants out with a long metal rod with a hook on the end. Giles walked over to Sibyl's table, and Kent came around from behind it and appraised Nora in her bib overalls, her curly brown hair tied back by a red and white bandana handkerchief, then said, "What rules? You weren't here to ask."

"My cat was sick, and I had to take it to the vet. All these farmers know the rules. Why did you get your big foot in the middle of it?"

Kent caught Giles's eye and smiled. Not wise. "I was just trying to help out, Nora, Andy being gone and all. Sibyl's been getting a rotten deal."

"You're here to take photos, Kent. Why don't you get on with that while I talk to Sibyl. I see farmers and customers arriving. You'd best get cracking."

Kent stalked off toward where Rosalind and Mark had just pulled in.

Sibyl's voice was low, but Penny had no trouble hearing Nora say, "That's why it's important for you to come to meetings, Sibyl. Don't be so childish. Be a grownup, for God's sake. In this market we help each other. People love your pies and cakes. They'll smell your hot bread and find you wherever your spot is. Be more understanding of your fellow farmers. It's called playing nice."

It looked to Penny like Sibyl was having none of it. Abbie had turned her back and was still intent on arranging the jellies at the other end of the table.

Penny did hear Sibyl's retort. "If you want to run this market, Nora, then be here on time. Then Kent won't have the worry and make everyone mad at him."

"Kent won't be back," Nora proclaimed. Kent jerked around from where he was bending Rosalind's ear. Penny heard him mutter, "Damn cow."

Rosalind laughed. "Instead of complaining, you'd better take your pictures. Nora's on the warpath."

But Nora had stopped to talk to Giles, who was fussing over his tomatoes. They kept rolling off the table. Herman came over and stood near Leroy and Penny. "See, his tomatoes bounce. They don't even bruise."

"Lethal," said Leroy and laughed. Leroy so seldom laughed that Penny was glad he had someone to talk to who could prompt that reaction.

Kent was still taking photos at Rosalind's table when Nora opened the gate for the customers and rang the bell. "Market's open, everyone. The Riverdell Market is open for your pleasure and enjoyment. Some very lovely vegetables and other goodies are for sale here today. Welcome."

Nora hurried back behind her table, where a line of customers was forming, and several people had come to their Greenscape table, asking about lettuce, eggs, carrots. All three items were proving a draw. She and Leroy were busy answering questions and taking money for half an hour. There were twice as many customers as the week before. The other farmers were drawing them, too. Sammie had sold nearly all her bouquets, and Penny heard George say to a customer: "This is my last columbine. Isn't it beautiful? Right out of the mountains, but it grows easily in Piedmont gardens with the right care."

"The eggs are selling," whispered Leroy when there was a lull about five. "Already six dozen. I may not have any to trade this week." He was happy, Penny could tell, though he never looked happy. This will put everyone in a better mood, Penny thought. She glanced down to Sibyl's table. It looked as if she had sold her big pies and cakes. She had her spot, and she was selling.

Then Penny saw Abbie standing by an olive green jeep, very close to Kent Berryman, whose head was bent next to hers. They were laughing about something. Nora had noticed, too. "He should be done with his damn photos. I don't want to see his ugly face here one more minute." Loudly she said to George, "Watch my table for a minute?"

"Sure, Nora."

Nora walked quickly toward the olive green jeep. Kent saw her coming, said goodbye to Abbie, slid into his jeep and drove off before Nora reached him.

"Nora's promised it will be first come, first served next week," George said. "Looks like Kent is running off. Scared of Nora? Sibyl better keep an eye on her daughter. What a looker."

"I can watch the table, Leroy," Penny said. "Have a look around. See what's new."

No sooner had Leroy left than Penny saw Henry strolling in through the customer gate. He still slouched, but he looked pleased with everything he saw. He walked straight up to Penny. "This is neat. I've never seen this market before."

"It's our first year," Penny said.

He looked genuinely interested. "Wow. Great lettuce. I had some in a salad Sarah made with radishes and onions. Power vegetables, my mom used to call organic ones."

Penny nodded and wondered if she'd misjudged him, or did he have two sides–an upbeat, interested side and a don't care, bored side? She smiled and thanked him. "Sarah's coming, too, then?"

"Yeah. She can walk from work. I've got the car. I'll take a look around. This is so cool."

He walked over to Nora's table and examined all her herbs, greens, tomatoes, European cucumbers. When Nora sighted him browsing, she hurried back, and soon they were engaged in a long discussion about healing herbs. Penny was definitely seeing a different side of Henry. He made the rounds of the market. Penny watched his progress when she had no customers.

When Leroy returned, she could give him the news that they'd sold all the lettuce and ten dozen eggs, plus all the carrots, spinach and radishes, and made $80.

"A little sun makes a difference," commented Leroy, on hearing the good news. "Think we could trade these onions?" It was going on six, and few customers were left. Penny looked around for Henry and saw him talking to Abbie near Sibyl's table. It had to be innocent, didn't it? He was interested in Sarah, right? Where was Sarah? All her skeptical feelings rushed back in. She had glimpsed what drew Sarah to him. He could be openly enthusiastic, but Sarah wouldn't be happy if she saw him now so totally engaged talking with Abbie. She could hear him saying, "That's so cool."

"Why don't you see if Sibyl has anything she'd trade for onions? By the way, the guy Abbie is talking to is Sarah's new boyfriend."

"Henry? I met him," Leroy said in a dull voice. "He seems lazy to me. I'll visit Sibyl." He picked up the last three bunches of onions and walked toward Sibyl's table.

Sammie came over to Penny's table. Only one or two customers remained. "You did well," she said. "I did, too, but that guy, Kent? He never did photograph me."

"He was sidetracked by the fight, I expect," said Penny.

"That, or he's not comfortable with black people."

"I hope not," said Penny, "but I don't think he'll be back, given Nora's determination to keep him out of the market."

"Maybe just as well," said Sammie. "He's kind of creepy."

Five

Friday Evening, April 12. "He's a disaster, Andy. He'll kill the market before it has a chance to take off." As Penny knocked on the carport door to Andy and Jan's house that Friday evening, she heard Nora sounding off within.

"I don't think …"

"Can you talk to him?"

No one responded to her knock so Penny slipped inside and into the family room, where Andy and Nora were standing beside a big table laid with a paper tablecloth of daffodils, plastic silverware and daffodil-patterned paper plates and cups.

"Hi, Nora, Andy. Am I the first one here?"

"Come on in, Penny." Andy walked over and took the big wooden salad bowl from her. "Our garden? Looks yummy."

"Kenneth will be here shortly. He'll bring the bread, but it hadn't quite finished baking."

Nora walked over and hugged Penny. "Hot bread, what a treat. It's so great to have you in the market. Our Riverdell market is going to be one of the best. I can feel it in my bones. If only we can ditch a few troublemakers." She waggled her eyebrows and laughed.

Two tall, but still young, children with curly red hair came walking slowly in from the kitchen. The boy carried salt and pepper shakers, and the girl brought a sugar bowl and creamer. "Dad, where do these go?"

It was hard to believe that little Penny and Kenny were eight this April. They were so intent on delivering their condiments to the table, they didn't see her or Nora at first. "Aunt Penny," cried little Penny. "We're having a party. It's Aunt Nora's potluck party, and all the farmers are coming."

Kenny ran over to hug Penny and allowed himself to be caught and hugged by Nora, but he was not long deterred from his mission of discovering what the supper choices would be. "Aunt Penny, what did you bring?"

"That salad. Nora, did you remember the cukes and tomatoes?"

"You betcha. They're over here." She retrieved a covered bowl from the couch where she'd thrown down her jacket and handed it to Penny. "Fix 'em any way you like, doll."

At a knock the twins rushed to the door. "It's the goat lady, Dad. Did you bring cheese, Miss Rosalind?"

"I most certainly did and a surprise, too. How are the two youngest farmers I know?"

"Seb is the youngest," explained little Penny. "He'll be here soon. What's the surprise?"

"Can't tell, or it wouldn't be a surprise." Rosalind walked to the table and set down a platter of differently flavored cheeses, each covered with a cellophane wrap. The children trailed her. She handed Penny a container inside a protective bag to keep it cold and gestured to the kitchen. "Put it in the freezer," she whispered.

"Ice cream?" Penny mouthed.

Rosalind nodded. Her hands free, she pulled the children to her and got down on her knees. "Now tell me about Seb."

"Here he is!" shouted Kenny. Penny turned to see Leroy in his familiar cut-off shorts and flip-flops, and her grandson, neatly dressed in matching blue shirt and shorts, his blond hair sticking straight up as usual, coming through the carport door. Seb ran straight to Kenny. "Want some 'tato salad? Daddy made 'tato salad. Yum."

Rosalind said, "Hello, Seb. I'm Miss Rosalind. Kenny tells me you're a farmer?"

Seb looked up at Kenny.

"Plant peas, Seb. Pick up rocks, pull up carrots."

Seb was nodding vigorously. "Plant peas, rocks, carrots. Me help Daddy."

Rosalind drew the children off into a corner while Leroy set down his potato salad garnished with hardboiled egg slices and parsley and sprinkled with paprika. "You think they'll all come?" he asked Penny.

"I hear cars outside. We'll see. Sometimes when people share a meal, they get along better. This group certainly has some odd ones, but then you and I are a little odd, too." She wouldn't mention the racism to Leroy, but maybe that, too, would be less problematic after they shared a meal. Hopefully.

Leroy pointed to himself and looked the question "Me, odd?"

As if on cue Herman Hicks knocked and then walked in carrying a big green, covered plastic bowl. Penny welcomed him. "Oh, great, Herman. Cole slaw. Did you make it?"

"No, my mom did. It's my great grandmother's recipe. I grew the cabbage."

"It looks good. You can put it here." Leroy moved over and began chatting with Herman, and Penny turned to welcome Sibyl and Abbie. Sibyl was carrying a large cake with thick, swirled chocolate frosting, and Abbie had a big apple pie sprinkled with sugar.

"Yum," said Penny. "We just loved your pecan pie. Two desserts tonight, you spoil us."

Sibyl looked pleased as she set down the cake. "I didn't know how many people we'd have, so we did both the chocolate cake–with Leroy's eggs, by the way—and pie using good pie apples from our crop last year, Gravenstein."

"If everyone comes, we'll be twenty at least," said Penny. "A few children and spouses. Have you met Andy's wife?" Penny had seen Jan come in with a gallon jug of cider earlier, and now she carried in a coffee urn and was plugging it into the wall near the end of the table.

"No, I never have," said Sibyl. "Pleased to meet you. We all love Andy." Penny had never expected to hear her say that, not after she had given Andy such a hard time at the first market.

"Me, too," said Jan. "Welcome."

Penny marveled at all that Jan balanced, working full time as an engineer for the Division of Air Quality, keeping up with her very active eight-year-olds, and still able to look relaxed as twenty people crowded into their family room. She beamed at Penny. "What have I forgotten?"

"Napkins?"

"Oh, right. Be back. I'm Jan, by the way, and I'm pleased to meet you …"

"Sibyl."

"Sibyl. Please make yourself at home. You brought the pie and cake? They look absolutely scrumptious."

Jan glided off. Penny tried to engage Sibyl by asking how she'd gotten into baking, but she seemed distracted.

"I believe I'll say hello to Rosalind," she announced and made a beeline for the corner where Rosalind and Abbie had gathered the children. Seb was on Rosalind's lap, and all the men had also gravitated, like bees to flowers. The adults were all laughing. The children looked happy, and the men were positively beaming.

Mark slipped in next to Penny. "Am I late?"

"Oh, no. Hi, Mark. Ah, you brought chard. It's so beautiful. You have to tell me the secret to your vegetables. I've never seen such vibrant vegetables."

Mark glanced toward Abbie. He didn't seem to want to talk about vegetables. He shrugged. "They're organic. I make my own compost and mulch them real good. Whose kids?"

"The little boy's Leroy's son and my grandson. The twins are Andy and Jan's. Come on, I'll introduce you."

"Abbie's so at home with children," he said. "That's the kind of wife I want."

"Of course, she is. She's a pediatric nurse," Penny said. "Here's Mark, everybody."

At that point Derek and Sammie arrived, each carrying a large casserole dish. Penny walked over to hug them as they set them down. "Smells heavenly."

"Just baked chicken and potatoes," said Sammie, glancing around. Was she worried?

"I see mushrooms," said Penny.

"Yes, the sauce begins with that old standby, mushroom soup, and I added a few fresh ones." She lowered her voice. "Any fights break out yet? Any racists show their colors?" Sammie grinned wickedly.

Derek slipped out of his jacket. "Things getting a little rough down at the new market, Penny? You let me know if you need help. Where's Kenneth?"

"He's bringing bread any minute now. Things were a little hot on Wednesday, Derek, but Nora seems to understand how to settle everyone's feathers. If there's racism, which Sammie and I are sure there is, it's very low profile at the moment."

"From what I hear Nora's good at ruffling feathers," quipped Sammie. "I've heard complaints about her, that she's late too much, not there when she's needed and a little on the strong-arm side when she settles disputes."

"These aren't easy people to manage, Sammie. They're a lot like writers, independent-minded, used to working on their own. Her tactics seem to work, as far as I can see."

"Maybe." Sammie sounded skeptical, and Derek raised an eyebrow.

"This will be a test," said Penny in a low voice when she saw Giles coming in the door carrying a crock pot and beaming. George was right behind him, a six-pack of beer under one arm and his other arm around a grocery bag of wine bottles.

"Welcome, Giles, George," said Penny. "You can put your contributions here."

Derek and Sammie moved off to join the group congregated around the children, whom they knew well. Penny had known the Hargraves almost as long as she'd known Kenneth. She and Sammie had worked together for years on community issues, like air pollution and nuclear safety. Derek, in his role as detective at the Shagbark Sheriff's Department, very occasionally consulted her. He tried to keep the knowledge of his cases from her, but she and Sammie usually got wind of what he knew one way or another and helped him out, despite his determination to keep them ignorant.

Penny helped Giles find a socket to plug in his crock pot of spaghetti, about which he bragged, "All fresh tomatoes. I have right many now, and I can't sell them all. I brought some to give away if anyone wants them?"

"Talk to Nora," said Penny. She wondered how popular his GM spaghetti would be. People should know the tomatoes were genetically modified, shouldn't they? George had opened a beer and joined her as Giles walked over to Nora, who was again bending Andy's ear in the kitchen doorway.

"What's in his crock pot?" asked George, as he lifted the lid.

"Spaghetti," said Penny. "The sauce is already mixed with the pasta."

"Eh?"

"Spaghetti."

"He make it?"

Loudly, Penny said, "Yes, from tomatoes he hasn't sold. He brought some to give away, too."

"I don't trust this GM stuff," said George, lowering his voice. "Mess with the genetic code, and who knows where it stops. They put all kinds of crazy things in the seeds, trying to protect them against herbicides so they can kill weeds with them. They fix the seeds so they won't reproduce, and there ain't no scientific proof they're any good for us. Hybrids I can see, but tomatoes that are still good after three weeks, and we don't know what they're doing to our insides? Pretty strange."

"You think we should let people know the spaghetti is GM?" She didn't want to yell but spoke close to his ear.

"Hell, yes. People generally, but especially farmers, want to know what they're eating. Herman would have a conniption fit if he ate GM food in error." He put the lid back on. "Too bad. It smells good."

"I don't want to offend him," Penny said. "I guess I'll tell Nora and Andy and let them figure it out. Andy's diplomatic."

"Nora's not," said George, "but she'll make sure people know. I mean we're not telling 'em what to eat, just what they're getting if they do eat it. I'd be worried most about the kids. We don't know what these GM foods do to us. We don't even know when we're eating corn oil or soybeans that are GM unless they're organically grown, the only safe food anymore."

Penny didn't have to ask Andy's help. As Kenneth walked in, carrying two loaves of Penny's whole grain rye bread fresh from the oven, Nora hit a spoon against a casserole dish and said, "Time to eat, everybody. Looks real good. Here comes some of Penny's good rye bread, and it's hot. Plenty of beer and wine, but don't get drunk. We got serious business to discuss tonight. Oh, and Giles's spaghetti looks fantastic, but it is made with GM tomatoes, and if y'all want more of his tomatoes, he has some in his truck to give away.

"My heirloom tomatoes are on top of Penny's garden salad. Line up, and dig in, folks. Not sure what you're eating? Ask the cook. All farmers are welcome at Riverdell Market, but we're all a little different. Adds spice to our mix, doncha think?"

People moved forward to serve themselves, waiting until Jan and Leroy served the children, who were to eat at the kitchen table. Only Sibyl and Giles served themselves to spaghetti, but the chicken and potato casserole disappeared quickly.

Once they'd all piled food on their plates, they clustered in pairs or small groups around the family room. Sammie and Jan stayed in the kitchen and ate with the kids, who were lively, not to say intoxicated, with the party atmosphere. Penny could hear Seb declaiming, "Me farmer, plant peas, rocks, carrots."

"No, no, Seb," insisted Kenny. "Plant peas, *throw* rocks, *pull* carrots."

"Frow rocks, frow peas, frow carrots," was Seb's response, which triggered giggles in the twins. Then, apparently to demonstrate, Seb picked up the raw carrot on his plate and threw it across the room. Penny saw it fly across the open doorway. This triggered both admonitions and more giggles.

Mark was sticking close to Abbie. So was Herman. He wasn't quite part of their conversation, but he was listening to everything they said. Leroy and Nora had retreated to the TV corner and were exchanging life histories, it sounded like. "You, too, huh? Yeah, I had a bad patch a few years ago," Nora admitted. "This is great potato salad, Leroy. Tell me how you got into chickens?"

The usually quiet Leroy was almost expansive as he talked about his life, his chickens and Seb, whereas the usually loud and raucous Nora sat quietly, looking entranced with everything he had to say. Sibyl and Giles, both with big helpings of spaghetti, had found two chairs off in another corner and were consoling each other. They seemed quite cozy.

Derek and Kenneth, the two detectives (Kenneth part-time these years both in Wales and in N.C.) were talking shop. Penny enjoyed watching them when she wasn't talking to anyone. They were from two different cultures but were not unlike. Derek was a proud and accomplished African American who had, after his four years in the Army and a Criminal Justice degree from State, been hired by the Shagbark Sheriff's Department, where he had slowly and carefully risen to his lieutenant position in the detective division.

Penny remembered how stiff he had been when he first interviewed her in Belle's and Kate's home across the way almost eleven years ago, when Belle's ex-husband had been murdered. It had taken Derek a while to warm up to Penny, although now he was quite at ease with her, enough to tell her frankly to lay off if he thought she had no business in his investigation. He had trusted Kenneth before he trusted her, but Kenneth was so easygoing and likable, most people did trust him right off the bat.

In the Swansea Police Department Kenneth had risen from being a lowly constable on the Gower Peninsula to detective inspector based in Swansea, and he'd been in charge of the murder of the German woman at the bed and breakfast where she'd been staying in the summer of 1991.

They were all old friends now, but the two police officers had their own bond, and sometimes she was left out. Mostly that was okay. Kenneth normally caught her up on whatever was going on, and if he failed to do that, then Derek's wife Sammie did a little sleuthing for them.

Penny settled near the food table, and Andy joined her after pulling up a chair. He obviously wanted to consult. "You think we'll avoid more fights tonight, Penny?"

"I hope so. You were aware of some racism on the board?"

"No!"

"It wasn't blatant, apparently. Some members fussed about Sammie's flowers, arguing she wasn't a farmer, just a backyard gardener."

"But that's absurd. I must have missed that part of the meeting. I did have to step out to answer the phone at one point. Did she have any trouble last week?"

"No, and I don't know who the objectors were. There was the fight over places, but Nora will have told you about that."

"Oh, yes, and I'll speak to Kent. Keep me posted, Penny, if anything as ugly as racism shows. We can't have that. Sammie will stick, won't she?"

"I hope so. She's tough, but that stuff is very insidious, and in addition to the fussing over the front spots, it worries me. This new market needs the good will and cooperation of all the farmers. But look on the bright side, Andy. At the moment everybody seems peaceful."

"I'm worried, too," admitted Andy. "I hope we can keep them in a friendly mood, but I wonder what Giles and Sibyl are plotting over there."

Once the ice cream surprise had been revealed and enjoyed, either with chocolate cake (a moist dark chocolate with a creamy and not-too-sweet butter frosting) or apple pie (just the right amount of tartness and another melt-in-your-mouth crust) or both, the children were led off to watch a children's video. Nora used the serving spoon again to clang them to order. They settled on chairs and couches around the room, Abbie and Mark cross-legged on the floor near Rosalind, with Herman on a chair he'd moved only inches away from Abbie. Penny and Kenneth stayed near the dining table on one side. Nora and Andy were standing near it on the kitchen side. Derek had gotten a call and had to leave.

"You want to speak first, Andy?"

"Go ahead, Nora. You're the manager. Call on me if you need to."

"I called this meeting, and I'm pleased as punch you came, all of you. We got ourselves in a right mess last Wednesday, and we need to sort a few things out. You asked me to be your manager, and I'm proud to be, but it takes every dadgum one of us to make this new market work. A small market like this can't afford to have farmers getting pissed and pulling out." She looked sternly at George. "Or being stubborn and not obeying the rules adopted by the majority." She stared at Sibyl. "Together we stand, divided we fall, so we need to stand together, folks. Enough of this petty junk. We work damn hard to grow our produce and haul it to market. We need to sell it at good prices and not piss this golden opportunity away that Andy helped make possible and several of us worked hard with him to make a reality–namely, Sibyl, Rosalind and yours truly. That's number one. Now number two."

Sibyl raised her hand. "I don't agree with the first come, first served rule. I think we should vote again. That's what started all the trouble last week."

Nora could not hide the look of exasperation on her face, and Penny remembered her choice words for Sibyl on Wednesday night, *bitch* and *Queen of the Mountain.*

Before Nora recognized him Giles stood up and said, "We should get to take turns at those two spots up in front."

Sibyl turned and looked at Giles in astonishment. They all did. Penny wondered, if he was so keen to take turns, why hadn't he given up his spot to Sibyl last Wednesday? It could have saved a lot of people a lot of grief.

Andy was shaking his head and restraining himself admirably, but Nora looked like she was ready to hit someone. She gave Giles a look so hostile it could have curdled milk. But then it was hard to know how Giles felt about Nora telling everyone his spaghetti was GM and pointing out, in effect, the safety of her own heirloom tomatoes.

Sibyl was waving her hand.

"Wait, Sibyl. Giles, just hold it a minute. We have how many farmers here tonight? Penny and Kenneth, Leroy, Rosalind, Herman, Sibyl, Abbie, Mark, Giles, Sammie, George and me. Andy?"

"Let me stay out of it," said Andy.

"What about Jan?"

"Leave her out of it, too."

"Okay, that's twelve farmers and bakers. Now we already voted this before, but I'm gonna ask you first if you want to vote again."

"No!" said George and Herman together.

"I didn't ask your opinion. I'm asking you to raise your hands if you want a new vote on this. All who want to vote again, raise your hand."

Sibyl and Giles did, but no one else. Abbie was whispering with Mark.

"Abbie," scolded her mother, "we're voting. You need to pay attention."

Abbie stuck her hand up and grinned at Mark, who did not. Penny doubted Abbie knew what they were voting on. Mark had a sly smile on his face and whispered to her something that made her jerk her hand down, but it was too late.

Nora noticed and grinned. "All in favor of staying with our original decision to follow first come, first served, and not re-vote on the matter, raise your hand." All the others did.

"Nine to three. That settles it, folks. So no more pissing matches over spaces. If you have a favorite spot, get there early. Andy or I, or Penny in an emergency, will be there at two-thirty to open up. Now, next item."

But Sibyl waved her hand.

Nora's "Yes, Sibyl," was steely.

"Why can't we assign spaces? Wouldn't that be better all around?"

"Sibyl, you're here this time. We voted again. The matter is closed. Get there early, or take what's available when you do get there."

Sibyl looked angry, started to speak, glanced around and saw no sympathy, and shrugged.

But Giles got up and walked over to his crock pot. He unplugged it while Nora went on. "Now the matter of Kent Berryman."

Giles swung around. "Leave Kent out of this."

"Kent inserted himself into this market's business, and we're going to discuss that. If you wish to contribute something constructive, please do." She glared at him. He turned away, wrapped the cord around his pot, and tucked it under his arm.

"You all don't listen to me nohow. I'm outta here. See you at the market." He left rapidly. Silence fell. Nora rolled her eyes.

Andy glanced at Penny, who smiled, wanting to reassure him that "this, too, will pass." She hoped it would.

Mark said into the silence, "That Franken-food spaghetti scares me. Giles's fields are only a few miles from where I have my tomatoes this year, organic and heirloom. His tomato pollen maybe be carried over and mess up my Purple Cherokees."

"Not to worry on that score, Mark," said Andy. "He's got terminator seeds. His tomato plants can't reproduce. More of a problem is how those seeds of his can resist pesticides and herbicides. So he can spray those poisons and not worry about harming the tomatoes, but then he's added some bad stuff to his farm and yours, too, Mark. Those poisons definitely travel by air and water."

"My God. I hadn't even thought of that." Mark jumped up. "I'm working so hard to have good organic crops and no pesticides or chemical fertilizers."

Meantime, though he hadn't moved from his chair near Abbie, Herman looked astounded, as if someone had just given him a blow to the head. He opened his mouth to speak but found no words.

Nora intervened. "There's always something, folks. Table that discussion. We'll deal with that hot-button issue later. Back to our second problem: Kent Berryman. He's been interfering in our market, and he's got to stop."

"He just came to take pictures," said Sibyl.

"But he didn't just take pictures," insisted Nora. "He butted in. You know that, Sibyl. He felt sorry for you because you made such a fuss, and so he knocked George out of the place he had claimed because he followed the rules. We have rules, and we all should know and observe them, else this two-week-old market is going to hell in a handbasket."

Sibyl raised her hand, but Nora ignored her. Finally Sibyl said, "But I sell hot bread."

Nora looked ready to explode, but Andy put his hand on her arm. "If I might say a word."

Nora shook her head, staring at Sibyl. "Go ahead, Andy," she said through her teeth.

"I was out of town. I had no idea that Kent's being there would be a problem. I've already told Nora I'll abide by your rules and talk to Kent. He's a good photographer, and I wanted photos of you all. I want this market to succeed, very much so. I should be able to be there from now on except for two weeks in August when Jan and I take our vacation. I don't think it will be a problem now. As we work together and support each other, we'll help our new market attract more customers. That's the goal, right?"

Penny was smiling at him when he glanced her way. The group relaxed. Nora said more quietly, "Anything else, folks?"

Sammie spoke up. "Maybe we can plan some special events to draw attention to the market. Then it would be easier to get the media to notice us and run stories."

"What, for instance?" asked Penny.

"What about a musician to come in and play?" asked Abbie.

"Good idea," said Nora. "Anyone know of any?"

"What about the guy who came by Wednesday? Isn't he your daughter's boyfriend, Penny? He seemed really nice, and he does gigs around–guitar and voice, I think," said Abbie.

"Henry?" She didn't want Henry there, but Henry would probably love to.

"Oh, yeah," chipped in Mark. "Great idea, and couldn't we set up a little science project for kids, bring seeds and let them plant them?"

"Fantastic idea," said Rosalind. "Get the kids there, and the parents will follow. Another idea is to bring live animals. Children love those. I could bring one of our new kids–baby goats, I mean."

"I could bring a chicken," contributed Leroy.

"Let's set up a committee to work this out. Rosalind, will you chair it, and Mark and Abbie, will you be on it? Anyone else want to?"

No one else volunteered, but when they all rose to go home, the whole mood had changed, and they had morphed back into happy farmers. As she picked up her empty pie and cake plates, not even Sibyl looked disgruntled.

Six

Wednesday, April 17, third market. Neither Andy nor Nora had been free to come unlock the gate, so Penny and Leroy opened the market that next Wednesday and were busy setting up their table when Henry walked in at about 2:45 p.m. Abbie joined him when she got there to help him set up his speakers. Their shelter had an electric box, and they were busy stringing his extension cord over a rafter and down to one of the plugs. It seemed to Penny that Henry loved having Abbie's attention, but Abbie seemed nonchalant. Maybe it was more fun hanging cords than stacking jellies. Perhaps Sarah needn't worry.

Penny hadn't wanted the responsibility of opening when things had gotten so out of hand only the week before, but both Nora and Andy thought they'd be there by three, and no one expected Kent this time. However, when Penny looked up from arranging the lettuce, she saw Kent stroll in, camera around his neck. He stopped briefly to chat with Giles, who was arranging his baseball tomatoes, then walked over to Sibyl's table. Abbie saw him, too, and headed that way. Does she like him, Penny wondered, or does she plan to warn him to leave? As long as he didn't start a fight or try to interfere, she wasn't going to do anything but keep an eye on him. Oh, where was Nora when she was needed?

The next time she checked Kent was chatting peacefully with Abbie while Sybil worked on her jelly display. The jars were beautiful, and the spring sunshine was giving their reds, oranges, yellows, blues and purples the incandescence of candles as if a light bloomed in their depths. Who could resist such beauty? But everything was calm, thank goodness, and then she saw Nora's old station wagon swing into the market drive. She barreled around the corner to back in abruptly next to Penny and Leroy and jerked to a stop. Nora must have spotted Kent. She was out of her truck in a flash and running down to Sibyl's table.

"Thanks, Sibyl. I really appreciate it," Penny heard Kent saying before he turned around and saw Nora hurtling toward him. He stopped in the center of the aisle and waited. He was a good eight inches taller than Nora, and he'd drawn himself up to his full height, well over six feet, and stood, feet firmly planted, like a soldier on guard duty. His body language declared that no mere woman was going to intimidate him. He stepped back, however, when Nora stopped so close to him that they were toe to toe.

"Did Andy speak to you, Kent?"

"What about?"

"Leaving these farmers and this market the hell alone."

"We talked," said Kent. "What we discussed is none of your business."

"This market is my business. I'm the manager, Kent, in case you haven't heard, and I'm asking you to leave now."

"Not very polite, are you? It's not good business to be rude to potential customers."

"We open to customers at four, Kent, but we'd prefer you leave this market the hell alone, period."

"I came to see if I had left out any farmers who need to be photographed."

"We don't need any more of your photographs, Kent. Please leave. Right now."

"Or you'll do what?"

Penny could imagine that Nora's small supply of patience was fully depleted.

Oh, where was Andy? Should she try to reach him at his office? Maybe someone had a cell phone. Or send Leroy to fetch him? Or go herself? He had a meeting until three in the ag building, she remembered, so he should be right out.

"Call the Sheriff," Nora said loudly. "I'll give you fifteen minutes to clear out."

Kent made the mistake of laughing, and then Giles came over, laughing, too. "Come on, Nora, ease up. He's not bothering anyone. Sibyl's all settled. George and I ain't gonna mix it up. Hang loose, woman. Kent's just jerking your chain. Hang it up."

Nora turned on her heel and stalked back to her truck. She jerked her tailgate down to start unloading and muttered to Penny, "I'll give him until three-thirty. Then I'm calling the Sheriff. Where the hell is Andy?"

"He's in a meeting, Nora, should be here any minute," explained Penny.

"Damned insolent man. I could cheerfully kill him."

George had wandered up. "Don't take it so hard, Nora. He says he's leaving, but he'll probably go faster if you ignore him. I got my spot; Sibyl's not fussing. It'll be okay. Can I help you unload?"

"Thanks. If you could lift out these crates of tomatoes, I'll set out the punch. It's already hot and gonna go up to ninety, they say."

"At least it's not raining," said Penny. "Here, I can handle the punch, Nora, and look who's coming. Andy's here." She saw him parking his green Toyota pickup near the front of the market next to Kent's jeep.

"About time," said Nora.

Penny poured the bright red fruit punch from the gallon containers into the big, five-gallon thermos and added ice from the bag, set out plastic cups and turned the spout so it was over the edge of the table. "You asking money for it?"

"Contributions. Where's the money box? Okay, here, just set this by it."

The box had "Contributions–25 cents and up" printed across it and a slot to insert the money.

George lifted down the last crate and walked over to the punch. "Farmers allowed?"

"Sure," said Nora. "The money benefits the market. We could buy an ad, have a party–who knows?"

George fished in his pocket for a quarter, dropped it in and turned the spout to fill his cup. Leroy joined him and got one for Penny, too.

"Good punch, Nora," said Penny. "What's your secret? Tastes like real fruit juice."

"That's the secret, doll. None of this cheap Hawaiian punch drek they sell at Food Plus. It's got apple, grape, orange, cranberry, even grapefruit."

They were all chatting when Kent walked up, said hello and also helped himself to punch. Nora probably wouldn't have been able to contain herself if Andy hadn't walked up right behind him. Nora saw Andy, walked to her pickup and climbed into the cab. She was facing away from her vendor table. Smart move, thought Penny.

Andy asked Kent if he could speak to him a minute. Kent set his cup down, saying to the others, "Watch my cup. I'll be right back." He and Andy walked over to the customer entrance out of hearing range. Meantime Mark, Sammie and Rosalind had arrived and parked, and Giles had come up, wiping sweat off his ordinarily pale face that was now a blotchy red.

"Don't mind if I do," he said, and picked up Kent's cup.

"That's Kent's," said George quietly and handed him a clean cup. Giles looked at Penny. "Nora's not too good at handling men." He glanced uneasily around.

George said, "Kent's belligerent. I hope Andy can persuade him to leave, but I don't know. Customers will be here soon. We don't need any more bad vibes in this market."

"He ain't bothering nobody today," Giles said. "He's a county agent, ain't he? Deserves respect."

"Eh?"

"Kent deserves respect," shouted Giles.

"Maybe so, but it's stupid to fight with the market manager, and that's bad vibes already even if he doesn't do another thing.

Why did he return anyways? What business is it of his to come here?"

Leroy said clearly to George, "Probably to talk to Abbie. He acts sweet on her."

"We're all sweet on Abbie," said George. "I'm heading back. Tell Nora not to let him get under her skin. He ain't worth it."

Leroy seemed suddenly to have noticed that Nora wasn't there. "Where is she?"

"In her truck," Penny said.

Leroy walked around to talk to her. Soon she was back at her table, trying to ignore Kent, when Andy and Kent strolled back. Kent picked up his cup of punch and without looking at any of them walked toward Sibyl's table.

Andy came over and stood by Penny. "I think he'll go now," he said quietly. "Whew. I never thought about all this stuff when I worked so hard to set up the market."

"Politics is in everything," said Penny. "These farmers spend so much time alone. They're not used to kowtowing to others. It'll be okay, Andy. He acts subdued now. Earlier, he was quite defiant."

Nora came up behind them and put her hands on their shoulders. "Finally gone? Damn the man anyway. You're a blessing, Andy, but Kent has no business being a county agent."

Andy glanced toward the front of the market. Kent was talking to Abbie again. "He's on his way, Nora. He does okay with the chicken farmers, and that's what matters in his job. Let's cross our fingers. I told him he was making the organic vegetable farmers uncomfortable, that he'd help the market and the county extension service the most by leaving and letting me and you see about the market. He objected to being tossed out, but I think he'll go."

"What a shit," said Nora and went back over to her table.

Penny looked at her watch. It was only minutes to four. People were lined up outside the customer gate. She wondered if

Nora was aware of the time. She couldn't seem to take her eyes off Kent.

Sammie walked over to buy some of Nora's tomatoes, since farmer vendors could buy early, and that brought Nora's attention back. Sammie was in purple and blue today and had with her bouquets of huge purple and blue iris. They were as exotic as orchids, especially one white one with a pale blue fringe.

After she handed Sammie her tomatoes and change, Nora looked again toward where Kent had been, saw him getting into his jeep and rang the cow bell. At first her voice was not quite loud enough, but the old Nora sound returned rapidly. "The Riverdell Farmers' Market is open for your buying pleasure. Welcome, everybody, and stop by for some real fruit punch."

By the time she'd put down the cow bell, Kent was gone, and Nora had her hands full selling tomatoes.

That Wednesday's market had been their best yet. Andy dropped in on Penny and Kenneth about seven-thirty to talk things over and exult. Penny was exhausted, but Kenneth's good "fry up supper" (fried new potatoes with onions, tomatoes, mushrooms, bacon and eggs), their pinch-hitting favorite, had eased the worst of her fatigue, and now she could sip Darjeeling tea and keep her feet propped. Sibyl had given away some little lemon-iced spice cakes that added just the right touch, and tomorrow she could stay home all day. Maybe she and Kenneth could have the heart-to-heart talk they needed to have about how much time to spend in the U.S. and how much in Wales. So much was going on, she kept forgetting. Then she'd feel guilty, but something else would distract her. She had to clear some time for him soon. It was too important.

For the moment she was just happy they'd brought home one hundred thirty dollars and sold everything. They'd take more next week. It was working, and there were no more farmer problems after Kent left. Most of the vendors had had good sales, and everyone was in a placid mood when the market ended, as far as Penny could tell. Andy said he'd better get back to read the twins a bedtime story, as promised, when someone knocked at the door. Kenneth got up. "Probably Leroy come to gloat," he said, smiling.

But it wasn't Leroy. It was Derek, and he looked very somber. "Come in, Derek. Can we offer you a cuppa? Andy was just leaving," said Penny.

"I can't stay long. Andy, could you stay a minute, too? We have a big problem."

They all sat down again. "What is it, Derek?" Penny asked.

"Kent Berryman is dead, and he was apparently poisoned, got deathly ill shortly after he left the market."

"Oh, no!" Penny immediately thought of Nora's anger, but surely she hadn't been angry enough to kill him. That market fight wasn't that bad, was it? Had it set off a farmer killer?

Kenneth was asking for details. "I can't go into everything," Derek said, "but it looks bad for the market. I wanted to alert you. Apparently he ate or drank something at the market. He went from there back to his office. His secretary said before she left at five, he asked her to leave the air conditioning on, said he was too hot. Then she looked in on him, and he said he must be catching a bug. He'd vomited and was having diarrhea. She said he'd better go home and rest, and he said he would. She said the sweat was pouring off him, that he looked sick, but she also thought it was a virus, and he's known to be stubborn, so she left the air conditioning on and went home.

"The lady who comes to clean found him in the men's room about an hour later, vomiting and acting crazy, saying, "You stupid bitch. You're trying to kill me, aren't you?" So she called 911, thinking he was either sick or having a mental breakdown. He was taken to the ER, and they did what they could. They didn't know what he'd eaten, and he died an hour ago. We went by his office. There was a plastic cup that had had something red in it in his trash basket, and he'd been eating a peanut butter sandwich when he got sick, but we don't know exactly what it was that poisoned him. We'll have to wait for the autopsy, but this wasn't your run-of-the-mill food poisoning. Someone was definitely out to kill him."

Penny felt sick, and Andy looked worse. Kenneth was the calmest. Nobody had wanted Kent to stay at the market, but somebody had made sure he'd never be at the Riverdell Farmers' market again.

When Andy and Derek had left, Andy having given him a list of all the farmers and their contact information, Kenneth and Penny sat down with a fresh cup of tea to think it through.

Penny had told Derek about the resentment of several farmers against Kent, explained about the punch, which a lot of people had drunk to no ill effect, including Penny and Andy. Derek repeated they'd know more after the autopsy, and he'd asked Kenneth to rearrange his schedule so he could be at all the markets and farmer gatherings. It wouldn't be undercover as most people in Riverdell knew that he helped out the Sheriff sometimes. But he could be in plainclothes and watch for any strange behavior, and perhaps by being there prevent another poisoning. Andy had also cautioned them that it might be necessary to close the market.

"What do you think, love? You were there. Any ideas?"

"I can't believe it's Nora, but she was the angriest. Anyway, when Kent came up to her table, she went and sat in her truck. I remember he carried his punch away with him after he talked to Andy. But a lot of people drank that punch, Kenneth. Leroy and I had some, most of the other farmers, Andy and many customers. It was so hot."

"Think carefully, love. Could someone have dropped something in his cup?"

"He had just helped himself to punch when Andy asked to talk to him, and they walked off."

"Did he take the punch with him?"

"No. Now I remember. He said, 'Watch my punch,' and he picked it up again when he came back."

"Super. So someone could have added something to it when it was unattended?"

"I guess. Several of us were chatting. This was around three-thirty, as I remember. Let's see. George, Leroy and I. Oh, Giles was there briefly to get some punch, and he and George argued about Kent. And Nora briefly, very briefly, before Kent reclaimed his cup and left."

"So if the poison was in his cup, George or Nora could have put it there?"

"Or Leroy, Giles, Andy or me."

"You or Andy seem very unlikely. I've never known you to poison anyone, Penny." He smiled his warm Kenneth smile. "I'm sure Andy's innocent."

"Of course, you're right, love. Andy and I wouldn't even think about it. But that Kent was worrisome. He didn't listen, couldn't believe that other people really wanted him to leave."

"He learned the hard way, and too late, then," commented Kenneth.

Seven

Friday afternoon, April 19. The phone was ringing when Penny let herself into the apartment in mid-afternoon on Friday. She dropped her book bag, grabbed the phone and sank down on the couch.

"Penny?"

At first she didn't recognize the voice, which was faint and sounded strangled, desperate. "Who is this?"

"Nora."

"Hi, Nora. Are you okay?" She sounded terrible. Penny could hear voices in the background, phones ringing, a door slamming, a siren.

"No. They arrested me. I'm at the jail." Her voice dropped. "You're my ..."

"Speak louder, Nora. I can barely hear you. Who arrested you?"

"Cops. Sammie's husband and some other guy. They think I killed Kent. I didn't, Penny. Honest. He was a real sh ... a real sleaze, but I never killed anybody. You believe me, Penny?"

She did. She didn't know why. Something must look bad, though, if Derek had arrested her. He was very careful not to jump to conclusions. "I believe you, Nora. What can I do?"

"I need a lawyer who won't take shit. This stinks."

"My neighbor, Kate Razor's, good. I'll ask her."

"I need somebody who goddamn believes me."

"She will, Nora. She's good and very smart. Friends of ours have been wrongly arrested before. Kate always helped." Penny was thinking how it had never been Derek doing the arresting before, not of someone innocent. What was he thinking? What pushed him to do it?

"Okay, but doll, my cats need feeding, and I have four-week-old chicks that need looking after, and the tomatoes. Hell, I'm a farmer. I can't sit around in jail. My tomato crop will go to hell."

"Don't worry, Nora. Andy and I will find other farmers to help."

"I don't trust 'em all. Somebody in our market's really sick."

"Who do you trust?"

"You, Andy, Rosalind, Leroy–he's a good guy. Maybe he could see about the chicklets and the cats."

"What about George and Mark, Sibyl and Abbie?"

"I guess. Not Giles. He accused me this morning of killing Kent. The nerve he has. That's probably why I'm here. What? Listen, Penny, they're gonna cut me off."

"We'll take care of everything, Nora, and I'll come down as soon as I can and send Kate. Don't say anything until she gets there."

"Thanks a bunch, Penny, I gotta ..." Her voice trailed off, and the line went dead.

The apartment was warm from the sun beating on the living area windows, but Penny was shivering when she got off the phone. First things first. She was starving and needed to think. She went into their kitchen and put the kettle on, pulled out the peppermint leaves and cut herself a piece of bread, which she covered with butter and her homemade peach marmalade. As she waited for the kettle, she decided to call Sammie next and see if she knew what Derek was up to. She should be home shortly. That would help her see what came next.

She had just poured boiling water over the peppermint leaves and settled the quilted cozy over her old blue teapot when the phone rang again.

It was Sammie. "Derek just called me in the car. I'm almost home. He says he arrested Nora, and they're processing her now down at the station."

"I just talked to her and was going to call you, then Kate. I'm trying to think what to do next. She didn't kill Kent, Sammie. What's Derek thinking?"

"He says he had to. He has a witness who says she put something in Kent's punch, and several witnesses say she hated Kent and said she was going to kill him."

"Hadn't we better pull some of the farmers together to help her? She needs someone to see about her chicks, her cats, her vegetables."

"Why don't we call some folks now and have a meeting tonight? I'd say here, but let's leave Derek out of it. This may be the dumbest thing he's ever done."

"Okay, over here. Kenneth should be back by five, and let's say at seven. I'll ask Andy and Leroy. She also mentioned Rosalind, Mark, George, Sibyl and Abbie. That's plenty."

"Okay. I'll call George, Sibyl and Abbie. You get the others. I'll bring snacks. You do tea and coffee. Our market is off to some rocky start. You think someone's trying to sabotage it?"

"I have no idea," said Penny. "It's all crazy. It's been crazy since Kent got involved. Even dead, he's still making trouble."

At least they'd stopped worrying about who was racist.

"See you in a bit, girlfriend."

"How can you be sure she's innocent, Penny?" demanded Kate. She'd found Kate Razor relaxing in her ironed jeans and a spotless white tee shirt in the living room of the large house next door. Their garage apartment was part of the house complex. Kate was reading and had a cup of steaming coffee on the table in front of her where her very white tennis shoes were also resting. She didn't seem a bit disturbed or energized by what Penny was saying.

"A gut feeling, Kate. I was standing right there when she was accused of dropping something in the man's punch. She wasn't even there most of the time. Kent was nearby. He had gall, for sure. She'd just told him to leave the market or she'd call the Sheriff, and he walked right up to her table and helped himself to punch. But Andy was right behind him, and Nora went and sat in her truck. She only came back to her table shortly before Kent left. Yes, she was angry, but she seemed quite content to leave him to Andy. It doesn't fit, Kate."

Kate picked up her coffee. "Kent Berryman sounds like a real jerk. I'll do what I can, Penny, but there must be some good reason Derek hauled her in. He's not impulsive."

"I know. Someone's accusing her. She thinks it's Giles, the modified seeds man."

"The modified what? Something's wrong with his sperm?" She grinned.

"No, no, Kate." Penny laughed, even though it was all so terrible, and it was her job to get Kate off the couch and down to the jail. Kate must be very tired. She didn't act like she wanted to move.

After Penny had explained exactly what Giles was doing with his genetically modified vegetables, Kate grinned even more. "Penny, you've given me so many impossible jobs, and I can't remember that I ever got paid, or only a pittance. Hell, I defended a Commissioner and God knows what all. Now we have an aging and sassy farmer accused of poisoning a county agent. How do you do it, Penny? You get yourself and me into these nearly inextricable situations, and you are always convinced they're innocent."

"Haven't they been?"

"Mostly, yes, or in effect. You really think she was simply pissed off, not out to kill him?"

"I do, Kate. I appreciate your help. I can't think who else could take this on and reassure Nora. She feels framed. She needs serious help."

"Don't they all?"

"It must be a terrible feeling if you're innocent."

Kate put her feet on the floor and stood up. "I'll do this for you, Penny, for nobody else. Let's hope she's as innocent as you're convinced she is. Guess I'd better put my suit back on."

Penny hugged her and left to call the farmers. It was already going on five.

The first person to arrive for their meeting was Herman, about whom they'd forgotten. Nora hadn't mentioned him, and neither she nor Sammie had called him. How had he learned about it? "Oh, hi, Herman. You're here for the meeting?"

"What else? I want to help Nora. Why didn't you call me? I had to learn it from Rosalind when I went over to trade vegetables for cheese."

Hopefully Rosalind knew what she was doing. He was on the board, and the others had known Herman longer than she had. Penny ushered him in, and Kenneth took his jacket and offered him coffee or tea. He obviously wanted to be there. He seemed fine with Nora as market manager, and Penny hoped they could keep him off the subject of politics. If he was one of their racists, she hadn't seen any signs.

Everyone they had asked came except Rosalind and Sibyl, who had cheese-making and baking preparations to do for the Saturday Sanford market. But Rosalind offered to manage the market in Nora's absence. Sibyl said she would send Nora some food, if she could receive it. She'd probably have cake or cookies left over as rain was predicted for Saturday morning.

Once they'd settled in the small living room, with Mark and Abbie on the floor, Andy explained to them Nora's situation at her farm. He and Leroy had been over to check on things. Leroy would see to the animals, but she would need her tomatoes, cukes and greens tended, and the ripe or mature ones picked, plus making sure everything had enough water. Mark and George volunteered to see to her vegetables and to sell hers along with their produce and plants.

Penny explained the legal situation and said maybe they could raise some money. Kate was good about *pro bono* work, but she shouldn't have to cover her miscellaneous costs, like copying.

Herman said, "I can't think who of us has any money unless Giles does. We're all scraping along, trying to keep ahead of our debts. Who has any extra money?"

Andy said, "Let's take it a day at a time. We'll figure something out about the money. I'm worried the customers will stay away. We need to stay upbeat. What do we have planned for Wednesday? Anything extra?"

"Henry's coming again," said Abbie. "At least he said he was."

"Good. None of us believe Nora did it, but if she has to be in jail, maybe people won't be scared to come," volunteered George. "We'd better not have punch though."

Herman laughed, and they all stared at him. "It's all from this genetically modified stuff and agribusiness. That's what Kent was all about, bigger and better and to hell with the little farmers trying to grow healthy food and feed their families."

Penny thought he had made his contribution and tried to get them back to the business of helping Nora, but Herman kept going. "Small farmers used to be the backbone of Shagbark's economy. Besides tobacco, cotton, corn, soybeans, chickens and cattle, both dairy and beef, we had loads of truck farmers. I remember as a child in the seventies, they'd set up along the road or in Riverdell. You could buy sweet corn, melons, tomatoes, cukes, several kinds of beans and peas, you name it. When my father was growing up on our farm during the Depression, there were no crop subsidies, but the people on farms survived best. They could grow their food and sell some of it, the ideal Paleo-Conservative economy. I don't hold with all this welfare and subsidies. It's pushing the good farmers out."

"Herman," Penny said. "We need to get back to Nora's problems and what we can do to help her." She glanced at Andy, who lifted his eyebrows.

"Nora's problems all came from people like Kent and Giles. These genetically modified crops will drive us all out. Don't you see it? Don't you want to know the truth? It's staring us in the face, and it will bring us all down. You'll realize when it's too late." Herman's face was red. He looked close to a stroke.

"Herman," said Andy firmly, "that's a different problem we can discuss another time. Let Penny …"

"No, it's all the same problem."

Penny saw Abbie and Mark exchange amused glances. Mark was still smiling when he said, "Maybe we'd better go for bottled water this week."

They all laughed. Then Penny seized the moment and said to Herman, "What can you do, Herman, to help Nora?"

His flow of words had stopped. He looked around at them suspiciously. He'd seen Abbie and Mark laughing the loudest. Maybe he thought they were all laughing at him.

George said, "I think we've covered the bases, but if we think of anything, Herman, we'll let you know." Herman scowled at him and stared at Abbie, who was whispering to Mark.

At this point someone knocked and pushed open the door. Kenneth, who was sitting at the kitchen table, jumped up and ushered in Sarah and Henry.

"Where's Seb?" asked Kenneth.

"With Grandma Belle. We can't stay, but Henry wanted to check about next Wednesday. You all want him to play again?"

"Definitely," said Andy. "Come on in. It really helps, Henry, to have an extra, like your music. It went down very well. Sadly, we have other problems." Then Andy explained about Nora's arrest and how they were all pitching in.

"That's awful," said Sarah. "What can we do?"

Penny said, "I think we have the bases covered, but if Henry comes and plays music, that's a lot."

"Will she have to pay a high-priced lawyer dude?" asked Henry.

"She has a *pro bono* lawyer, my friend Kate, but she'll need help with copying and other costs," Penny explained. She could see that Sarah was sincere about helping. But Henry didn't strike her as altruistic, so she was surprised when he looked at Sarah and said, "I could contribute any money I raise at the market."

Sarah beamed at him, and so did Abbie, whom he glanced at next. She also looked very happy with him and said, "Way to go, Henry." But it was Mark to whom she turned and whom she hugged.

Kate had said they'd have a better chance of seeing Nora if they went down to the police station and jail early that Saturday morning, so they left the house at 8:00 a.m. It was a ten-minute drive. Kate said she would also make an appointment to talk to the Assistant D.A. in charge of Nora's case and then drop Penny back at the house afterwards.

Penny dressed as she did for her teaching job in a black pantsuit and her relatively new blue turtleneck. Kate looked dressy, no matter what she wore, but she had swept her dark hair up and wore a white silk blouse with her navy suit and heels.

They waited a full half-hour before Derek came out and took them into an interview room. The decor was depressing: sheetrock, painted grey and peeling in places, an old, scarred wooden table chained to the concrete floor, and several folding chairs covered in chipped, brown paint. "I'll stay with you," he said. "The Sheriff is very anxious to clear this case, and he's nervous about all the procedures being followed to the letter."

"We understand, Derek. Thanks for arranging it. How does she seem to you?" asked Penny.

"Depressed," he said. "Once she stopped cussing us out, she hasn't said anything, and she's not eating much." Penny sat down on one chair, on the farther side of the table from the door.

"Jails are depressing," said Kate.

"Especially if you're innocent," added Penny. Derek lifted his eyebrows but forbore to comment. "I'll go get her. Be right back."

Nora seemed to have shrunk. Her complexion was pasty. She was wearing jeans with holes in the knees and an old windbreaker jacket that was torn in places, probably what she wore to garden in. Had she been gardening when they arrested her? Her tennis shoes were dirty and worn down at the heels. Her shoulders slumped as she slid into a chair opposite Penny and Kate while Derek waited at the door. There was a large window that looked black across from Penny, probably a one-way window. Penny wondered if anyone was observing them.

"Hi, Nora," Kate began cheerfully. "I've brought Penny to see you. She and the other farmers met last night, and they'll be taking care of the chicks, cats and vegetables. Right, Penny?"

Nora didn't look up, just examined her hands as if they might have a message for her. Derek had taken off the handcuffs he had used to lead her from her cell to this room. She rubbed at her wrists.

"Right," said Penny. What could she say to help Nora get a grip? Finally, she simply explained how they'd divided up the work the night before. She mentioned that Henry would contribute his income from singing to help pay Kate's expenses.

At that Nora looked up. "How will five dollars and seventy-five cents a week help you, Kate?" She sounded bitter, a new note in Nora. Usually she was jubilant, or if she was upset, angry.

Kate looked surprised briefly. Then her professional demeanor returned. "It all helps, Nora, but don't worry about it. I've had some fat clients lately. I can afford to help you."

"I ain't got shit," said Nora. "Sorry."

"It's okay, Nora," said Penny. "What can we bring you? A change of clothes, hairbrush? Tell us. Sibyl offered to send cake later today." She looked at Derek. He nodded.

"A cake with a knife in it?" Nora snorted.

"We check everything you receive," said Derek. "We'll check the cake. The sooner it arrives, the sooner Nora can have it. Also a comb is better here than a brush."

"Real food would be nice," said Nora. "Some tomatoes and cukes, fruit. This jail food is crap."

She seemed a little livelier for a minute but not much. "Tell Leroy and the others thanks. At least I don't have to worry about my babies dying or the tomatoes rotting on the vines." Then she slumped again.

"If you think of anything else, Nora," urged Penny, "tell Kate. We'll get it to you if we possibly can."

Derek gestured to his watch that her time was up. Nora staggered as she got to her feet. Weak from hunger? "Don't stop eating, Nora," said Penny. "Keep your health up, and do your meditation."

"What the hell good will it do here?" Nora said as Derek clipped on the handcuffs. "Just make sure everybody knows I didn't bump off Kent. I'm a Buddhist, for God's sake. I don't believe in killing anything, not even insects like Kent."

Eight

Wednesday, April 26, fourth market. Another perfect April afternoon, and the market went extremely well, considering Kent's death and Nora's arrest. Kenneth had been there, acting like a customer who found everything so interesting that he couldn't drag himself away. Sarah and Seb arrived just before six to pick up Henry, who was singing in a soft croon one of Sarah's favorite Jim Morrison songs, "Light My Fire." But when Sarah saw the way he looked at Abbie as he sang, she handed Seb to Penny and marched over to where Henry had set up his mike.

Abbie was sitting cross-legged at his feet. She had been there for at least half an hour. Seb started crying, sensing his mother's anger even before she started yelling, "You told me that was my song, Henry! Why in the hell are you singing it to Abbie?"

If Henry hadn't shrugged, and Abbie hadn't jumped to her feet guiltily and gone back to her mother's table, things might have played out differently.

"Mama!" wailed Seb. Penny carried him away, walked around Leroy's van and headed out onto the open field next to the market shelter. Where could she take him to get out of earshot?

"It's okay, Seb. Mama's talking to Henry. She'll be back in a minute." But talking was hardly the way to describe the screech Sarah's voice had become.

"Just get out! I'm sick of you, Henry Sutton. Get out of my life, and stay out."

"It's only a song, Sarah. What's wrong with you? Abbie just likes to hear me sing. She was just listening. Is that a crime? You're the one acting like a bitch."

"And you're a two-timing bastard. I never want to see you again!"

Seb was still wailing, and Penny couldn't walk fast enough to get them some distance away. She'd gotten part-way down the road away from the market when Seb got very quiet, and his sobs gradually subsided as she murmured to him. She had circled around and almost reached the entrance gate to the market again when Seb lifted his head and said, "Mama!" in an entirely different voice.

Penny turned. Sarah was coming up to them. Seb stretched out his arms, and Penny handed him over.

"Sebbie, it's okay. We'll go home and eat supper. Thanks, Mom. I hate Henry. I can't trust him. I came to give him a ride, but forget that. He can find someone else to give him rides and feed him, put a roof over his head."

Realizing she'd been right about Henry's tendency to sponge didn't help now. Penny wished Sarah and Seb hadn't had to suffer.

"I'm sure Henry will cope, Sarah. You and Seb go on home. It will be okay."

"Thanks, Mom. If he asks, just say I told you I never want to see him again–ever. I mean it, Mom."

"I can tell," said Penny and kissed them both before heading back to help Leroy pack up.

Leroy walked from behind his van to meet Penny. "Is she okay?"

"Yes. Sounds like she's done with Henry though."

"Just as well," said Leroy. "He didn't take any notice of Seb. I've got us packed up. We sold everything but one dozen eggs. I'll give them to Sarah. Oh, and Kenneth caught a ride back with Andy. He said he'd start the tea. He means your supper, right?"

"Right. Okay, I'm ready. Let's go home." Penny looked around their spot, which was whistle clean, and waved to Sammie and Rosalind, who were waiting in their vehicles for Penny and Leroy to pull out.

She'd just shut her door and Leroy had let out the clutch when Henry ran up to her window. "Penny, can I catch a ride? Sarah was supposed to take me back, but she's left."

He was pleading. Did he not understand what had just happened? She wanted nothing more to do with him. "Sarah told me she doesn't want you at her place anymore."

He looked astounded. Hadn't he heard Sarah when she shouted at him to get out of her life? Did he tune other people out that easily?

Leroy gunned his engine. "Other farmers are waiting for us so they can get out, Penny."

Henry reached in his pocket and pulled out a fistful of bills and change. He thrust it toward Penny. "Here's for Nora's lawyer."

Penny looked at Leroy. "Can't we give him a ride?"

"Not to Sarah's."

"Henry, you can ride home with us, but that's the best we can do, and we need to leave now. We're holding up Rosalind and Sammie."

"Thanks." Henry grabbed his guitar case and portable amplifier and pulled open the door while Penny squeezed over to the center of the bench seat. Henry had just pulled the door to when Leroy let out the clutch again.

Penny took the money and put it into the central pocket of her purse so she wouldn't mix it up with their market money. Leroy was looking stonily ahead.

"I don't know why she's so mad," began Henry. Leroy shook his head but his eyes didn't leave the road. Penny couldn't think of anything to say, and she didn't want to help him understand Sarah. Sarah had been very clear, yet he genuinely sounded bewildered. He must be pretty self-absorbed or dense if he couldn't follow what had happened to set Sarah yelling.

"My take was pretty good," he said. "I think people like my music."

Ordinarily Penny would have agreed, but all she could manage as she remembered Sarah's fury was, "Um," that wonderfully ambiguous British expression. Leroy said nothing.

Henry must have interpreted their silence as encouragement because he added, "I thought the market was the best yet. Maybe it helped that Nora wasn't there. She really stomps people, doesn't she?"

Leroy said angrily, "Leave Nora out of it if you don't want me to put you out."

They all subsided into an uncomfortable silence.

"Problem is," Henry said a few minutes later when neither Penny nor Leroy had picked up the conversation. "I did give you my take for Nora, but I'm broke now. I thought I'd have supper with Sarah. Abbie's mother gave me some cake, and that skinny guy with all the tomatoes gave me a bag of them."

"There you are then. You've got your supper," said Penny.

"Want to go potluck?" asked Henry. Leroy stiffened and drove faster.

"Sorry, Henry," Penny said. "You're on your own. We'll drop you at Whitfield Mill Road. It'll be up to you from there."

"Could I call Sarah from your place?"

"No, Henry. She doesn't want to see you or talk to you. She was very clear about that, and I'd advise you to respect her wishes."

The van lurched around the last corner and swung into the No. 7 Whitfield Mill Road driveway. Leroy braked abruptly.

"Doesn't Andy live next door here?"

"Why do you ask?"

"I might drop in."

Penny wanted to tell him to leave Andy alone, too, but that wasn't her problem. Andy and Jan would cope with him just fine. "They may not be home." She wished they weren't, but probably they were. They'd passed their vehicles as they drove in. She wished she hadn't persuaded Leroy to give him a ride. She could tell that Leroy was thoroughly fed up with him.

Leroy snapped, "Hop out. Penny and I need to unload."

Henry got out and walked across to the Styles' front door.

"He'll mooch off Andy," said Leroy as he pulled forward, then backed up to Belle's and Kate's garage. Penny had seen the front door open next door and Henry go in.

"Shall I call and warn them?"

"Nah. Let's unload. I'm going over to Sarah's to take her these eggs, make sure they're okay."

Penny and Kenneth were having lapsang souchong with the first strawberries and cream after their Wednesday night fry-up special when Derek and Sammie turned up. "Mind if we pick your brains? I want to hear Kenneth's thoughts and get both your impressions of the farmers," explained Derek. "Are we interrupting your supper?"

"No, and of course, you're welcome. Tea? I'm afraid we've eaten all the strawberries."

"Tea is great," said Sammie.

They settled around the kitchen table. Kenneth started. "Everything seemed to go well today as far as I could tell. Nice day. Steady stream of customers until about five-thirty. All the farmers were very pleasant to me and their customers."

Penny agreed. "The only fight was when Sarah arrived to pick up Henry when he was singing to Abbie, but most of the farmers were packing up by then. It was right before six."

Kenneth added, "He asked for it. He was acting far too enthralled with Abbie, and she with him. I think Sarah has finally wised up to what a moocher he is. I left with Andy right after she left. We followed her home to be sure she was okay."

"So that was why they disappeared so fast." Sammie looked worried. "She's okay? You're sure?"

"I expect so," said Penny, "with all the people checking on her." She got up to put the kettle on again. "Leroy went over, too, and Henry's at Andy's. He rode home with us. He gave me about ten dollars he raised playing today, then said he was broke.

Leroy and I wouldn't share our supper, so he ended up with Andy. I'm pretty sure they fed him."

"A bit of a flim-flam man," commented Sammie. "Where did he come from anyway?"

"Sarah hasn't said, and she may not know. She brought him over a few weeks ago. She was quite taken with him, but I admit I was skeptical." She looked at Kenneth, who nodded.

"Very skeptical," he said. "Your intuition was right on target again. He took me in, too."

"Leroy and I both noticed how he ignored Seb, and Seb ignored him."

"What's his full name? I'll run him through our computer," said Derek.

"Henry Sutton." Penny poured more boiling water into the tea pot and replaced the cozy. "He seems harmless enough. He plays the guitar well, but he's a moocher. I'm glad Sarah finally saw it."

"You don't think he could have had anything to do with Kent Berryman's death?" persisted Derek.

"No," said Penny slowly, sitting back down. "Although he was there, but it was only for the first time, and he came to play. He'd been there briefly the week before. What possible motive could he have had?"

"Tell me more about how you and Kenneth see the other farmers. If not Henry, it must have been one of the farmers because Berryman left before any customers came in, right? Who was around when he was there?" He reached for the pot and offered tea to Sammie and took some for himself. "I've been over this ground before, but I'm missing something."

Penny thought how things had changed over the years between her and Derek. He still didn't like her to get involved and was furious when Sammie did, but she had figured out the killer too many times for him not to want to pick her brain, if not share his key information with her.

He caught her eye. "Penny, I'm not asking you to investigate, just share your insights."

"He's smarter than he once was," quipped Sammie. "He talks to you first now."

"Not true," said Derek. "Let her and Kenneth talk, woman. You've already had your say, several times."

Sammie rolled her eyes but didn't say anything. She was wearing a chartreuse tee, navy blue shorts and bright green sandals. Normally, she was irrepressible. She looked far from compliant now. Her dark eyes sparkled with mischief.

"Let Kenneth go first," Penny said. "It was his first market. I've been telling him about the various farmers, and he has been at two of our meetings."

"I don't know much, Derek. I've been observing, that's all. I'm not sure what it all means yet."

"Just talk, man," said Derek.

"I discount Andy, who came late, and Kent left pretty soon after Andy tried to persuade Kent to leave. I like Rosalind very much. She's kind, and the children swarm to her. No way she could be a poisoner."

"I also leave out Andy and Rosalind," said Derek. "What about Herman Hicks? What do you make of him?"

"Let's see. Is he the Paleo-Conservative, Penny?"

"Yes, very much so. He distrusts Giles, the modified seeds man. He didn't like Kent either. He associates them both with agri-business and driving out small farmers."

"Could he have done it? Was he there near the punch?" pressed Derek.

"I guess he could have," said Penny. "He always gets there early, and he was drinking punch and standing around when Kent was at Nora's table and left his cup there for a short time. But I doubt very much he'd try to poison anyone. He sounds off a lot, but he's basically pretty shy, I think."

"Poisoners can be shy and sly," said Derek. "Basically, they're sneaky, as a rule."

"Suspect him if you wish, but I doubt it, Derek. And I'm sure Nora didn't do it."

Sammie nodded when Derek wasn't watching her.

"Nora won't talk to me, even when Kate's present," Derek complained. "She acts depressed to me. If she didn't do it, why doesn't she help me?"

"Of course, she's depressed, Derek. Why should she help you if you charge her with the murder? Try letting her out. It's terrible to be accused when you're innocent."

Derek shrugged. "I have a witness who says he saw her do it."

"Who's your witness?"

"I can't tell you."

"Giles? Kent's friend?"

"I can't tell you."

"He might be lying, Derek, if it's Giles. He doesn't like Nora. He told her he thought she did it."

Kenneth asked, "More tea, anyone? Let's move to some of these others. George the plant man. What about him, Penny? He was around that punch table, wasn't he?"

"Yes, but he's a very nice man."

"I thought you told me he was upset when Kent made him move so the bread and jam lady could take his spot."

"True, he didn't like that, but he had his spot back the week Kent got poisoned. I mean, Kent did make people angry, but you need someone with a bigger grudge than that, Derek. A lot of people get angry, most of us, but very few people kill other people. It's either a diseased mind or a huge sense of resentment, injustice, jealousy–something."

Derek sipped his tea, holding her eyes. "I know that, Penny, but sometimes we don't know what all is going on in someone's mind. I have to consider all the possibilities. I'm trying to be fair, Penny, in case Nora didn't do it. If not Nora, then who?"

"Giles also seems unlikely, and Sibyl, because they got on well with Kent," said Penny, "and Kent played favorites with them against George, for instance."

"Could Giles have done it and be covering up by accusing Nora?" asked Kenneth. They now all knew who was accusing Nora to Derek. Had Kenneth known all along and been sworn to secrecy by Derek? If so, it hadn't worked.

"Possible," said Derek. He glanced at Penny. What he meant was: help me here. "I don't know these folks well enough."

"Abbie was helping Henry set up that day about that time," said Penny. "She seemed drawn to Kent. I remember she was talking to him that afternoon, but mostly she was with her mother or Henry. Something's bothering me, some detail that may be important, but I can't get hold of it. Does anyone want more tea? Shall I make a fresh pot?"

Sammie shook her head. Derek stood. "We won't keep you, but if you think of anything else, please call. You'd do her and us a big favor, Penny, if you could persuade Nora to talk to us. I mean, of course, with Kate present. She's not helping herself."

"You said she was depressed, Derek."

"It sure looks that way."

"I'll go see her. If you let her go, she'd probably be very helpful." Penny grinned.

Derek bristled. "I can't do that, Penny."

Sammie put her hand on his arm. "Penny knows that." She made a face at Penny, which Derek couldn't see as he turned to the door and felt in his pocket for his car keys.

Then he turned back. "I'm just asking for observations, Penny. Don't start some harebrained scheme to uncover the murderer. Whoever this is, you don't want his venom turned on you. This isn't someone to mess with." His voice was brittle with worry.

"I'll walk you down," said Kenneth and followed him out the door.

"It's driving him crazy, Penny," said Sammie. "He needs help, but he's trying not to grovel." She laughed and hugged her friend. "I think we might have to figure this one out our own selves. What say?"

Penny smiled. "I was thinking the same thing. I'll see if I can get Nora to talk to me tomorrow."

"Call me."

"I will."

Nine

Wednesday afternoon, May 1. fifth market. There hadn't been a Maypole in Riverdell since Penny had moved there over eleven years earlier, although she remembered them from her grade school days. There were streamers attached to a pole, and the third grade girls in pretty dresses danced around the pole until it was wound entirely with their pastel crepe paper streamers.

It had been Sammie's idea to invite all the children at Riverdell Elementary to come to the market, and those who wished could dance around the Maypole. She said she didn't want to lose the tradition. Henry had refused to provide any more music, so Sammie brought a CD of some lively traditional tunes like "She'll Be Coming 'Round the Mountain," "Daisy, Daisy" and "Oh! Susanna."

Sammie was early, and when Penny, Kenneth and Leroy drove in, she already had her CD player plugged in and the extension cord looped over the rafters with Andy's help. She waved happily at them. "I need you guys to help me rig this pole. Andy said we could put it here, just inside the customer gate, but how do we make it stand up?"

"Do you have a post-hole digger?" asked Leroy, who had walked over.

"No. What's that? I have a shovel, but the dirt's rock hard."

"A digger makes it easier," Leroy explained. "I have one back at the garage. If you'll help us unload, I'll go back and get it."

Today Sammie had bouquets of daisies, Gaillardia and Cosmos in white, red and yellow. Her shorts and sleeveless top matched, of course. Her shirt was yellow and white, and her shorts the reddish orange of the Gaillardia. She wore yellow and white daisy earrings and red sandals, and today her hair was cut close to her head, no wig. "I tried digging a hole with my spade, but I can't even dent this clay."

"I'll bring a pickaxe, too," said Leroy, and soon he'd driven out to get his tools while Penny organized their lettuce, bunches of carrots, beets and plastic bags of sugar snap peas.

"It's gotten so warm, the lettuce will bolt soon," she said to Sammie. Kenneth had gone down to the front of the market to talk to Giles and George. As soon as he was out of earshot, Sammie asked, "Have you learned anything?"

"Not really. It's a busy time for me and you, too. I'm trying to get all my grades averaged and the extra credit papers marked before I give exams next week. At least I've finished classes. I have tomorrow and Friday off. If it weren't for Nora, I wouldn't be very motivated to find Kent's killer. What a pain he was."

"I know what you mean, but Derek says Nora has closed down completely. She's no help at all. If she would try to remember everything that day, he might be able to let her go, but keep that to yourself. He'd kill me if he knew I told you he's beginning to agree with you that someone else poisoned Kent."

"But who?" Penny adjusted the blackboard of their prices where she'd hung it from the wire over their table.

"For all we know, Nora knows, and there she is, rotting away, hiding from all of us."

"I went to see her last week, but she barely talked to me. She's so passive. It's not like her." Penny was about to say, "Let's go see her tomorrow," when Giles walked up.

"Afternoon, ladies. You all have sugar snaps already?"

"We do," said Penny. "Leroy got them in early, and it's been such a warm spring. Organic, too." She wondered if he'd react. He shrugged.

"You one of them sustainable folks?"

"Yes," said Penny quietly. "We live next door to Andy, and he's taught us how to farm without dangerous chemicals. Of course, Leroy's chickens give us a rich compost, too, and we do a cover crop through the winter."

"I thought so," sneered Giles. "The smart way to go is to get these seeds they have now where the chemicals can be sprayed, and it doesn't hurt the vegetables, like my tomatoes and collards."

Sammie had left. Penny didn't want to take on Giles's attitudes toward farming. They saw things so differently. He made her want to argue. She couldn't resist saying, "It doesn't keep the poisons out of the soil, air and water, though, and we hope we'll be able to live a few generations more on this earth and not leave our children a polluted environment."

"Too late. It's already polluted," Giles said, "but what do you and these other new-fangled farmers know about sustainable? I come from a long line of farmers. My great, great granddaddy got his start in 1866, soon as the Civil War ended and he could plow again. We been in Shagbark ever since, through recessions and depressions, and we're still here. That's sustainability, the only kind that makes any sense."

Penny was aware that Leroy had backed in and walked past her with his double-handled posthole digger and pickaxe.

She was glad Herman hadn't arrived. He'd have a fit if he heard Giles, but then she heard the sound of a large engine and turned to see Herman backing in his big blue pickup next to them. How could she get rid of Giles? She looked down to the front of the market. Kenneth was chatting with George and Sibyl, who'd just driven in. He had the art of getting people to talk to him. So did she, but what she needed now was the art of making Giles *not* want to talk to her or stay on this theme of his version of sustainability. His views were rather a slap in the face to all the organic farmers present who were so conscientious about avoiding pesticides and chemical fertilizers, not to mention genetically modified seeds.

"I'd better see how the Maypole is coming along," she said. "Excuse me, Giles." It was cowardly, but if he had no one to harangue, maybe he'd leave. If she kept listening, Herman would get pulled in. They didn't need another fight.

But Giles followed her over. Sweat was pouring off Leroy as he worked the digger into the clay. She could see where he'd used a pickaxe to get the hole started.

Giles watched a minute and then said, "Seems a little silly, a Maypole at the market." Leroy ignored him. So did Sammie, who walked back to her table to arrange her bouquets. They all heard Giles say, "They must think Nora killed Kent. They sure are hanging onto her."

Leroy kept digging, but now he was jabbing viciously at the ground. Penny and Sammie exchanged worried looks.

Sammie said lightly, "The idea of the pole is to draw the children and pull their parents in to buy our veggies, flowers, eggs, cheese."

This did not distract Giles, who said, "I didn't think colored had Maypoles."

Sammie looked shocked, then furious. "The correct term is African American, and yes, we did. Shagbark schools were desegregated in 1970. We all danced the Maypole."

She turned away to her table.

Giles shrugged. "I don't get all this political correctness stuff."

Penny said, "It's not political. It's called being considerate of other people. She's drawing customers for you, too, Giles."

He shrugged again. "Maybe." Then he added, "As for me, I'm danged sure Nora killed Kent. She hated his guts. What's holdin' up the trial? That's what I want to know."

Penny thought of Shakespeare's character Cassius and his "lean and hungry look." That's what Giles had, and he was determined to stir them up one way or another. She blurted out, "Nora's innocent, that's why, and they have no evidence against her, Giles. Don't go around bad-mouthing her. That doesn't help anything."

She knew she had little chance of changing his mind or his behavior, but he offended her, and she wasn't the only one. Suddenly Leroy dropped the digger handles and turned on Giles. "Just shut up. Leave Sammie alone. Nora, too. Nora's got enough troubles without you talking behind her back. We're working our tails off to attract customers here. The least you could do is shut your mouth and stop harassing the rest of us."

"I don't take insults lying down," Giles said. "Step outside this fence, and I'll take you on right now."

Leroy picked up the digger where it had fallen. He spat on the ground, nowhere near Giles, but Giles jumped back. "Son of a bitch." His face turned beet red and his fists were clenched. He was shaking with anger.

Leroy said nothing, just spat again, as if making his point, then turned and focused again on the digging. Giles apparently saw no interest on anyone else's face. Penny walked back to their table. Rosalind and Mark were arriving. Maybe their presence would help calm things down. But where was Kenneth? Herman, however, had heard something. He set down a crate of broccoli and walked over to Penny. "What's coming down?"

"Giles is trying to start a fight with Leroy. Best to ignore him."

When would she learn enough about the male animal to understand what set off the rage component of their testosterone? Herman didn't even hear the "ignore him" part. He walked straight over to Giles. "Leave Leroy alone, Dunn."

"He insulted me. I only said what's obvious. Nora's in jail, ain't she? It ain't only me thinks she killed Kent."

"But you're probably the reason they arrested her. What you got against Nora?" demanded Herman.

"She's a bitch, that's all, a loud-mouth bitch, can't appreciate a good county agent, hell, can't appreciate a good man when she sees one." He looked over at Leroy as if hoping to stir him up again. The man was like a kid poking a stick into a hornet's nest to see what would happen.

Leroy stopped digging and stared at him. Herman had no similar impulse to be quiet. "Probably those modified seeds destroyed your brain, Dunn. Nora's a good person, and she's a fantastic organic grower. You ever noticed how many people line up for her tomatoes? It's because they taste good, and they're soft like tomatoes are supposed to be, not hard and tasteless like yours."

Giles smiled, though Penny was sure he was furious. His red face now had white blotches in it. Herman walked right past him over to Leroy. "Want me to dig for awhile?"

"No, I've almost got a deep enough hole."

As Herman turned back to return to setting up his table, Giles erupted. "You sustainable people are all alike. Hell, you don't know peanuts about real sustainability. My farm's been in the Dunn family five generations. That's your dang sustainability."

Herman turned, shaking with rage. "You are full of shit, Giles. Go back to your billiard ball, tasteless tomatoes and leave the rest of us and Nora the hell alone. You know as much about organic farming as—as a rat. That's what you remind me of. Even a rat wouldn't want to eat your tomatoes. Probably kill them in no time like white bread does."

"You wanna fight, Hicks? I've had enough."

Kenneth appeared as Andy drove up and parked just outside the customer gate.

"What seems to be the problem, Mr. Hicks?" asked Kenneth.

Andy strode through the customer gate and stopped on the other side of Giles. "What's happening, Giles?"

"Hassel insulted me, then Hicks took his turn. I'm fed to the teeth. Hang it." He stalked away.

Slowly the farmers who had walked up to see what was going on, turned and went back to their tables. Sammie, shaking, held the Maypole while Leroy and Herman tamped in the dirt with their boots. Kenneth and Andy turned to Penny. "What exactly happened here?" asked Andy. She told them. One racist and a false witness identified.

Leroy and Penny arrived at the Riverdell Police Station and jail at eight the next morning. On the way home from the market, Leroy had proposed they visit Nora. He'd steal an hour or so from his current carpentry job. Penny was free. They were allowed to see Nora after a fifteen-minute wait. Penny had seen her the week before, but she was shocked at how sick she looked. She'd been in jail only ten days, but her normally tanned face was pasty. Her brown eyes looked dull and bloodshot. She had clearly lost weight off her slightly plump frame, and her short, curly hair was matted. Had she even run the comb they'd brought her through it? She now wore the standard issue orange jumpsuit.

Penny glanced at Leroy, who looked shocked. He said nothing, so Penny plunged in, trying to disguise her worry. "Hi, Nora, we came to check on you. Are you getting enough to eat? Can we bring you anything?"

Nora didn't say anything at first. Penny waited. Then, "No, thanks. Did Lieutenant Hargrave tell you when he's letting me go?" She said *Lieutenant* savagely.

"He says you could help him more."

"That's his excuse. I didn't do a damn thing but tell Kent to take his sorry ass off the premises."

"What can you remember? We're all trying to remember the exact sequence that afternoon."

"My mind's shot, Penny. Yours would be, too, in this hell hole. I can't sleep. The food's garbage."

"I brought you some hardboiled eggs, spinach, sugar snaps and carrots," Leroy said. "They're checking them now."

"Do they think you put a weapon in a pea pod?" asked Nora. "I complain, but no one listens. Derek came and asked me a lot of questions. He's talking about a probable cause hearing, but he hasn't told me when. How am I supposed to help them solve it if I'm stuck here?"

"You could talk to Derek or even to Kate. You might remember something that would help find the real killer."

"Sounds like a lot of work," said Nora and examined her dirty fingernails.

"We're all trying to help, Sammie and I and the others. Don't despair, Nora. We know you didn't do it. Keep your spirits up." Easy to say, thought Penny, but not so easy to do in Nora's situation.

"Maybe this will help," said Leroy, and he pulled a small, sleepy chick out of his pocket.

Nora put out her hands and held the chick close to her cheek. "A baby. Yours, Leroy?"

"Just hatched yesterday. Her name's Nora."

"My chicklets doing okay?"

"They're growing fast, Nora. We got to get you out of here." He looked around at the bleak, stained walls and down at the ground-in dirt on the warped linoleum.

"It's awful being stuck here," said Nora. "I'm just rotting away. I feel blind. No light at the end of the tunnel for me, but thanks for bringing the chick, the veggies and eggs. Real food is so amazing after this jail slop."

"I can bring more," said Leroy.

"Only if you have time. I know you've got extra now taking care of my place and yours, too."

"Mark and George took your tomatoes and greens to yesterday's market," said Penny, "and the money's going to your legal fund, unless you want to do something else with it, Nora."

"Let Kate have it. She's good, Penny, but everything's stacked against me."

"Don't say that, Nora. You can help yourself here. Try to think back and reconstruct what you remember. There must be some detail that could make all the difference. Okay?"

"Penny, my mind is shot. Lay off."

The guard knocked, and Nora handed the chick back to Leroy, who quickly tucked it in his pocket. How had he smuggled it in?

"Time's up, ma'am."

Nora shook her head, and tears glistened in her eyes.

Penny hugged her impulsively, and Leroy said woodenly, "I'll bring you food every day. Please eat, Nora."

The most hopeful sign they'd had was the small smile she gave Leroy before she walked out the door.

Ten

Thursday Evening, May 2. It was one of those perfect spring evenings that made you glad you lived in North Carolina. They'd gone onto Daylight Savings Time in early April, and it was light now and often still in the seventies until eight in the evening.

Kenneth had gone down to work with Leroy and Andy in the garden. They were cultivating and creating the rows for the summer garden's tomatoes, peppers, cucumbers, bush beans, and crookneck squash. Penny had taken her tea to the end of the couch near the window that looked down on the driveway and the garden beyond. The men's voices and the sound of the rototiller drifted up along with the fragrance of honeysuckle in bloom along the orchard fence.

She felt so relaxed and contented. The problems were still out there, including Nora's depression, Sarah's fight with Henry, and the tensions that still plagued the market, but her semester's teaching was done. Only finals remained to give and grade, starting on Monday. She could sit and drink her tea. She could write. She didn't have to move.

Then someone knocked on the door. She hadn't heard a car drive in. She pushed herself to her feet just as Sammie opened the screen door and stuck her head in. "Can I drop in unannounced?"

Besides Kenneth, probably only Sammie was truly welcome at that moment. "Come on in. I'm sitting here glorying in doing absolutely nothing."

"I'll drink to that. Sit down. Tea still in the pot?"

"Yes, help yourself. I don't know how hot it is."

"It's fine." Sammie sank into the armchair closest to the window and to Penny. "All done, bar the shouting?"

"Yes, just exams left."

Sammie grinned wickedly. "I did my exams this week and turned the grades in today."

"You're kidding?"

"No. Quite a few of us do. Lets us and the kids out early. You're so 'by the book,' Penny."

Penny sighed. "Probably. I want to give them one more chance to do well."

"Was I right when I told you last year that the kids would end up loving you, even strict as you are?"

"I don't know how they feel, with a few exceptions, but I know I've fallen in love with them."

"You're a real asset to the college, Penny. Keep your standards high."

"Maybe they're too high?"

"Never. But listen, we've got to get our market murder solved. Morale is low, even if we did get right many children to come dance and sing yesterday. Lots of parents were there, some who'd never been to the market before. I think most farmers had a reasonable take."

"Nora's morale is scraping the bottom of the barrel, for sure. She looks terrible, Sammie, and she won't try to remember the sequence of events. She's frustrating Derek."

"You got that right, girl."

"What can we do?"

"Let's talk to everybody again."

"Even though Derek doesn't want us to investigate?"

"Oh, we're not investigating, Penny. He wants us to observe, but in order to observe, we have to talk to people, right? And observe their reactions. Forget Nora. If we can give Derek some new ammunition, he'll let go of Nora in a hot minute. As for us and our observations, you know he never carries out his threats. He just thrashes around for an hour or so and then forgets all about it. You should know that by now."

"So what's our next move? More tea?"

"Absolutely."

"Let me put the kettle on and make a fresh pot."

"While you do that, I'll make a list of people we need to talk to."

"Let's leave Giles alone. He stirs up the others, and he's convinced Nora's guilty. He's like a broken record."

"Okay, for now. Maybe I'll tackle him later, depending on what we learn."

"You can stand him?"

"I can tolerate him long enough to find out if he saw anything."

"Okay, then he's all yours. He unnerves me."

The kettle whistled. Penny rinsed the pot, tossed the old tea in the sink, added boiling water to the pot to warm it, threw that out, spooned in some lemon ginger tea and filled the pot.

"Smells great. Okay, which farmers you want?"

"I'll take George and Herman. They were right there at Nora's table."

"Can you take Henry, too?"

"I think we've lost Henry. Sarah tossed him out, and I haven't seen him since last Wednesday."

"I saw them down at Food Plus this evening about five-thirty."

"Together?"

"Yes, ma'am."

"Rats. I was hoping he'd left town. I don't think he's good for Sarah."

Penny carried the pot in its cozy over to the window sill, and they sat down again.

"He must be hard to resist." They both laughed. "I heard your Sarah telling him off last week. She can really let it fly when she's angry. Where does she get that?"

"Me, probably," said Penny.

"Mild-mannered Penny?"

Penny poured them each some tea. "I lose it sometimes, you know that, Sammie. More often when I was Sarah's age. Anyway, I'll talk to Henry. I don't like him, but if he's back with Sarah, I'll probably be seeing him. Okay, who else?"

"I'll call Mark, Rosalind, Sibyl and Abbie."

"Sibyl wasn't there early enough, was she? She usually gets there later."

"I can find out. I do remember that Abbie and Henry were setting up his speakers, and that was pretty early. I can't actually remember exactly when the others got there. Derek talked to everybody, but I'll check all that."

"Good."

"Listen, I'll go home and do this right now. Derek has some meeting tonight."

"You've revved me up. It's nearly dark, but I think Kenneth is going with Leroy to check on Nora's animals, so I'll have a little more quiet time. I'll see if I can get a few calls in."

Sammie stood and stretched. "I'm off then, girlfriend. Call me."

The only farmer Penny reached by phone that Thursday evening was Herman.

"Oh, I remember it all, Penny, clear as a bell. You and Leroy opened the gate. I was right behind George and Giles–well, nearly. You and they were there when I got there."

"Do you remember when Kent showed up?"

"It was before Nora, 'cause when she drove in and saw him, she tore down there and laid into him, told him to leave. Then him and Giles laughed at Nora. Them two, Berryman and Dunn, are thick as thieves. They are thieves, too, so help me God. Those modified people shouldn't be allowed to farm, much less sell food. Their pollen shouldn't be spread around, and that weird food they grow, more like plastic than food, can't be healthy. It's disgusting."

She wanted to steer him back to the sequence of events at the third market. "Do you remember when Sibyl and Abbie got there?"

"I saw Abbie helping Henry set up. I was worried about her. I don't trust that Henry. When was that? She was down at our end for awhile."

"Henry came not too long after we did, I think," said Penny. "Andy and Nora were late. So Nora came after Kent, but I think Sibyl arrived a little before Nora. I think Kent was talking to Sibyl when Nora barreled down there. Am I remembering that right?"

"Abbie did help Henry, and Henry was still setting up after we started drinking Nora's punch. Giles is the one I'd arrest. I hate his guts. He'd do anything to protect his precious killer seeds. Growing that stuff should be illegal. It's a lot more dangerous than marijuana."

"But isn't Giles a friend of Kent's? He's the one accusing Nora of killing Kent," protested Penny.

"People have been known to kill their friends," said Herman. "Thieves fall out, you know." He sounded smug. What was he implying?

Then Herman launched into another long invective against Giles. Penny waited for him to pause and then said quickly, "Thanks for talking to me, Herman. I'll call again if I have any more questions."

Penny was more confused than ever. She decided to write down what she knew about who had arrived when. It was nine already, and when the screen door opened, she thought it was Kenneth returning, but in walked Henry and Sarah, carrying Seb.

Penny was tired, and she didn't want to see Henry. Why had she agreed to talk to him, sponger that he was? He looked not the least bit abashed, even gloating, as if he knew she didn't like him and had outwitted her and her daughter. Sarah seemed embarrassed. She didn't look at her mother. Penny had no idea what to say to her. It was her grandson who kept her from saying, "This isn't a good time."

Once his mother set him down, Seb ran to where Penny was sitting on the couch and climbed up beside her. "Story, Gamma?"

"What's up, Sarah?" Sarah came farther into the room, Henry waiting by the door. Probably Sarah had picked up on her mood.

"You look tired, Mom."

"I am. What can I do for you?" She must want something. She didn't usually come by this late on a week night.

"Sebbie's got a sore throat and a little fever. He's not real sick, but I don't like to take him to daycare when he's got a sore throat. They'll probably call and tell me to come get him. Could you keep him tomorrow? I know it's last minute."

Penny had looked forward to a free Friday. She could catch up on things neglected in the last busy weeks of school and help get the summer garden in, a day to choose what she'd do instead of moving pell mell from one item on her list to the next.

"Froat hurt," Seb announced, pointing down his throat.

"I guess, Sarah. What time will you pick him up?"

"I'll bring him at eight and get him at five-thirty, if that's okay?"

Penny nodded.

Seb asked, "Story, Gamma?"

"Come on, Seb. We'll have a story at home. You'll see Grandma in the morning." Sarah scooped him up.

Penny remembered she was supposed to question Henry. What she wanted to ask was why he didn't stay away from her daughter and grandson, but instead she said, "Have a seat for a minute. I want to ask you something, since you're here."

Sarah walked back into the living area, but Henry turned to the door. "Stay a minute, Henry. Come sit down. We're trying to understand what happened at the market right before Kent Berryman got poisoned. I wanted to see what you remembered."

He shook his head and shrugged. "I can't remember anything. Which market?"

"The third one, the first one you sang at."

"I went and I played, starting at four. That's all I remember."

"Abbie helped you set up, right?"

"Yeah? So?" He hadn't moved. He didn't want her asking questions. Of course, Abbie was probably a sensitive subject. He was looking at Sarah.

"Was Kent Berryman there when you were setting up?"

"Who?"

"The man who got poisoned. Tall, red hair, bald."

"Old guy Abbie was talking to later?"

"Probably. He wasn't a farmer. He was a poultry agent. He left before you would have started playing."

"I'm not sure. I was doing my set-up."

"You were right across from our table, Leroy's and mine. When Nora got there, she had punch for us and the customers."

"I guess. I didn't even know about the punch. When was that?"

Surely he had seen the punch. Nora had announced it when the market opened. "It was a little after three when Nora arrived. I helped set up the punch, and some of the other farmers were standing around drinking it, and Kent Berryman, too."

He shrugged again. He was still standing by the door. Sarah looked worried, glancing at him and then at her mother.

"I didn't drink any punch. When I do a gig like that, I don't pay attention to much else. Sorry. Sarah, let's go."

Sarah stood and shifted Seb to her hip. "See you at eight, Mom. Thanks so much for keeping him." They were gone before Penny could think what else to ask, but she didn't believe that he hadn't noticed the punch.

Penny was walking into the bathroom to take a shower when the phone rang. "Penny? Sammie. I just got off the phone with Sibyl."

"Henry and Sarah just left. It's as if they'd never had that fight at the market."

"She'll wise up eventually," said Sammie. "We all learn at our own pace."

"I guess." Letting your children learn the hard way the lessons you had learned the hard way was the toughest part of parenting. Penny sank back down on the couch. "What did Sibyl have to say?"

"She says she saw Kent when he was leaving. Was that about three forty-five?"

"Roughly. It wasn't long after he left that Nora opened the market. Wait, she was watching him and waiting to open until he drove off, so closer to four."

"She says she didn't pay much attention before that. She was busy setting up her jellies. She didn't even know about the punch. She got there too late to get George's spot, so she took the one next to him. She agrees Abbie was helping Henry set up his music, but that's all she remembers."

"Did you talk to Rosalind?"

"She's supposed to call me back. She was midwifing a nanny. What did Henry say?"

"He remembers less than Sibyl. It makes you wonder, doesn't it?"

"Not surprising. No one knew Kent was going to go off and die. Farmers get focused on getting their displays ready."

"No one knew but the poisoner. I got Herman, but he thinks Giles did it. He gave me a lecture on killer seeds and plastic vegetables."

"Let's call it a night."

"I was doing that when you called. Maybe when I get caught up on my sleep, I'll remember more. I was right there."

"Don't be too hard on yourself, Penny. I'll try the others tomorrow."

"Me, too, when Seb's sleeping."

Eleven

Friday, May 3. What was it about dirt? Penny liked to get her hands in it, crumble the clods in her fingers, sniff its damp, rich smell, see the earthworms wiggle free when she loosened a big clod. The sun was high enough at mid-morning to warm her through her long-sleeved plaid shirt. Kenneth was running the rototiller, and she and Seb were planting Blue Lake bush beans. He squatted near her, a few beans clutched in his fists, waiting for her okay before he dropped a bean into the hole she'd made.

Kenneth came over. "There are easier ways, love."

"I know. I just like to work the soil through my fingers. Plus, Seb's happy."

"Seb plant beans, Gampa." Several beans fell out of his fist. "Uh oh."

They both waited while he retrieved them one at a time.

"Put it here, Seb. One bean. Just one. Now one here. That's right."

"I'll work on the marrow bed then," said Kenneth. "I bet I can plant fifteen hills of squash, as you Yanks call it, while you and Seb do one bean row."

"Probably." Penny smiled up at him. "Make yourself happy. We are."

He bent and kissed them both. Of course, Seb dropped his beans again. Before she could help him retrieve them, Andy came striding out the back door, letting the screen slam behind him. They all looked up. Andy never slammed doors, and he looked stricken.

Penny stood up. "What's wrong?"

"Everything. This will kill our market." He waved the morning's *Moon* at them.

"What, Andy?"

He handed her the paper folded to an editorial with the headline, "Close the Farmers' Market Now."

"Oh, no." Derek had managed to keep the details of Kent's death from the media, but it was out now. She glanced at the first paragraph as Kenneth came to read over her shoulder. "They're demanding the state close the market before anyone else is poisoned, but the *Moon* editor is always demanding something. He's against sustainability, for one thing."

"It's no good, Penny." Andy looked bleak. "My boss called. The state ag department is also now demanding we shut down. My boss insists, since we got off on the wrong foot, that we should start all over again next year, because by then this poison problem will be solved and forgotten."

"He's not a believer in getting back on the horse as soon as possible after you fall off then?"

Andy shook his head. "I don't know what to do."

"Let's have a sit-down," said Kenneth. "We can sit at Belle's picnic table. I'll bring down the coffee pot." Belle had a sandbox for her grandchildren, among whom she included Seb, since she'd been part of Sarah's support system during her pregnancy while Penny and Kenneth were in Wales. The box was on her patio next to the concrete table and benches, and Penny persuaded Seb to leave his beans and play with his small shovel and bucket in the sandbox near them.

"Who has authority?" asked Penny. "Is it up to you to open and close the market, or is it up to the farmers? Don't we have some say so?"

"Yes," said Andy. "At least I thought so, but I'm not sure now. The markets are approved by the state ag department, like meat is approved by the U.S. Department of Agriculture. The state makes sure we only sell certain things, and if meat or baked goods are sold, these operations have to be approved by the state inspectors. But we wouldn't even have a market if I hadn't helped the farmers set it up."

"Everything's been going splendidly," said Kenneth, coming up with the coffee pot and three mugs. "We've had two markets since Kent's death, and both went off like a charm. I was there. Do they know I'm undercover there, more or less? The farmers know me, but the customers don't. No one else has been poisoned. We only sell bottled water now."

"I think this newspaper story is causing everyone to panic. It panics me. How will we hold onto our customers with screaming editorials like this? If the people don't come, the farmers won't come either. We'll be dead in the water. Food contamination of any kind can ruin a market forever. I'd hoped against hope we could solve it before it went public. I can't think clearly. What in the world am I going to do?"

"They haven't acted yet, have they?" asked Kenneth.

"No, it's just a threat now. That's bad enough. If the poison case isn't solved fast, my boss says, he'll have to close it. He'd rather do it than have the state force his hand. I told him everything was okay now, but he yelled and said, 'No, it isn't. We can't have people getting poisoned at the farmers' market.' Then he slammed down the phone. He's never been mad at me like this before."

Penny put her hand on his arm. "It isn't you. You've done a good job, Andy. It's the pressure from higher up that's worrying him."

"I've worked so hard on this. I thought I'd done a really good job, but now?" He picked up the mug of coffee Kenneth had pushed over to him. "I don't want to give up without a fight. I know that."

"The farmers are with you," said Penny, "and Wednesday was a good market. We had the Maypole, a lot of new people came, and we sold well."

"We need to find our poisoner fast," said Kenneth. "Derek's not getting anywhere. I haven't seen anything suspicious. Giles is very argumentative, but even he has calmed down. He was Kent's friend, so no wonder he's upset."

"I think Nora may know more about what happened than she realizes," said Penny. "I'll go talk to her again. I have Seb today, but I'll go in the morning."

"I'll come, too, love, if you want me to." Penny smiled at Kenneth. They still hadn't talked about their Wales dilemma, but he was trying to be helpful even so. They'd have to talk soon, no matter what else happened.

"But what do I do now?" lamented Andy.

"Why don't you call the old reliables like Rosalind, George, Sibyl. They'll stand behind you. They may have ideas."

"I guess," said Andy. He looked over at the garden. "I hate that the summer planting is falling so much on you guys and Leroy."

"Don't worry, Andy. You do what you need to. We'll get the garden in. We're happy to plant beans, aren't we, Seb?"

"Plant beans?" Seb stood and threw down his bucket. Andy laughed and walked back to his house.

"More san'ich, Gamma." It was going on five-thirty, and Penny hoped it was okay to feed Seb supper. After an active morning planting beans and playing in the sandbox, he'd eaten only a little of the scrambled eggs she'd fixed him and then slept three solid hours. Now he was a bottomless pit, and she'd been feeding him peanut butter and honey sandwiches made with her high protein rye bread. Sarah was due any time. His throat wasn't hurting, and he hadn't had any temperature all day. No sniffles either. Sun, sleep and happiness seemed to have cured his cold.

When she heard someone on the stairs, she didn't expect Leroy, who cracked the screen. "Is Seb here?"

"Daddy!" Stuffing the last piece of sandwich into his mouth so that his cheeks bulged, he climbed down and ran to Leroy, who lifted and hugged him. Penny was so glad for their mutual affection. Sarah loved Seb, but there was a steadiness about Leroy these years that gave Seb an extra sense of security.

"Come on in. I'm giving him supper, though Sarah's due any time."

When Leroy sat down on another kitchen chair, Seb squirmed down from his lap and climbed back onto his chair, made higher with several local phone books. Penny put another small square of sandwich on his plate.

"I came to tell you Sarah asked me to keep him overnight. I do have to go check on Nora's animals, but he likes to come with me. By all means, feed him. I'd been wondering what I had on hand that he would eat."

"He loves these sandwiches. You can let that be his supper. He's eaten more than I thought possible. Leroy, let me ask you something. Is Sarah's spending time with Henry again bothering you?"

She looked at him to gauge his response. His face rarely showed his feelings and didn't now as he replied. "Don't worry about it, Penny. It's her business. I gave up on her ever marrying me. Perhaps it's just as well. I never did believe I was the marrying kind."

"What's the marrying kind?" asked Penny. She hadn't been sure she was either after her failed marriage to her first husband. Not until Kenneth, and that had hit her out of the blue.

"You know, sharing everything, helping each other, making a real home like you and Kenneth have, and Andy and Jan, Belle and Kate, too. You all have solid connections, can give and take. I'm too much of a loner, I think. I love Seb, but he's easy for me, at least part-time. If I was married, too, it would be harder, I think, working out care for him that we could both agree on, you know?"

It was a long speech for Leroy. "Maybe, but Kenneth and I were loners in a lot of ways when we met."

"But then you really connected, from what you've told me."

"Well, yes. I couldn't imagine being separated from him after that. It's like Carolyn Heilbrun says in one of her detective books, something like this: sometimes you can't get unmarried, and if you're lucky, you laugh."

Penny put some slices of apple on Seb's plate and pushed his two-handled sippy cup of milk closer. He stuffed the apple in his mouth and said, "Down." At least she thought so. His full mouth made him inarticulate. "Finish your apple and your milk first, Seb."

"Penny, I've never once felt I couldn't get unmarried, but something new is going on with me. I can't figure it out. I haven't changed really."

"Since I first met you, Leroy? You've changed a lot. You were very much a loner then. It was hard for you even to be a neighbor. Remember when you cooked spark plugs on the stove and left your totally black and disgusting work clothes in the washer we were all using?"

Leroy laughed. "I remember you used to tear me up. You civilized me, Penny. Thank God. I was so miserable back in those days–wow, ten years ago."

"Down," repeated Seb, banging his cup down with a flourish. He smacked it on the table so hard it would have spilled if it had had any milk left in it. Penny took the damp sponge, wiped his sticky hands and face, and let him climb down.

"It wasn't hard, Leroy. You bore up well when I lectured you."

"But you didn't just lecture me. You believed in me. You actually liked me. Penny, I think you were the first person actually to like me."

"Not hard to do. You're a good friend and neighbor." Leroy reached down and grabbed Seb. Was he hiding tears? Dear goddess, she'd never seen him cry. "You said something new was happening. What's that?"

He hugged Seb tight a long minute and then let him scramble down, watched him go pick up his dump truck, and turned back to Penny.

"I know you can keep a secret, Penny."

"Of course."

"I think Nora likes me, and ..."

"And?" Penny watched Seb rolling his yellow dump truck along the edge of the living room rug.

"I like her a lot. But I don't know, not being the marrying kind."

Penny laughed. "Sounds like that phase of your life may be ending, Leroy. I think that's wonderful. She wouldn't appeal to some men, she's so independent and outspoken. I thought I was bad, but she's louder and more persistent than I am."

"But she's right most of the time, Penny, and she cares about people, about her farming, and she's shyer than I thought."

"I never considered shyness to be Nora's problem," said Penny.

"Underneath. If her loudness doesn't work, that's when she gets shy and too quiet. Look how quiet she is now, and depressed, too. I went to see her this afternoon. I think your earlier visit helped some, and she perked up while I was there. She said she was trying to remember what happened and when like you wanted her to."

"Good. That helps her, and it certainly helps us."

"Would you come with me in the morning to visit her?"

"Yes, I was going to go with Kenneth anyway. Maybe the two of us? What about Seb?"

"I'll ask Belle and Kate to watch him for an hour or so."

"Okay, sure." They both stood, and Penny was gathering up Seb's clothes when Andy leaned his head in.

"Can I come in?"

"Welcome, Andy. What's wrong now?" He looked white, his freckles dark against his pallor.

"Sit down, Andy. What's happened?" Leroy turned from gathering up Seb's toys.

Andy sat down at the table. "I've been meeting with the state ag people. They're closing the market in ten days if the Sheriff's Department can't solve the poisoning."

Twelve

Saturday, May 4. Nora had washed and combed her short, curly hair, and her brown eyes were alert, not dull and dead as before when nothing had seemed to matter to her. She even smiled at Leroy as she was ushered into the interview room. Derek joined them, as did Kate, whom Penny had urged to come with them. They had to solve this and clear Nora.

When Penny told Nora that they had only a week to solve Kent's death, as the state was threatening to close the market, she was loud in the way of the more self-assured Nora Penny was used to. "Dang. They can't do that! Where do they get off?" Nora glanced out the small, barred window at ceiling height. Then she looked at all her visitors. "What's coming down? Why the hell are you all here so dang early?"

"Because," Penny said, "we think you can help us solve this before we lose the market, and yes, Nora, the state ag department can close the market if there's even a chance of food poisoning. We're all sick about it. We want you out of jail." She looked at Derek, who looked away. "We want to save the market."

Nora stared at her hands. She had to wear the cuffs now when she was with them. She folded her hands together. When she looked up, she was crying. She raised her hands to wipe the tears but couldn't do much more than smear them. Kate pulled a packet of tissues out of her pocket and handed her a couple.

"Sorry, I'm just so fed up. I didn't poison Berryman. I yelled at him. Is that a crime? I tried to get him to leave our market alone. He messed up everything the week before. He was talking to Abbie when I drove in, and he wasn't even supposed to be there. Andy told him nicely to stay away after I asked him to, and there he was, big as life."

"Nora, this is exactly what we need you to do," said Penny. "Just tell us everything you remember from that afternoon. Okay? You drove in. I remember you parked right beside us, then jumped out of your truck and went immediately down to where Kent was standing." Penny stopped.

"He was right by Sibyl's table, talking to Abbie. He had no business bothering Abbie, but I just wanted him gone. I'm the manager, even though I can't do squat in jail."

"You can remember it all, Nora," Leroy said quietly. Nora looked at him, Penny thought, as if he were a miracle. Leroy was right. She did like him. She could see the good heart he had. Few could. His shaved head and wooden expressions didn't throw Nora, thank goodness. Would Leroy be able to cope with Nora's love?

"I've been trying to remember everything," Nora said.

Kate leaned forward. "You're doing great, Nora. Keep going. We're all listening."

Derek looked like he wanted to speak, but Kate held up her hand. "We're all listening, Nora," she repeated. Derek pulled a small notebook out of his pocket and began taking notes.

"I know I shouted at him. I was so dang pissed." Nora took a deep breath. Then she looked at Leroy and kept her eyes on his eyes while she talked.

He wasn't smiling. Did he know how? But his body was motionless, and his focus was totally on Nora as if he were willing her to keep talking.

"I asked him to leave. He fussed, said he'd come to take more photographs. I said we didn't need any more of his photos. Just leave. He said I was being rude. He was a customer. I said just leave, period. He still challenged me."

She stopped and took a deep breath. No one moved. "I said I'd call the Sheriff. Andy wasn't there yet. I didn't know what to do. So he laughed at me, and then Giles came over and laughed at me, too. Giles said to cool it. So I did. I went back and started unloading my stuff. I didn't go near the punch. It was fruit juices from cans and bottles, nothing else. I mix grape, apple, orange, cranberry, like that. Penny poured it all in the big thermos and set out the cups, and some of the farmers came by and bought a cup of punch while I was still unloading."

Penny interjected: "Leroy bought us some, George had some." Kate gestured to Penny with her fingers on her lips.

Nora went on. "I was at the other end of the table from the punch. I didn't touch the punch after I'd pulled the gallon jugs out of my pickup. I was getting ready for market. So then I looked up, and here comes Kent. I could feel my blood pressure going up. He couldn't get it through his head he wasn't wanted, or else he enjoys torturing people. Hell if I know.

"Penny said Andy was here, and so then Andy came up quickly, and when I saw him, I went and sat in my truck. I think Andy talked to him. I used my meditation exercise to calm myself down and lower my blood pressure." She smiled.

"When I tuned back in, everything was pretty quiet. Then Leroy came around and asked if I was all right. He said Andy was talking to Kent, and he'd help me finish setting up. So I went out. I was pretty much ready. I didn't even look where Kent and Andy were talking. I arranged my displays. I didn't go down to the end of the table where the punch was. Out of the corner of my eye, I saw Kent come back and get a cup of punch that was already poured and walk back toward where he was parked. I thought Andy must have persuaded him to leave, so I went over to where Penny and Andy were talking. Kent was still down at the front of the market talking to Abbie, but Andy thought he'd really leave this time. I doubted it. But it was time to open the market, so I decided to wait until he left. When he got in his jeep and drove off, I rang the bell for the market to begin."

Then tears rolled down her cheeks again. Leroy leaned toward her, but Derek held up his hand. Kate handed her more tissues and said, "That was great, Nora. Are you tired? Do you feel like answering questions?"

"I want to save the market, Penny. I want to save myself."
She looked at Leroy.

Penny caught Derek's eye. "Is it okay if we catch her up on
our observations about the other farmers?" He looked startled
but nodded.

"The other farmers, leaving Giles out of it—we figured he
wouldn't be helpful." Derek closed his eyes like he couldn't
believe what she was doing. He'd probably rake her and Sammie
over the coals for talking to them at all about the murder.
"Anyway, no one else remembers anything different. I talked to
Herman, George and Henry."

"I forgot about Henry," Nora said.

"He was there that day. It was the first time he played for us.
He was setting up across from your table. He claimed he knows
nothing about any punch, never had any, didn't even know it was
there."

Kate raised one eyebrow. Derek made a note on his pad.

"Sammie talked to Rosalind, Mark, Sibyl and Abbie.
Rosalind, Mark and Sammie got there about the time Andy did,
and they didn't notice anything. They were too busy setting up.
Sibyl and Abbie must have arrived before Kent, because Kent
was talking to Abbie when Nora drove in around three-fifteen, I
think. Abbie had been down near us before that helping Henry
get his music set up. None of them had punch or hung around the
punch table. Only Giles, George, Leroy, Herman and I had
punch, and it didn't hurt any of us. We might have missed
something during those minutes when the punch cup was left on
the table and we were all trying to get set up, but I don't think so.
Derek, the upshot is I don't see how Nora could have put
anything in Kent's punch in any case. Most of the time she was
sitting in her truck."

Nora smiled at her.

Kate followed her and Leroy back to the Whitfield Road
house, and they all dropped in on Belle, who was stirring a bowl

of batter in the kitchen while Seb, draped in a bath towel, stood on a dinette chair with its back to the sink, his hands splashing in the soapy water. When he saw them, he said solemnly, "Seb wash dishes, Gamma."

"And Belle?" asked Penny, having a look in the bowl.

"Pancakes. Hungry?" Belle gave Penny a hug.

Kate walked past them. "Let me change. I'd kill for pancakes. Do we get bacon?"

"Ham and eggs," said Belle. "Blueberry pancakes."

Leroy had gone over to inspect the dishwashing. "He's wetter than the dishes," he reported.

"It's Penny's fault. She taught me this babysitting trick, but I think there's one more change of clothes in his bag."

"Should be," said Penny, "unless he went through several sets last night. I'm starved, too. I was up at six. The good news is Nora's feeling better, and she finally started talking to Derek. She might actually talk her way out of jail, right, Kate?"

"I'm pushing the DA to do the probable cause hearing right away. They've got only one witness who says she did it, and if he's lying, it all falls apart. I can't tell you who, but I know. They have to tell me what they've got and, believe me, it's all gonna fall apart pretty fast now that Nora's fighting. I can't figure out why she got so depressed before and now she has suddenly snapped out of it."

Penny glanced over at Leroy, who had turned from the sink to listen. He had his hands in the water now and was apparently washing the dishes Belle had been piling up beside the sink. He looked happy. He caught Penny's eye and smiled. He had glad eyes. She'd never seen his eyes look happy. The rebirth of Leroy. Amazing. She wouldn't tell Kate yet. Time enough for Leroy and Nora to figure out how they felt. Kate didn't tune in sometimes to those subtle undercurrents, or maybe Penny was the unusual one, but it made her happy to see that some happiness lay ahead for Nora and Leroy. They could both use a big dose.

"Thank God she's helping you now," said Belle. "Hey, Leroy, give a shout to Kenneth and Andy and whoever else is out there in the garden. Pancakes in ten minutes. I've got the ham in the oven, and I'm starting the cakes now."

"Can I help?" asked Penny.

"Nah, go sit down, you and Kate. Take a load off. I got it."

Kate patted the couch beside her. "Tell me more about the vendors, Penny. I've got to get every scrap of info I can. Tell me about this Giles Dunn guy. What's his story? Kenneth told me he was a friend of Berryman's."

So Penny told her everything she knew about his enthusiasm for genetically modified seeds, which most of the other farmers were leery of, his family's farming history and his hostility to sustainable farmers. "I don't like him. Something about him makes me uneasy. He seems underhanded, fake. He's hostile, too. He defended, still defends, Kent Berryman. They were good friends. Did I hear they always go hunting together? Maybe. Herman doesn't trust either one of them. Plus, he made some racist remarks to Sammie when we were setting up our Maypole."

Penny saw that Andy and his twins, her godchildren, had come in. They were all in the kitchen, Andy admiring the pancakes, and little Penny and Kenny with their hands in the dishwater, too, now. The eight-year-olds were continuing Leroy's dish washing, but Seb was splashing and squealing.

Leroy grabbed him up. "Clean clothes, Seb. Get ready for Grandma Belle's pancakes," and he carried him, towel and all, through the living room to the family bathroom beyond.

"Tell me more about Herman," said Kate.

"He's pretty strange, too, but it's more awkwardness. He's not mean like Giles feels to me. Herman talks politics even though no one wants to listen. He's very distrustful, but he seems to like me, and Leroy gets along with him. He likes Nora, and he's another admirer of Abbie, but I think they're all half in love with her."

"Who does she like?"

"She seems to like Kent. She stood around talking to him a lot, but he knows them, and Rosalind, I think it was, said that he's been kind of a father figure to her. Apparently, Abbie's father committed suicide, and Sibyl had to pull the farm out of debt and make enough money from it to support them. Kent must have been helpful."

"So who else does she like?"

"I've seen her talking to Mark. He's about her age. Then she was quite entranced by Henry, which set off Sarah, who was furious at Henry for a while, but they've made up."

Kate smiled. "I don't think you're wild about Henry."

"No."

Leroy returned with a dry, clean Seb, and Kenneth wandered into the kitchen as Belle set a big platter of thickly sliced ham on the counter, which gave off the aroma of cloves, and went back for a huge stack of pancakes.

"Shall I scramble all the eggs?" She was looking at Penny.

"Sure, Belle. Sounds great." They all hovered around the counter.

"Kenneth, Andy, Leroy, let the kids get what they want and settle them in the dinette. I'll bring them some eggs in a minute. Kate, can you grab the syrup, butter and OJ from the fridge?"

It had been awhile since they'd gathered for a meal at Belle's. So many crises and happy times they'd had in this same room, helping themselves to potluck dishes, trying to solve something or celebrating having solved it. More than once Belle had been furious, but now how lovely to see her happily cooking eggs and telling them to go ahead and fix their plates

They'd all eaten to satiety, and Kenneth, Andy, Leroy and the children had returned to the garden work. Belle poured herself another cup of coffee, lit a cigarette and sank into the armchair beside the couch. Kate and Penny both had their feet on the coffee table, and Penny was finishing her report on the vendors. "But what you should do, Kate, is come to the market. If we can't solve Kent's death, this next Wednesday may be our last one this season."

Belle set her cup down. "So from what Kate tells me, this jerk was poisoned by someone putting something in his Koolade."

"Punch, Belle," said Kate.

"Okay, punch."

"But we can't figure out how it was done," said Penny.

"Maybe that's not how it was done," said Belle. "The guy drank some punch. Did he eat or drink anything else either before he came to the market or while he was there or after he left?"

Thirteen

Wednesday, May 8. sixth market. Since their market on the following Wednesday might turn out to be the last one, it had brought out all their vendors and the biggest group of customers they'd had yet. A notice in *The Moon* said they welcomed children and would provide seeds for them to plant, and a local singer would entertain. Henry had agreed to sing again, but when they let in customers at four o'clock, he still hadn't arrived. Rosalind, as Acting Market Manager, confided in Penny right before she rang the bell that she was worried. He had always been on time, even early, before.

Penny found it hard to worry about Henry. Anyone that good at talking other people into filling his needs could certainly take care of himself. Mark had the seeds table set up near his own to let the children plant various vegetable seeds in paper cups full of "sustainable dirt," as he called his homemade potting soil mix. Abbie had abandoned her mother's table and was standing ready beside him to help with the children. Penny had never seen Mark look so happy. In the competition for Abbie's attention, he seemed to be winning.

Among the customers now streaming in were Penny's landladies, Belle Jones and Kate Razor, with Seb and Belle's twin grandchildren in tow. She and the children headed straight for Mark's table. Kate walked over to see Penny and Leroy's display. Between them and Mark, Herman was offering peas, turnips and their greens, and beautiful, large, firm cabbages.

While Kate bought some of Penny's carrots, onions and lettuce, she quietly asked Penny to point out Herman, Giles and George. Since Kate and Belle did very little in the garden, they had agreed to buying the neighborhood produce, either at home or at the market, though they got a discount. "Those were the other three who were around the punch table, right?"

Penny nodded. "Plus, Henry was right over there, though he denies even knowing we had punch that day."

"Where is Henry? I thought he was singing today."

"Theoretically," said Penny, unable to keep the sarcasm out of her voice, but Kate knew how she felt about Sarah's new boyfriend.

Kate smiled. "Theoretically. Okay. I'll start with these others, do the farmers' market equivalent of window shopping. See ya."

Penny and Leroy had a rush of customers. When she was able to look around again, she saw Derek talking to Sammie, who today had bouquets of daisies along with yellow, purple and pink cosmos. She was in gold and purple, with a fetching straw hat and dangly gold earrings. Apparently Derek was also wanting to visit George, Giles and Herman, as Penny saw Sammie pointing out their tables. George and Giles had their usual spots in front, and Sibyl had the one she'd had to accept next to George. She was doing a brisk trade in her bread and cakes, and Penny saw several customers carrying her jam around.

Two women, rather formally dressed in pantsuits and wearing name tags, came to Penny's table. Leroy was discussing his chickens' pasture-raised lifestyle with a young and very earnest man and woman, so the two women fell to her.

"May I help you?" she asked. Their name tags had NCDA on them, which stood for North Carolina Department of Agriculture. Oops, these were the people who wanted to close the market. At least, if they looked around at all, they could see that the market was doing well. They had more customers than usual, not fewer. That fear-mongering newspaper editorial hadn't scared people off so far.

"We're from the North Carolina Department of Agriculture, here to inspect your market. We'll be talking to all the vendors, but could you point us to your manager?" They didn't smile. The older woman, her grey hair stylishly cut short, was clearly in charge, but the younger one, in a similar suit and with her blonde hair also cut short, looked solemn.

"Our regular manager isn't here today, but Rosalind Mann, the lady selling goat cheese right over there, is manager today. Her operation is the Gum Springs Goat Farm. She'll be happy to help you."

Actually, not happy, but Rosalind would be up to these tough customers. Then Penny forgot about the two inspectors as little Penny, Kenny and Seb rushed over from Mark's table, each holding two paper cups of dirt. "Aunt Penny, me and Kenny planted peas, beans, cucumbers and squash, and Seb planted watermelons in his cups."

"See, Gamma?" Seb stretched up his cups, and she bent down to see them. Belle hovered just behind him and rescued one cup when it tipped, and the dirt started sliding out. He was poking now in the other cup. "See the little seed, Gamma?"

"I think you're supposed to let it sleep under the dirt, Seb, so it will grow."

"See, Gamma? My seed? Melon."

"Yes, Seb. Now put it back and cover it up again, so it can grow."

"Grow!" he said to the seed as he pushed it back into the dirt.

Little Penny came over as he was about to dig it out again. "No, Sebbie. It has to go to sleep a long time before it grows. Let it sleep." She patted it down again.

"Sleep!" ordered Seb to his seed.

Belle grinned at Penny and rescued the second cup. "I'll let Kate shop for us. Gamma's tired and wants to go home. Come on, kiddies."

By the time Belle had corralled the children and hauled them and their cups of dirt into her car, and Penny had handled several more customer needs for lettuce, carrots and sugar snaps, she saw that Rosalind had taken the NCDA women down to the front of the market and was going with them vendor to vendor. They were all in front of Sibyl's table. Sammie had apparently been left in charge of Rosalind's cheese shop, as she was working both tables.

It was nearly five when she looked for the NCDA ladies and saw them nowhere, and Rosalind was back selling her cheese again. "I'm going to take a little break, Leroy. Okay?" He waved her off.

As she approached Rosalind's table, curious to know how the inspectors had reacted, Henry slouched in the customer gate with his guitar slung over his shoulder and followed Penny to Rosalind.

"Henry, where were you? I was worried." Rosalind was filling a paper bag with cheeses for an elderly, white-haired gentleman.

Henry shook his hair. "I fell asleep. Sorry. You want me in the same spot?"

"Yes."

"I don't have my mike, but I'll sing till six, no problem."

"That will be fine."

As he walked languidly off, Rosalind shook her head. "Ah, Penny. You want to trade eggs for cheese? If you have any left. Looks like your eggs are going fast."

"Of course we want to trade. Leroy, Kenneth and I all love your cheese. Have you any more of the raspberry-flavored one?"

"Coming up. I'm so glad the inspectors are gone."

"Did they find any problems?"

"Not really, but they're very picky. So Sibyl didn't do her bread and cake labels the way they wanted them. She has to redo them. They gave her till next week."

"Does that mean they'll let us be here next week?"

"They didn't say. They looked at everything, but they didn't tell me anything. They didn't even mention the poison incident. You know we have our cheese-making room and equipment inspected at least once a year, and our milking barn, but I've never seen them at other markets, like Sanford, where I've been going for years."

"It's the poisoning."

"They did look at the bottled water very carefully and spent most of their time with the meat people and Sibyl."

"They only browsed here," said Penny, "very briefly."

"Yes, and that's what they did with the other vegetable people. At least they're gone now. It was upsetting to Sibyl though. She tries so hard to get everything just right. You know her story, how she had to pull them out of debt when her husband died? Abbie was only five years old."

"You told me some of it. Her husband committed suicide?" The strains of Henry's music reached them. Penny hoped she didn't acquire him as a son-in-law, but he certainly made beautiful music.

Rosalind also stopped to listen. "He's good, isn't he?"

"Yes. I just hope Sarah tires of him. He seems to have no determination to provide for himself, much less anyone else. He's basically a bum."

"Don't be too hard on him, Penny. Maybe it's the best he can do. I watch Sibyl fussing over Abbie." She looked across to Abbie kneeling on the ground with three small children squatting in front of her. "Doesn't Abbie look happy helping these children and working with Mark? Mark seems to like her a lot."

"I agree," said Penny. "He told me how much he admired her and how good she was with children."

"But Sibyl doesn't like him. She doesn't want Abbie marrying a dirt farmer, as she calls it, especially not one of these newfangled sustainable folks." Rosalind laughed. "She makes sustainable sound like a cuss word."

"Mark is so nice and such a good farmer," said Penny, "and Abbie has her profession, pediatric nursing."

"Sibyl wants her to marry a rich doctor, someone like that, so she can quit her nursing job. Sibyl has to struggle to keep up with her bills. She wants Abbie to have money and an easier life."

"Mark could end up doing very well. Andy says organic food is where we as farmers are all headed, if we want to survive economically. The customer base for local, fresh food produced without chemicals is growing fast."

"I doubt Sibyl can believe that, but she's rather old-fashioned. She says Mark doesn't even own a tractor. You see how she views things?"

When a customer came up for goat cheese, Penny took the cheese and went over to collect the eggs from Leroy, who was chatting with Kenneth and Derek. She relayed to them that the NCDA inspectors had been and gone and found nothing wrong except with Sibyl's labels. Then she remembered she wanted to ask Derek about anything else that Kent could have eaten before, during, or after the market and before he died. She beckoned him to walk a little ways off with her.

"It's possible he ate something before, but unlikely, the pathologist says. He still had traces of that red fruit punch in him. He'd eaten a sandwich, too. The poison worked fast. He thinks it was something in the nightshade family, going by his symptoms. Whatever it was must have gotten into his system as soon as he left the market, and it started having its effect immediately. They estimate he died within two hours of taking the poison. Now, Penny, keep this information to yourself."

"Of course," said Penny. "I'll take over the eggs, Leroy, and here's Rosalind's cheese. Do you want to look around, or shall I see what else we might buy or trade?"

"You go ahead, Penny. It's slowed down a lot. I still have two more dozen eggs we could trade."

"I'll have a look then. Herman has some nice cabbage, and I'm sure Sibyl would trade eggs for cake. Do you have a preference?"

"See if you can get several of the small cakes, and then we'll share them."

After she had traded for the cakes–spice with lemon frosting–she bought more beautiful chard from Mark and cabbage from Herman, then stopped to chat with Rosalind and Sammie, who were both nearly sold out.

Rosalind was saying, "She needs to let go of Abbie. Children will go their different ways. So many parents have trouble with that one."

"I guess I do, too," said Penny, thinking of Henry and how much she wanted him out of Sarah's life.

Sammie nodded. "I can't blame you. I wouldn't want Henry in my family."

"But that's the point," insisted Rosalyn. "If you let them have their head, especially by Sarah's and Abbie's ages–mid to late twenties, right?"

Penny nodded.

"They make their mistakes, but so did we. The end result is better, though. I'm sure of it because they're deciding for themselves, not to please you or make you angry."

"You think Sarah might be choosing men to make me angry?" asked Penny, astounded.

"It's just a thought," said Rosalind, "but it does happen."

Sammie left to take care of a customer who wanted both of her last bouquets, and Penny found herself confiding in Rosalind, who was a little younger than she was but had been farming for twenty-five years or so. She projected her vibrant health and sense of well-being, even when clearly tired, as now.

"I'd like to hear more of your thinking about how I could be adding to Sarah's problems. I don't want to be. She was very miserable in her marriage, and it took her forever to let go of that."

"Did she know you didn't like him?"

"Yes. When she left, she moved in with me, and she couldn't understand why I wasn't happy when she left him. She said she knew I didn't like him. I was surprised that my opinion was clear to her."

Rosalind regarded Penny thoughtfully, twisting a strand of her braid that had come loose. Her blonde braid on top of her head gave her real customer appeal. She looked like a Dutch milkmaid, and she greeted everyone with a smile that made them feel both noticed and valued. "Children read us so easily," she said. "I'm surprised you hadn't caught onto that."

"Oh, the little ones, yes, but I hadn't thought of it when they're grown. It makes sense. My kids all do seem to figure me out in ways I never expect, even as adults. They get angry, even when I haven't said a word to criticize them."

"It's more complex when they're grown. Their major job is to establish their own lives, but they've been such a big part of ours, and we want them to be happy. So in my experience, while we're worrying over them and wondering how we could have been better parents, they're trying to figure out ways to keep us out of their lives, even while they're asking for help or rescue. Funny, isn't it?" She grinned.

Penny stared across at Abbie, collecting what was left of the seed-planting supplies and handing the box to Mark. She watched Abbie walk toward where Henry was singing.

"So when they beg you to help them, they actually want you to urge them to figure it out themselves?"

"Right. At least mine were like that. What infuriated my two daughters was my hovering over them. Fortunately, Rex had gone through it already with his grown sons, and he distracted me while my girls sorted out what they wanted for themselves. There were a couple of hair-tearing years, but now they call us and come visit, and I even get the oldest grandchild for visits in the summer. But it was excruciating for me a few years back."

"Kenneth thinks I don't want to spend so much time in Wales because Sarah still isn't settled. I can't believe it's that simple. I love teaching, and now farming and coming to the market. I didn't think Sarah had that much to do with it."

"Did you used to go to Wales for longer stretches?"

"Yes, for six months at a time, as soon as we could afford to. One time she was pregnant, but we went as planned, and my friends helped her out."

"How did she do then?"

"Fine, but she fussed that we didn't think enough of her to change our plans. I did come back for Seb's birth, but I still felt guilty."

Rosalind laughed. "Oh, of course, but she did fine, and even though she fussed, she learned she did fine without you."

"I guess."

"So maybe it's time to spend another long time, some months, in Wales. She may fuss, but then it really will be her problem whether she takes up with a less reliable person." Rosalind glanced over at Henry, Abbie sitting cross-legged at his feet. Was that the song Sarah liked that he was singing to her?

"Or while you're gone, and she can't move back in with you or blame you for not understanding, maybe she will figure out what she really wants versus picking someone sure to annoy her mother," Rosalind added.

Fourteen

Thursday, May 9. Penny laid down the last exam triumphantly and stretched.

"That's it then, love? You've marked all your examinations?"

Kenneth stood up, put down on the coffee table the Tony Hillerman novel he'd been reading, and set his glasses on top of the overturned book. "This calls for a celebration."

"I'm ready," said Penny. "This spring has been a little too busy, and you're a dear to put up with me."

He had pulled a bottle of good Chablis out of the refrigerator and was pouring it into two wine glasses. "I love you," he said simply as he handed her the first glass.

"I love you. I realized yesterday at the market that we'd never gotten back to talking about Wales and your *hiraith*. Why didn't you say something? I meant us to talk again long before now. I've been so obtuse and distracted, Kenneth. Why didn't you remind me?"

He studied his glass of wine and then raised his glass to her, still standing in front of her, solemn. "I knew you'd come back to it. We've both been busy, and then Nora's problem, and the danger of the market closing. I decided to wait. But here's to us, to our love and continued happy partnership. To our both being as happy as possible."

He settled beside her on the couch and put his arm around her. She leaned into him and rested her head against his shoulder. "I do want us both to be happy, Kenneth. I want you to have your Wales time, and I miss it, too. When I'm here, I always get so busy. Something about our American culture, I guess. There's so much I see that needs doing, and that I want to do. There aren't enough hours in the day. But some things that Rosalind said yesterday about letting your adult children go, letting them make their own mistakes, threw some light for me. It hit me that Sarah might do better if we weren't here so much but got back to our regular time in Wales."

"How so, love?" She heard the puzzle in his voice. "I did feel you were worried about her, and that made you want to be here. I don't understand."

"It's a paradox." She took hold of his free right hand and squeezed it. "It is hard to understand, but it makes sense. See, Sarah's real job these years is to live her own life, feel good about her bringing up Seb and her life partner, the man she wants to live with and share Seb with. But there's a part of her which doesn't want to let go of me. She used to make me feel guilty about being off in Wales with you, but in fact, she did quite well on her own. When we're here, she can afford to have babysitter and boyfriend crises because we're here. Rosalind even thinks maybe she picks unreliable men to get back at me."

"That doesn't make sense, love." He sat forward and poured more wine into their glasses.

"Maybe, maybe not. It's true I haven't liked any of the men she's gotten close to. I'm good friends with Leroy, but I didn't think he'd be right for Sarah to marry. What if she would pick better if I stayed out of it, if I were off in Wales?"

"I want to sweep you off to Wales for a little while, but I can't see how that helps Sarah. She needs us, Penny."

"She may not need us as much as she says she does. You're as bad as I am." Penny laughed. "Anyway, I'm going to see if Leroy, Andy, Kate and Belle, and whoever else they can round up, can take over the farming and the market August first. Don't you think August is one of the nicest months to be on Gower? That would give us until mid-January."

"You mean it, don't you?"

"I do. She'll miss us, and so will Seb, but she has plenty of good support here, and yes, it's a gamble, but it resolves my own sense that I'm neglecting you and at the same time leaves her free to grow in new ways. I'm pretty sure she's angry that she still needs me. This forces her to grow up more, see? We'll have less money, but I can spend more time writing poetry in my favorite Gower haunts."

Kenneth was shaking his head and looking bewildered when the telephone rang. He jumped up to get it and handed it to her.

"Rosalind, hi. What's up? Oh, no, just what we were afraid of." She turned to Kenneth, who was looking very worried. "Rosalind says the state people will definitely close the market. Can we do anything, Rosalind? Good idea. Okay, Andy's at seven tomorrow night for a potluck and meeting. Kenneth and I will be there, and I'll tell Leroy. We've got to do something. This is ridiculous. I can bring bread, and we can contribute a salad. Okay. See you then. Meantime, Leroy, Kenneth and I will brainstorm on it."

She set the phone on the coffee table. "If they close it, we won't be able to reopen it this season. Maybe we'll be off to Wales in June, the way things are going."

Kenneth did not look happy. "Don't be cynical, Penny. It doesn't suit you."

"I'm just discouraged. It feels like Murphy's Law: everything that can go wrong does go wrong, and all at once. Nora's still in jail. We've barely gotten started with our new market. It was a good market. Lots of customers. It all feels so stupid."

Kenneth pulled her to him. "It might be stupid, or it might be smart. Somebody poisoned Kent, and we don't know who. We have to find out."

Before Penny could reply, someone knocked at the door. It was nine already, and they didn't usually have people coming by so late. Kenneth opened it to Sarah.

"What's wrong?" Penny jumped up and went to hug her daughter, who had tears rolling down her face.

"Where's Seb?" asked Kenneth.

"He's asleep in the car. I just had to talk to you, Mom. Henry's moved out." She started sobbing again.

Penny felt both relieved and sad as she looked into Kenneth's eyes. He gestured to the door. "I'll go stay with Seb. You talk to her." He slipped out quietly.

Penny led Sarah over to the couch and hugged her until she stopped crying. She handed her a paper towel that Kenneth had used to set their wine bottle on. "Tell me about it, Sarah."

"When I got home from work, he wasn't there. His guitar and all his clothes were gone, and there was no note or anything. I mean, I was sure he'd moved out, but I told myself maybe I was wrong, and he'd just gone to the laundromat or something. So I fed Seb and waited, but he hasn't been back. I do get mad at him sometimes, but why didn't he tell me? I don't even know what I did to make him mad."

"You might not have done anything, Sarah." She couldn't tell Sarah she was better off, but it was hard to comfort her in a convincing way. Sarah needed Henry like a hole in the head.

"I loved him, Mom."

"I know."

Kenneth reappeared holding a bright-eyed and bushy-tailed Seb. "Sandwich, Gamma?" He stretched his arms to Penny, and she took him onto her lap.

"I'll make us a milky drink," said Kenneth. "Sarah, whatever feels so bad now, things will look better before long. You're a beautiful young woman, and the man who latches onto you is going to be very, very lucky."

When Penny, carrying a huge, fresh garden salad, and Kenneth, holding a warm loaf of bread wrapped in a clean towel, entered Andy and Jan's family room through the garage door, to their surprise, Nora walked up to them.

"Nora, you're out! What happened?" Penny put her salad down on the food table. Nora still looked pale but cheerful.

"Thank God for Kate, or I'd probably still be rotting in that cold, miserable cell."

"What happened?"

Kate walked in from the kitchen and put a big platter of meatballs on the table next to Penny's salad. "Probable cause hearing this morning."

"They got no dang evidence," said Nora, triumph in her voice. "Maybe now they'll concentrate on finding the real murderer."

"Come on, let's sit down. I want a full report, Kate." The room was empty. Kenneth had gone into the kitchen. It wasn't quite time for the meeting. Penny led the way to a couch at the other end of the room.

"The D.A. has no evidence. Nora's punch being the culprit for Kent but for no one else doesn't prove she did it, and her argument with Kent isn't proof of anything either. People argue all the time and don't go killing each other. I've been pushing this, but I think Derek finally got the picture. Anyway, she's free and clear."

Nora grinned. "Now I can look after my cats, my tomatoes and my babies. I've been home, and Leroy has done a fantastic job looking after things, and I found a note from Mark and George with their sales receipts. I haven't lost much money, not anything worth shaking a stick at."

"Good," said Penny. "You look good. I know Leroy will be so glad you're out. He has worried so about you." She watched Nora's face and saw a little half-smile before she turned away and said gruffly, "Where is he anyway?"

"Oh, he'll be here. You heard why we're meeting?"

"The dang staties have lost their mind."

Kate didn't know and looked puzzled.

"The state inspectors are closing the market, Kate. I don't know if we can stop them, but we're going to try."

Nora stood up suddenly. "We're gonna save our market. Period. I'm here now. Where do they get off, anyway?"

Her declaration seemed to pull people into the room, first Leroy, then Herman behind him, and Rosalind and Sibyl behind them.

Penny saw Leroy's eyes actually light up when he saw Nora. Something was healing him at a very deep level. Could love do that even when someone was as transparently wounded in his psyche as Leroy? Apparently. Nora walked straight to him and hugged him. He looked astounded but let her help him put down the bottle of wine he was carrying and lead him off to discuss, what, her cats and chickens? Or their feelings? Wouldn't that be something? Penny went to welcome the others, and when she looked next, Nora was laughing happily. Good medicine all around.

Herman sidled up to Penny, holding a pan of golden brown cornbread. "My mama's famous cornbread," he said. "Where should I put it?"

"Over there on the food table."

"I don't want it to get cold. Could I put it in the oven, if they have one?" He looked around.

"Of course they have one. Go into the kitchen. Ask Jan. She'll be in there, a tall, dark-haired young woman."

"You mean Andy's wife?"

"Yes." She pointed him toward the kitchen door.

"Rosalind told me Henry moved into the apartments where they let their hired help stay."

"Are you serious? He moved out of Sarah's apartment, but I hadn't heard where he went."

"Rosalind said he offered to do farm chores if he could stay there. He doesn't act like someone who would know one end of a cow from the other–I mean, goat. What good can he do on a goat farm? What else does he know how to do besides play the guitar?"

"Shovel manure?" asked Penny. "Don't worry about it, Herman. It's his problem, right?"

"Not if he hurts Abbie." Herman looked angry and had a tight expression on his face.

"What makes you say that?"

"Didn't he ditch his other girlfriend? Rosalind told me."

"My daughter," said Penny.

"Right, and Rosalind said Abbie was with him when he moved in last night."

Penny thought, that explains that. She flashed on Abbie sitting cross-legged in front of Henry, her blonde hair falling down her back and catching some of the sun where it lay on her shoulders. Then on Sarah, tears running down her face, wailing, "I love him, Mom."

She didn't want to give Sarah's vulnerability away, and she didn't want to say what she thought of Henry, so she said lightly, "Henry seems to get around."

"It's like Nora said about Kent. He goes after young women and corrupts them, treats them all nice at first and gets their hopes up. Then he drops 'em, smash. He's a skunk. So was Kent. They didn't ought to treat women like that."

"I agree," said Penny, "but Abbie's grown, Herman. She can figure out what she wants. I'm surprised though. I thought she was interested in Mark a while back."

"Mark?" Herman jerked to attention. They both looked across to the refreshment table and saw Mark and Rosalind in close conversation. Was Mark learning about Henry and Abbie, too? It would have been just as well if Rosalind hadn't spread the word so effectively, Penny thought. Best to distract Herman.

"Come, I'll take you into the kitchen, and we'll get your cornbread warmed up."

Penny left Herman to Jan and went to say hello to Sibyl, who was sitting alone on a straight chair. "I'm glad you could come. What goodies did you bring us tonight?"

"Chocolate cream pie and carrot cake with lemon icing." She gestured to the laden table. It could be said to groan: fried chicken, baked beans, steamed broccoli, and collards that had been chopped and well-seasoned, no doubt. A bowl of strawberries. Even fried pies. Sammie must have arrived. In fact, she came up behind Penny and hugged her.

Penny whirled around. "You made pies."

"We deserve a treat. It can't get much worse, can it? You think we can stop the state?"

"I doubt it," said Penny quietly, "but fighting them has Nora all fired up, so I'll keep my doubts to myself. I was just chatting with Sibyl. She seems so sad."

Sibyl smiled as they turned toward her. Had she heard them? "I'm sorry Abbie couldn't come. She has to work tonight. Glad I could make it. I'm just about ready for the Sanford market in the morning, and I would hate for us to lose our brand new market." She brightened.

"Nora thinks we can save it," said Penny. "What do you think, Sibyl? You're more experienced than we are."

"Oh, those state people aren't so bad. Their bark is worse than their bite. They barked at me, of course, about my labels. Typical. What can they do though?"

At this point George joined them. He was holding a full paper bag.

"What did you bring, George?" Penny peeked into his bag. "Oh, wine and chips. Very good. Maybe we can put the chips out on the coffee table. I'll get a bowl and a corkscrew."

Once provided with a bowl, George emptied the contents of the bag into it and said casually to Sibyl, "I stopped by the bookmobile on the way over and saw Abbie and Henry going into Pizza Tower. How come she's not here tonight? Doesn't she care about the market?"

Sibyl turned white, even though her face was tan from being outside so much. "With Henry?" was all she said. Herman had been drawn to their corner by the chips bag being torn open and heard George, too. Herman nodded gloomily, like the worst had definitely come to pass where Abbie was concerned.

So Abbie had jilted Mark, and Henry had jilted Sarah. Some unhappy undercurrents tonight, but Penny was determined to stay out of it, especially where Sarah was concerned. She hadn't, however, reckoned on Kenneth, who came up to her as they were lining up to fill their plates. "Mark wants to date Sarah," he said. "Now you have to be happy about that, love. He's such a nice bloke. You've said so yourself."

"He is, Kenneth. He is, but remember I'm trying to stay out of Sarah's romances."

Kenneth grinned at her. "Then I shouldn't have promised we'd babysit for Seb tomorrow night?"

Fifteen

Sunday, May 11. Sunday morning was Penny's favorite time of the week. Normally they let themselves sleep in. Kenneth made them a big Welsh breakfast, which lasted them until suppertime, and more than not, they made love in a leisurely way and then caught up with each other, especially if it had been a hectic week. They postponed everything else–people, work, problems–until noon, and their friends and Sarah had learned to respect their Sunday morning privacy.

Of course, in the last month or so since the market opened, Kent had died and Nora was arrested, which had made it harder to preserve their Sunday morning ritual.

Penny knew when she woke that it was already mid-morning by the way the sun flooded in. Their lively yellow curtains intensified its radiant presence. She lay quietly, not wanting to wake Kenneth, whose arm was flung protectively over her back. Sometimes it was good to enjoy all that was hers: a loving man beside her, her daughter and grandson okay. Sarah and Mark had seemed happy with each other and enjoying Seb when they picked him up the night before.

She and Kenneth could return to Wales in two and a half months, but she would enjoy the farming and the market until then. No, wait. Would they have a market? A fly in the salve of happiness. They would just have to find the poisoner. Fast.

Kenneth stirred and turned onto his back. "A Penny for your thoughts."

She laughed. "The old dog's up to his old tricks?"

He leaned over her and nibbled her earlobe, and then they didn't say anything for a while, but all the sounds were happy.

It was eleven when Kenneth started the sausages and Canadian bacon, which was the closest he'd found to the lean "rashers" served in Great Britain. Penny made coffee and then slipped on her jeans to go retrieve their Sunday edition of *The Moon*.

When they'd feasted in leisurely fashion on the sausage, bacon, eggs, tomatoes, mushrooms, toast and peach marmalade, Penny noticed it was noon. "Shall I turn on the ringer and check the messages?"

Kenneth looked up from reading the international news. "If you're determined to find out what's going on in the world, then by all means, love."

They both heard Rosalind's message on the answering machine. "Penny, something terrible has happened. Please call me as soon as you can."

Penny immediately dialed the goat farm number. She knew it rang in the house, the barn and the cheese-making room.

"Hello?" Rosalind's voice sounded hollow.

"Rosalind, it's Penny."

"Oh, thank God. We've had a bad morning here."

"What happened?"

"First, Mark discovered at daylight that his vegetables had been mowed down–you know, his beautiful chard and curly kale and spinach. The carrots and onions are there, but the tops got mowed. He's so upset. You know he was out with Sarah last night?"

"Yes. We kept Seb. Poor Mark. Such wonderful vegetables. He must be sick. Who would be so cruel?"

"Herman did it, Penny. It makes me ill. Mark saw the tractor tracks and followed them to Herman's farm, which is next to ours, you know."

"I know."

"Then Mark came over here, and we called the Sheriff. Your friend Derek came out. He found Herman out behind his house, burning his trash in a big barrel, and in with the trash was Henry's guitar."

"Oh, no." She didn't like Henry, but she knew his guitar was his most prized possession. "Does Henry know?"

"Yes, Derek took him over to identify it. Henry's bunking with us now. So Herman's in jail, and Henry just sits on his bunk and stares into space. We hired him to do chores, but he's useless today, and I haven't the heart to push him. Mark is devastated, of course, and he has gone off to see Sarah. Maybe you can help him talk about it. He's too quiet. I know he likes you. I can't think of anything meaner that anyone could do to a farmer or to a musician, for that matter, than what Herman has done. I don't get it. What could have possessed him?"

"Where is Herman now?"

"In the Riverdell jail. I've tried to be nice to him, Penny, for years, but something is very wrong with him. It's crazy what he did. It's all gotten crazy lately. But if they let him go, what else will he do? We farmers have to trust people, especially other farmers, not to destroy our livelihood. Why? Why?" Penny could hear tears in her voice.

"I don't know, Rosalind, but I've noticed he hangs around Abbie a lot, and she told me he pesters her. Could he be jealous of Mark and Henry? They've both had more luck getting Abbie interested in them than he has. He's not very skilled at attracting women."

"You're right there," admitted Rosalind.

Kenneth sat down beside Penny, but she didn't stop to explain. She'd wait until Rosalind was ready to hang up.

"What can Kenneth and I do, Rosalind?"

"Talk to Mark, if you see him. Maybe some of it can be replanted, but it's late to start spring crops like that. Just get him talking. I don't know. Everything gets worse and worse. What is wrong with us, Penny? Whatever it is, we have to stop it. All this is destroying us and the market, too."

When Penny knocked on Sarah's front door an hour later, Sarah answered it, wearing her favorite robe made from an old patchwork quilt. Seb came running up behind her to peek through her legs at them. Sarah said, "Go back and finish your cereal, Seb." She turned back to them. "It's not a very good time. Mom. Mark is here, and he's miserable. Could you come back later? I'm not even dressed yet. I'm giving Seb his breakfast."

Penny would have left. She had promised herself to stay out of Sarah's affairs, but Kenneth stepped forward and into the house. He scooped up Seb. "I'll see to his breakfast, Sarah. Your mom might be of help to Mark. We know what happened."

Penny followed him in. Sarah yielded but didn't look at Penny. Mark was sitting on a sofa in the small living room. When he saw Penny, he smiled briefly and then seemed to shut down. All expression left his eyes, and he didn't speak.

Penny could feel Sarah standing, hostile, beside her. Kenneth had carried Seb off to the small kitchen and was saying, "Milk on your Cheerios, Seb?"

It was too late to leave, and maybe she could be of help to Mark, if he'd talk to her, and maybe later Sarah would forgive her. She wouldn't be able to forgive herself if she kept Mark and Sarah from continuing to see each other. He was the first man Sarah had been interested in whom she could be genuinely enthusiastic about, so she'd better not show it openly–at least not yet–or seem too interested in their new relationship.

She walked over and sat down on the armchair, facing Mark across the coffee table, and Sarah sat next to him on the couch. She wasn't looking at her mother.

"Mark," Penny said gently. "Rosalind called me and told me what Herman did. Kenneth and I feel really bad about it, and we'll do anything you can think of that would help."

Mark didn't say anything. He kept staring at his hands as if they held some clue as to what had happened and why.

Penny felt awkward. He was giving her no signals, and he wasn't talking at all, just like Rosalind had said. He did need to talk, but she couldn't think of anything else she could say. Maybe she shouldn't have let Kenneth push her on this. Sarah was sullen while Seb was babbling to Kenneth in the kitchen. Mark continued to stare at his hands.

Probably only five minutes had passed, but it seemed an eternity when Mark looked up. "Thank you, Penny. I just … I don't know what so say. It's so horrible. My first big season, and it's all ruined."

"You still have the carrots?"

"Yes, and the transplants in my glassed-in back porch, but I've got nothing to sell now except maybe baby carrots and green onions with no tops." He sounded disgusted.

That was true. She wasn't sure what she could do to ease his pain, but some instinct told her to keep him talking.

"Can we help you set out your summer crops?"

"Will he come back and mow down the tomatoes and peppers, zucchini and eggplants? It was so awful. Nothing left of my beautiful garden." He looked up, tears in his eyes.

Sarah put her arms around him and her head on his shoulder.

"But the gardener is still here," Penny said, "the farmer who knows how to grow beautiful chard and spinach, kale and carrots."

Mark shook his head. "Do they put people away for very long when they destroy your crops?"

"I don't know," Penny said. "Do you have any idea why he did it?"

He stared at Penny as if she'd lost her mind and shook his head. "He might as well have killed me. It hurts so bad."

"But you're okay, Mark. You're alive." She looked at Sarah. "People care about you." Sarah hugged him tight. "The other farmers will help you out."

"It must be Abbie," said Sarah, her anger at her mother temporarily dropped. "She was dating Mark and then Henry, and he went after them both. He's such a weird bastard."

"Abbie told me he bugged her all the time," added Mark. "When we were together, like at meetings and the market, he was always hanging around. What a creep, but I had no idea he was dangerous. He came out of left field on that one. Crazy Herman suddenly goes on the warpath because he can't get a date with Abbie and burns Henry's guitar and destroys my whole spring crop? I feel jinxed. I'm afraid to plant anything else."

Suddenly Sarah got a stricken look on her face. "What if he's the one who killed Kent? He's mean enough." She hugged Mark tightly again. "Like my mom says, you're alive, Mark."

When Penny and Kenneth arrived home, they found a message from Derek, who asked if they could drop by the police station. All he said in explanation was, "I have some questions about Herman."

By the time they found Derek in his tiny office, it was nearly three o'clock. He lifted a stack of papers off his extra chair and invited Penny to sit down, then offered Kenneth his rather beat-up swivel chair. Kenneth shook his head. "I'd rather stand. Sit, Derek."

Derek sat and pulled over his clipboard. He stared at it. "Where to begin?" He sounded both exhausted and exasperated.

Penny said, "We've just talked with Mark over at Sarah's. He's pretty devastated. Herman is here?"

Derek nodded. "But what in the Lord's name am I supposed to do with him? It's clear-cut property damage, but it's hardly a felony. He'll go before the magistrate in the morning and be free to go as long as he attends court when his case comes up. But if I let him go, all the farmers will be down on me like a ton of bricks. Then who knows what he'd do next?"

"We're wondering," Kenneth said, "and I'm sure you are, if he's Kent's killer. Pretty strange behavior. I had him pegged for eccentric, but this is beyond that. Maybe he's mentally unbalanced. He has acted in a much more hostile way than I could have imagined from talking to him."

"I'm stymied," admitted Derek. He smoothed his mustache. "Even if he is the killer, and that's a very good reason for not letting him go, I have no evidence, nothing. He offends me, but I can't figure out how to hold him here beyond tomorrow. I've interviewed him, or at least tried to, but he won't talk, and his father won't hire him a lawyer. He doesn't ask for one anyway. His father won't even talk to him. That was his one phone call, to his father, and it didn't pan out. No one has been to see him."

"Derek, you must have thought we could help in some way if you invited us down. What can we do? Do you want us to talk to him?" asked Penny.

Derek looked at Penny. He always had trouble asking Penny to help him, despite the fact that she was nearly always willing and had often been quite useful to him in the past, even when he hadn't wanted her help. "You, Penny. Maybe you can get from him some idea of what's going on with him. If I had some hint of how he might have poisoned Kent ..."

"He's strange and insecure, Derek, and he's obsessed with Abbie, but I don't think he killed Kent. He may be a grown man, but he acts about thirteen or even younger. I'm happy to talk to him, but I'm not sure I can get you anything relevant to Kent's murder, because I don't think there's any connection."

"But you said Kent was talking to Abbie that afternoon. Jealousy there, too?"

"Yes, Kent flirted with Abbie. Everyone likes Abbie. All the men grow wishful when she's around. I've seen it in their eyes. Herman's not the only one."

"Remember that Herman had no use for Kent," added Kenneth. "You told me that, love. He put him in with that genetically modified lot he hates, like Giles."

"True, but I don't feel the kind of anger in Herman that makes a person want to kill."

Derek was aghast. "Not anger? Penny, he destroyed all of Mark's vegetables and burned a valuable guitar. Wasn't that anger?"

"Let me talk to him," said Penny. "Put a guard at the door, but stay out in the hall, you two. I'll try. He may not talk to me either."

Why was she angry with Derek? Everything he and Kenneth said made logical sense. But murder wasn't a matter of logic, was it? What pushed people to that edge was emotional.

Herman seemed to have acted like a small child, had a tantrum, in effect. She wasn't sure she could be much help to Derek or to Herman, for that matter, but she would try.

Sixteen

Sunday, May 11. The room Penny entered was the same interview room where she'd visited Nora. When Herman was led in, he looked worse than Nora had. Normally sturdy, even jaunty when he walked, he looked gray and on the point of collapse. He shuffled in, suddenly an old man, although Penny assumed him to be in his thirties. He hadn't shaved. His nails and hands were dirty, and he looked cold in his orange prison suit. The room was chilly. It was May, but the old building took a while to change temperature, Derek had told her.

"Hi, Herman. I hope it's okay with you if we talk a little."

He stared at her as if he'd never seen her before.

Derek said, "Sit down, Hicks. Ms. Weaver's trying to help you. I'll be right outside the door." Derek looked his skepticism at Penny but left them alone. He was looking in the window at intervals, Penny noticed.

"I learned that you mowed down Mark's vegetables, Herman. Do you want to tell me why you did that? It hurt Mark a lot to lose his whole spring crop."

Herman lifted his head but stared at her without saying anything. Penny waited. The whole fifteen minutes might pass, but she'd see if he'd talk. She wasn't going to bug him. It was up to him whether he talked to her or not, but no matter why he'd done that, he had put himself in a difficult spot. Anger and jealousy had probably been replaced now by embarrassment, maybe shame, too, given his father's refusal to help him.

Several minutes passed. Penny watched his face and waited. She couldn't read anything there. He showed no emotion.

Then he shifted his position, took a deep breath and said, "I'm sorry, Penny. I know it was wrong. Tell Mark I'm sorry. He can have Abbie. She'll never look at me now I've been in jail."

Had he thought destroying vegetables would get Abbie's attention? "Abbie seems to be dating Henry now, not Mark, Herman, but did you want Abbie to date you? Was that what you thought would happen?"

"I don't know. I don't like Henry either. She's a nice person. Mark and Henry just want her body. I want to marry her and make her a happy woman."

Inside Penny cringed. "But she has to choose who she dates, who she marries, right? Just like you get to choose who you ask out?"

"I asked, and she said no. Worse, she laughed at me. She doesn't understand. I really love her. I'd take care of her. I'm not like these other assholes."

"So then you wanted to get even?"

In a low voice he said, "Stupid."

"We all make mistakes, Herman. I've made a lot. But mistakes can be ways we learn and do better next time."

When he looked up, he was crying. "I always make mistakes."

"Not always. You grow wonderful cabbages, Herman."

He stared at her, unbelieving. "You're not mad at me?"

So her opinion mattered after all. "No. But you're in a spot, Herman. Farmers don't do things like this to other farmers."

"My dad's mad at me. He says I'm no son of his if I do shit like that."

"What about your mother?"

"She's scared of Dad, or she'd probably be down here. Could you go talk to them?"

"What should I say?" She saw Derek gesturing at his watch through the window in the door.

"Tell them I'm sorry. I know it was stupid."

"And Mark?"

"I'll help him plant or whatever he wants. He can have my market money, what I've saved for a greenhouse."

"That's a good start, Herman. We're trying to save our market, too, and help each other, not make things harder than they already are."

"I know. I just liked Abbie."

"All the men seem to," admitted Penny.

Derek knocked and came in. "Time's up, Herman. Let's go."

Herman got to his feet and looked at Penny as if she were the shoreline, and he was having to board a boat to take him he knew not where. "Say hi to Leroy."

"I will." What else could she say?

"Say hi to Leroy?" asked Derek when he came back to collect Penny. "Is that all you got out of him?"

"He's feeling bad now. It was jealousy over Abbie. He asked her out, and she laughed at him."

"He's a grown man, Penny, for God's sake."

"He is, technically, but emotionally he's about eight years old. He offers to give Mark money or help him plant, but I doubt Mark will trust him enough to want him helping. I hope Herman's father lets him go home. It's pretty sad, Derek."

"He acted in a criminal way, Penny, and you feel sorry for him?"

She could tell Derek was fed up with her. Penny remembered suddenly an old cat she'd had who had always seemed indifferent to affection as long as his food bowl was full, but after he was hit by a car and his leg was amputated, he had crawled up in her lap to be comforted. Herman reminded her of that cat.

Kenneth stood up as they re-entered Derek's office and looked at Penny expectantly.

"I do feel sorry for him, Derek. I don't excuse him, but I'd hate to be in his shoes now. About all he had going for him was his wonderful vegetables, and now none of the farmers will trust him, and his father may not either. I hope he has some place to go when you release him."

"Did you talk about Kent?" asked Kenneth.

"No. We didn't get to that, Derek, but I'm sure he didn't kill Kent."

Kenneth didn't say much until they got home that Sunday evening. Penny could tell he didn't believe her intuitive feelings about Herman, even though it had been her insights into people which had, more often than not, zeroed in on a killer when Derek—and sometimes Kenneth, too—had been busy trying to build a case against someone else. She couldn't explain why she was convinced Herman hadn't poisoned Kent. He'd certainly demonstrated that he could be violent, but burning a guitar and mowing down a garden were quite different from slipping poison into someone's punch. She just couldn't see Herman doing that, though she'd have trouble explaining it. She knew he'd ask her to.

They worked together to prepare a simple high tea. It included some leftover minestrone, warmed up in the microwave, with chunks of cheddar cheese, toast made with Penny's rye bread, and sugar snap peas to eat raw. She'd gone down to the garden to pick them while Kenneth made toast and tea and warmed soup. The quiet garden, with the warmth of the day fading, had comforted her. She nibbled peas as she picked them. She had always loved to pick the food she'd eat, whether in the wild or in a garden. She remembered other places she'd lived where she had endured chiggers, briers and steamy July weather to pick wild blackberries. Once in California she'd found a limb of ripe apricots hanging over a fence and helped herself.

When they'd settled to the soup, Kenneth asked gently, "Can you tell me why you believe so strongly in Herman's innocence as far as Kent's murder?"

He genuinely wanted to know. She wished she could explain. Sometimes there was a hard knot of truth that she could feel inside her. It wouldn't budge, even when other people were very persuasive and had many good and reasonable arguments on their side. It was usually impossible to articulate.

"I'll try, but it's hard to explain."

"You were right about Nora. Maybe you're right about Herman, but Derek can't go to his boss with your intuition. He needs logic, Penny, and evidence."

"But logic fails me, and I have no proof."

"Talk about him, then, what you see and know and feel. Maybe the two of us can pull out something that will help Derek. Herman's anti-vegetable and guitar campaign seems part of the whole farmers' market case somehow."

"It may be related. Both are outgrowths of the market. I guess that's why Derek wants to connect it up with Kent's murder, but I think the two events are quite different. Herman's a good farmer but inadequate in people stuff and very inexperienced with women. I told you it's a child's revenge. 'If you won't play with me, I'll smash your toys,' or, 'If you date the girl I like, and I can't get her to go out with me, I'll ruin your guitar and your vegetables.'"

"What was he like when you talked to him?"

"Very pitiful. Sorry now. Feeling stupid and scared of his dad like a little boy who's sure his father will beat him."

"Maybe he will."

"Or used to?"

"Certainly, he has the rage necessary to kill, love."

"But he didn't go after the people, Kenneth. He went for what they loved, not counting Abbie. He's got Abbie on a pedestal like a lovesick teenager. He's suffering and scared now. Kenneth, if he had killed Kent, he wouldn't have continued to act in his normal mode, talking politics, following Abbie around and bringing his vegetables to market. He's so proud of his vegetables. He couldn't have acted so very normal. I'm sure of it."

"But nobody seriously suspected him, right?"

"He was questioned informally by both Derek and me. No, I think he would have acted quite differently back then and now, too, if he'd killed Kent." She stood up to make a fresh pot of tea. "Does that help at all?"

"I'll pass it along to Derek. It helps me see a glimmer of what you see, but Derek's in a very tough spot, and the market is, too. It would be nice to close the case."

Penny reached for the darjeeling cannister. "Of course I want to find the poisoner, but not by picking a scapegoat. Herman has such low self-esteem. It's almost as if his unconscious drove him to do those stupid things so he'd get caught and punished, even if it wasn't for what he did. It's too easy, Kenneth." She rinsed the pot with boiling water, then spooned in tea and filled the pot.

"Fancy another piece of toast?"

"Yes, thanks, with peach marmalade."

"I was thinking the same thing, and we have cream cheese."

"Even better."

As he stood by the toaster, he said without looking at her, "It does worry me, love, all this violence, and our still not knowing where it's all coming from."

She gave him her full attention. "What do you mean? I don't believe we're in any serious danger."

He took the toast onto a plate and then gave her one piece. He set the marmalade and cream cheese on the table between them. "How can we fail to be, especially you? You always get into the thick of things. Someone in that market–one of those farmers, we assume–is a killer, and you're there every week and also trying to find out what happened. I mean, supposing Herman is a murderer, and there you go, sitting alone with him in that interrogation room, and Derek outside the door instead of in there with you. You're precious to me, love."

He was slathering marmalade on his toast and topping it with a big slice of cream cheese. She poured their tea. "We've been through this before, Kenneth, though not recently. I'm not a prehistoric woman you can drag off to your cave and club anybody who gets too close, right?"

She hoped to stir his sense of humor, but it didn't look like it was working. He wasn't smiling as he poured milk in his tea and stirred it round and round. "I'm serious. You have your intuitive feelings. I have mine. I want you to pull out of this market and all its problems. We can afford to lose those few dollars a week it brings in. I don't want you to get hurt. The whole thing is running away downhill. Even if the state doesn't close it–and, frankly, I wish they would even if you hate me for saying that–I won't rest easy until you're out of it. We could go to Wales in a week, not wait for August. Then we'd be right out of it."

Monday morning Penny was still depressed over Kenneth's sense of urgency about getting her out of the market. He left early, and she wrote in her diary for a couple of hours, trying to sort herself out. No, she did not want to pull out of the market. Not yet. Everything she was doing right now, including helping find the killer, if she could, felt right. That core of truth inside her made her sure she should not yield to Kenneth's fear for her. His over-protectiveness was an old issue, but they'd always gotten through it before. Surely, they would this time, too. She loved him, but she couldn't dodge or deny the clarity inside her. It hurt her that he didn't see things as she did. It always had.

She wondered sometimes what made people accident prone and why some, herself included, seemed "accident-unlikely." Several times over the last ten years or so she had confronted a killer, but she'd always emerged unscathed. She'd been in car accidents a few times, too, or stumbled and fallen. The summer before she met Kenneth, she had sprained her ankle very badly walking alone in a remote part of Gower, but she thought of that as one of the few times in her life when she hadn't followed her intuition. When she did, any minor problems she ran into were just that, minor. The car had a flat tire, but it was in the driveway at the time. She fell flat on her back picking peaches from a high limb, but she didn't break anything. It wasn't exactly a charmed life, but she did believe that her strongest intuitions, the ones that came at her out of the blue or stuck like the one inside her now about not giving up, were the reason she was relatively safe. If she was listening to what she needed to do, then she was, if not exactly protected, yet in her best possible place for coping with whatever came along.

She felt slightly better by eleven, though she still didn't know how to bring Kenneth around so he wouldn't worry so about her. She would arrange it so they could leave August first, but now she had to focus all her energies on saving the market. She was in their big, half-acre garden, down on her knees weeding, when Sammie walked over to her.

"Need some help, girlfriend?"

"I didn't hear your car. Sure, you can weed that row of tomato plants, and I'll keep on with these peppers. Can you stay and have lunch? I could use your perspective."

"I picked up some strudel in the bakery at Food Plus for us, hoping I could stay awhile. I'm so mad at Derek, I could spit."

Penny stopped to mop her face with a paper towel. Even with a sweat band, she was dripping. It must be close to ninety degrees already. She laughed. "I'm not exactly mad at Kenneth, but I can't get him to understand why I need to stick with the market and also find this killer we've got."

"Don't tell me. He wants to whisk you away to Wales, away from all these dangerous Americans you keep getting hooked up with?"

"Exactly. He's on his protect-his-wife-at-all-costs kick, like a caveman, I told him. But I refuse to be a cave wife, and he has no sense of humor at the moment." She flung a handful of weeds onto the pile she was collecting to feed to Leroy's chickens.

"Meantime, Derek is still chasing down all the wrong suspects, at least as far as I can see. I mean, he finally saw the light with Nora, but now he's sure Herman did it. Herman's a creep, but I can't see him as a sneaky poisoner. He's so out there. Sneaky? No, he runs right over you with all his opinions and hostilities. Derek is being stupid."

"Kenneth thinks Herman's guilty, too. I talked to Herman."

"Derek told me. He spent ten minutes telling me that intuitions, including yours, Penny, could be way off base. Then I called Nora, and would you believe it? She thinks Herman's the one, too."

Penny flung another handful of weeds. The pepper plants seemed as relieved as she felt as she rid them of the little weeds springing up. "I think we're right, whoever disagrees. Herman's a mess, but he's not a killer."

"Who else we got? You saving these weeds to cook or something?"

"The dandelions could be cooked, but no, they're for the chickens. They love them. I've gone over it and over it. I'm not going to tackle Giles, and he seems unlikely. That leaves Henry and George. I really like George. I don't like Henry, but ..."

"What if I talk to George again and you talk to Henry? See if we get any new zingy intuitions?"

Penny laughed and wiped sweat off her face again. "I don't see Henry now that he ditched Sarah again."

"That's okay. Then you can have George, and I'll take Henry. Be a pleasure to press him a bit. He could be the one, though I can't see why either of them would have plotted to kill Kent. Whoever did it was some devious plotter. Oh, and I found out something interesting."

"Think we should stop? It's getting awfully hot."

"Yes, ma'am. Let me pull up the chicken food on the rest of this row first. I bugged Derek to tell me what the poison was, but he wouldn't, said it 'wadn' my bidness.' You know how he gets, another variation on Kenneth Caveman. So I got up real early this morning and had a peek in his briefcase. Kent's file was there, along with the pathologist's report. The symptoms, plus the analysis of his stomach contents, yuck, suggest one of the really toxic nightshades, either Deadly Nightshade, which is *atropa belladonna,* or Black Nightshade, *solanum nigrum."*

Penny stood and straightened her back. "Sneaky of you, not to say devious, but very helpful to us, and Derek is getting nowhere, right? At the market he mentioned it could be a poisonous nightshade but gave no other details."

"Right. It's ridiculous. Where would he and Kenneth be ending up without their womenfolks' help? Where do you want this chicken lunch to go?"

Seventeen

Monday, May 12. Penny called George Gardiner, after Sammie left about two o'clock, and left a message on his answering machine. She felt restless. They knew now that it had been one of two poisonous nightshades. She and Kenneth didn't own an encyclopedia, but she got out her trusty Standard College Dictionary, out of date but very useful for both English and American vocabulary, and the derivations of words. Under *nightshade* she learned about Black or Common Nightshade which had white flowers and black berries. In the nightshade family also were tobacco, peppers, jimsonweed, tomato and potato. Interesting. Deadly Nightshade was also used medicinally in very small amounts as belladonna.

She had heard something about Kent's symptoms. He'd been vomiting. What else? Diarrhea? Then, yes, the woman who found him thought he was crazy. He hadn't seemed in his right mind. Where could she check the symptoms? Had it been Black or Deadly Nightshade? Oh, his secretary had left the air conditioning on for him since he'd been sweating a lot.

Who could help her? She could drive down to the library, but she didn't feel like changing out of her garden wear into going-out clothes. Then Andy drove in. Home early? It was nearly three. Maybe he had some comp time coming. The twins wouldn't be home for a while. She might be able to snag him for a few minutes. He might know about Black Nightshade. Ag agents had to learn a lot about plants. Did it grow in Shagbark? If a farmer poisoned Kent, and it could grow locally, it seemed likely it was growing here, maybe even on someone's farm in the county.

She tied on her old tennis shoes and hurried down the outer stairs. Andy was getting out of his Toyota pickup. She caught him before he slipped into his house through the garage door. "Hi, Andy, can I consult you for a minute?"

He turned and gave her a big smile. "Yes, Mama Penny, any time. I'd be honored. Usually we all consult you. Come on in. Jan has a late meeting, so I'm on kid duty, meet the school bus, give snacks, all that. Lovely day, eh? I thought I'd get the kids out to help weed."

"Sammie and I worked down through the peppers and tomatoes earlier. It is hot, though."

He gestured to their comfortable den couch. "Drink? I'm having some apple juice."

"Sure." She sat back on the couch and took a deep breath. She would be glad when all this turmoil was over. Would it ever be over?

When he returned with two tall glasses, she explained that she wanted to learn all she could about the nightshade family, especially Deadly Nightshade and Black Nightshade.

"Jimson weed can kill you, too," he said, setting down his glass. "A couple of kids in my senior class ate a spoonful of seeds and had really bad hallucinations. No one in the Emergency Room could figure out what they were high on. Finally, toward morning, one of them confided in his mother, thinking she was his girlfriend, that they had gone into the botanical gardens at the university and stolen some jimson weed seeds. They were lucky they didn't die."

"Would you have some kind of reference work about them? I guess it could have been jimson weed, and I have seen that around. It's a garden weed, right? But I think Black or Deadly Nightshade is more likely, if they grow here. My guess is that whoever poisoned Kent was growing it or knew where it grew somewhere around here."

Andy stood up. "So it's Kent's death you're trying to figure out. Aren't the police pretty sure Herman Hicks did it? Nora said they'd arrested him."

Penny hoped Andy wouldn't fuss at her like Kenneth had but would go ahead and help her. He must have access to books she could consult, but she didn't want him to spread abroad that she and Sammie were doing their own investigating. It wasn't quite a lie when she said, "I'm curious, Andy. From what I've heard, he had some hallucinations but also vomiting and diarrhea, and he was sweating a lot. It all happened fast. True, they've got Herman in jail, but he may not be Kent's killer, even though he certainly killed Miles's spring vegetables and Henry's guitar."

"Are you sure you want to get into this, Penny? I feel protective of you. Shouldn't you leave it to the police?"

Another quandary. She didn't want to lie outright to him, though she knew Sammie wouldn't have hesitated, but she didn't want him talking to Kenneth either. "It's my curiosity, Andy. I'd like to know more about these poisons. If they crop up easily as a weed, I want to be better educated. For instance, we give the weeds we pull to the chickens, but I'd never give them jimson weed, and I wouldn't want to give them another poisonous nightshade by mistake." Would he accept that? She waited, wondering what else she could say if he wouldn't help her. Who else would know? Maybe Nora. She grew a lot of herbs.

But Andy said, "Let's look in my study. I think I have a book on medicinal herbs. Of course, in medicinal plants a small amount can be helpful, but a larger amount can be lethal, as with poke, but you know that."

She nodded and followed him into what would have been a downstairs guest bedroom but was serving as office space for both him and Jan when they needed to work at home. She sat down in his desk swivel chair while he bent down to study the volumes in the bookcase next to his desk. Jan had a desk on the other side of the room which looked out over the front lawn.

They each also had a computer. Both their jobs involved heavy use of a computer and the internet.

As he stood up with a thick tome in his hands, Andy looked at his watch. "Uh oh, time for the kids' bus. Here, Penny, have a look. The index should have all the nightshade plants. I'd better get out to the bus stop." He hurried out.

She found the two entries. *Atropa Belladonna,* Deadly Nightshade, didn't grow wild in central North Carolina, but Black or Common Nightshade did. The first could be cultivated, and the roots were used to produce the drug atropine, or belladonna, which was used in very small doses to ease intestinal disturbances and to dilate the pupils for an eye exam. Her first husband had taken it to relax him so his incipient ulcer would get no worse. The symptoms produced by only a single leaf or a few berries of Deadly Nightshade were severe: dilated pupils and blurred vision, a slow heartbeat, loss of balance, staggering, headache, rash, slurred speech, confusion and hallucinations to the point of delirium and convulsions. The Black Nightshade, if unripe fruit or leaves were ingested, led to enlarged pupils, but also sweating, stomach pain and vomiting, diarrhea, an erratic pulse, slowed breathing, and again, delirium and hallucinations.

Curious how deadly one branch of the family was and how delicious and useful the potato, tomato and eggplant branches were.

It must have been the Black Nightshade that had killed Kent. Diarrhea and vomiting. In medicinal amounts it could be used to help people sweat, and he'd sweated profusely.

She closed the book and was kneeling to replace it in the bookshelf when little Penny and Kenny, flushed and sweaty, burst into the room and flung themselves on her. She pivoted and hugged them. "You guys look hot."

They nodded and threw down their school backpacks and lunch boxes on the rug beside her.

Andy turned up in the doorway. "Come and have some apple juice, Pen and Ken. First, put your things away. Let Aunt Penny finish her research."

She rose to her feet and followed them all toward the kitchen. "Thanks, Andy. I found what I needed. Apparently, it's Black Nightshade that's fairly common around here, and there's a good photo of it in that book. Can I have another glass of juice, too? Then I might join your weeding team."

"Of course, Mama Penny. Come on, kids, into the kitchen."

They were all seated at the kitchen table in a nook with long benches on either side when the front doorbell rang, and Andy hopped up to get it.

"We're doing research at school," little Penny was reporting, "and I have to interview someone, you know, some old person like you or my grandma." Penny smiled. She seldom thought of herself as old, but to eight, sixty-five could seem ancient.

"I'm sure Grandma Belle would love to be interviewed," said Penny, thinking they certainly started them early on the academic approach.

"Oh, Ken already has dibs on Grandma Belle. Can I ask you my questions?"

Penny looked at their young solemn faces and said, "What about Grandma Kate?"

Little Penny was insistent: "I want you, Aunt Penny."

"Okay. So what do you need to ask me?"

Andy had reappeared with George Gardiner in tow, also red-faced and sweating, his hands in his overall pockets.

"George, I wanted to talk to you!" She spoke loudly enough to be sure he heard her.

"I know. I thought I'd drop in, since I had to be in Riverdell, and see if I could get some of Leroy's eggs and maybe some of y'all's lettuce and suchlike. I'll pay, of course. You got extras?"

"Sit down, George, and have some apple juice." Andy gestured to the bench where he'd been sitting. Then he looked at Penny. "I think we can fix you up with veggies and eggs?"

"Oh, yes," Penny said. "We've got lots."

"Don't forget. I have to interview you." Little Penny was tenacious. To make her point, she grabbed Penny's arm as if her subject might escape.

"I will, little Penny, but I also need to talk to George and get him some eggs." Penny hugged her and started to get up.

Then George said he wanted to get the vegetables first. Andy halted at the back door as he and George were about to go out. He was carrying the big basket they used for harvesting vegetables. "Interview, Pen?" He looked puzzled.

"Ken and I have to do interviews of old people, over fifty years old, our teacher said. It's our homework, Dad. Ken is interviewing Grandma Belle when she gets home, and Aunt Penny promised me."

Andy looked from Pen to Ken. They both nodded solemnly. "Okay, you talk to Aunt Penny right now. Ken, you come with me and help pick veggies for Mr. Gardiner. Penny, where are the eggs? I'll get them so you can be interviewed." He lifted his eyebrows.

"We have two dozen in our refrigerator, and George can have both if he wants. Leroy hasn't gathered eggs today yet, and I know he has some in his egg refrigerator, but it's easier to get mine. The door's open."

When she and little Penny were alone, Penny saw that her interviewer had her tablet open to a clean page and a typed list of questions on a sheet of paper. "What do you need to know?"

"Did you grow up in Riverdell?"

"No. I moved here in 1991, long before you were born."

Penny watched her write down "No."

"Where did you grow up?"

"In a little town in Oklahoma. Norman, Oklahoma."

"Tell me about when you were eight years old like me. What year was that?"

"I was eight years old in 1945. We were still in a war. That was World War II, and my daddy was in the war. He was gone.

The war ended that summer, and my friends and I made a parade and walked around the block shouting, "The war is over. Our daddies are coming home."

Pen's next question startled her. "Were there any black people in your little town?"

"No. In fact, they had a very bad law in that town that no black person could be there after dark. They called Norman a sundown town. My mother explained it to me. I was about eight when she told me, and I was very upset. They were people, too."

Pen was listening with complete attention. She'd forgotten to write things down. "That's very mean."

"Yes, it was." She was thinking of Sammie and how racism died so very slowly, even fifty years after the Supreme Court's decision on desegregation. They'd never figured out who had tried to block Sammie, though Giles had shown his racist side at their May Day celebration market, but who else? Little Penny pulled her arm.

"Aunt Penny?"

"Yes, I'm listening. Sorry."

"So if Aunt Sammie had lived there–no, she couldn't even live there, and she couldn't come visit us after dark?"

"That's right. Of course, no black children went to school with us. Even the colleges for black people were separate from the colleges for white people. They called it separate but equal, but it wasn't equal education. It was very unequal. The college where I teach still has mostly African Americans, but now all American young people can choose the colleges they want to go to as long as their grades are good enough to get in and they have enough money. Now most children in our country go to integrated public schools. It means everyone is welcome, no matter their skin color."

Pen was lost in thought, staring into space. Penny waited. "You mean you couldn't even have a black babysitter, like we have Neill and Joe sometimes? Or play with black friends and go to school together?"

"That's right. It was very wrong, so finally they changed the laws, but black and white people had to work together to make it change, and it took a long time. That was called the Civil Rights Movement. It's much better now, but still some people are mean to our African American friends and neighbors." They were too little to understand how insidious racism still was. Maybe when they were in college, it would be better. She devoutly hoped so. "I'm happy you and Ken don't go to a segregated school."

"Me, too."

"Hadn't you better write some of this down?"

"Oh, I forgot. Thank you, Aunt Penny. I think that's all I need now." She bent her head over her tablet, and Penny eased off the bench and walked quietly to the back door.

George was putting plastic bags of vegetables under the tattered burlap in his big red pickup. He pulled out a pot with an orange columbine blooming in it as she walked over.

"Oh, George, that's lovely. I love columbine."

"Eh?"

"I love columbine!"

"I brought it to give you as a present. I thought you'd said you were partial to 'em." He smiled and handed it to her.

"Thanks so much, George. Come up a minute. I want to pick your brain."

"It's going to rain? I'd better get home."

"No, George." She pointed at the bright blue sky. "I want to talk to you, remember? Pick your brain." She pointed at her head.

"Sure thing, Penny. That's why I came over in the first place. You think the vegetables will be okay? They won't wilt? I'm about to wilt myself."

"Should be okay, with your burlap to shade them, and the shade of the house is moving toward your truck."

She led the way up the outside stairs to their apartment, very aware of George panting as he lumbered up after her. She slowed her pace, but it didn't help much. Didn't he ever get exercise? How did he manage his extensive nursery of exotic, wild, sun and shade plants without moving around? She found vegetable gardening very strenuous but healthy exercise.

She held the door. His face was so red, she was alarmed. "You okay, George?"

He nodded, too out of breath to speak, plodded into the room and sank onto the couch where she gestured.

"You look awfully red in the face."

"Sorry I have so slow a pace. I'm out of shape." He caught his breath. "Stairs kill me, and then the heat."

"I'll get you some water." Hopefully he wouldn't die on her. "Would you rather have Gatorade?"

"I have a hearing aid. My hearing's not much good."

She held up the Gatorade. Had he heard her? "Or would you rather have water?"

"Water's fine."

She handed him a glass and poured herself some Gatorade. It was hot. Now how should she get him talking? He knew the other farmers better than she did. "I keep trying to understand what exactly happened the day Kent got poisoned. Can you remember back to that market in April?" She said everything loudly and slowly, trying to enunciate clearly.

George took out a large white pocket handkerchief that had been clean but now was crumpled and damp, and wiped his face. "What do you want to know? I'll never forget that day. I liked Kent okay. He's been around these parts some years. Went to State after he finished his years in the Army. Started working here. I forget exactly, but mebbe ten years ago. Good man. Knew poultry. The big chicken farmers liked him. I waren't close to Kent or nothin', but we spoke, y' know. That time he made me move so Sibyl could have my spot? He had no right, but Sibyl's pushy like that. I don't like pushy women."

Penny figured she fell into that category, but there was no point calling attention to it. He was talking. Let him talk.

"I waren't happy to have to move and all, after I were all set up–takes me twenty minutes to set out all my plants, so I were pissed, but more at Sibyl than at Kent. Know what I mean? That Giles is a pain. Why did he have to get into it? He shoulda kept his trap shut. But Kent was only trying to help. Now the one I don't trust at all is Herman. I knew he was a loner, but I'm just boggled at what he done to Mark. Listen, if somebody ruined all my plants, I would take a shotgun to 'im, fill his britches with buckshot, yes, ma'am. That ain't right. Know what I mean?"

"That day," Penny said clearly and loudly, "the day Kent was poisoned, who else was there when Kent was there? Do you remember? Leroy and I were, and Nora. You and Giles. Henry was setting up, and Abbie was helping him. I think Sibyl was there, too, must have been if Abbie was?"

She didn't have a clear picture of Sibyl that afternoon. Then she suddenly remembered watching Sibyl stacking her jellies, and right before he left Kent had stopped at her table and been talking to Abbie. Yes, Sibyl had been there. Did that make a difference?

"Yeah, Sibyl was there. For a change she didn't fuss about her place. Herman was there. He's an oddball. I had no idea he could be so mean. Just a little strange, I always thought, but after what he done to Mark? He must have killed Kent. None of the rest of us is ugly mean, know what I'm saying?"

"Let me ask you this, George. Have you ever thought any of the other farmers was a racist? You know, might not want black farmers in the market?" She enunciated as clearly as she could.

"Nah, not really. Giles mebbe. He calls 'em colored folk still. Least it's better than niggers. He has a whole slew of 'em picking and weeding for him. Sibyl has her colored man, too. But you mean what might have kept out the cut flower lady, Sammie? Herman was agin her because it was only flowers, not food growing, but I ain't seen any problem. She's fitted right in, seems like. I ain't picked up any bad vibes about her."

Penny felt tremendous relief. Whatever had been, at least it wasn't as active or virulent as she'd feared. She'd tell Sammie. "Thanks, George. She's a wonderful woman and a good friend."

She chatted with George another ten minutes, but her mind was elsewhere. They still had no idea who had poisoned Kent. She was relieved when George pulled himself upright, his face slightly less red, and took himself home.

Eighteen

May 13, Tuesday morning. When Penny and Rosalind drove up to Sibyl's farm in Rosalind's small green van the next day, Penny suggested that, although it seemed so unlikely, Sibyl could have poisoned Kent. They were friends, yes, but Penny was determined to check out every possibility, and she needed Rosalind's help.

At first Rosalind was horrified and could barely consider it. Sibyl was a friend. Slowly she had allowed that Sibyl did have strong feelings in certain areas, for instance about Abbie and who she should marry, and she was very proud of her baking and her jellies. Penny hadn't seen much evidence of passion in Sibyl. She hid her feelings very well, but Rosalind had known her for years. They had been raising their children together through the eighties and nineties. "You must have talked freely," Penny said.

"No," said Rosalind, "not really. She's not one to confide much. Keeps her counsel, but she's a good woman and a wonderful baker. We were often together, helping each other with farm chores or keeping each other's children. She wouldn't kill Kent, Penny, and besides, he's been her friend for years, since before her husband died."

"I don't say she did it, Rosalind," said Penny as Rosalind braked and stopped before the farm gate. A large wooden sign announced in black letters painted on white: Kidds' Acres. Sibyl Kidd, Baker. To their right was a huge strawberry field, and to the left Penny could make out fruit trees planted at regular intervals. Peach, probably, apple, and the definitive, slightly lopsided shape of the native Kiefer pear which made such amazing pear preserves.

Penny got out to open the gate and latch it again after Rosalind had driven through. "When I called her," Penny said, "I said I wanted to see her place, especially her fruit trees and berry bushes. We might put in a few blueberry bushes for next season. Don't worry about my suspicions. I could be wrong. I hope I am. Let's enjoy the visit, okay?"

"I know you want to help Herman like you helped Nora, and I know Nora didn't do it. I was sure arresting her was all wrong, but what Herman did was so cruel. I've never seen Sibyl be cruel like Herman was. Mark and Henry are still devastated."

"I agree what Herman did was terrible, and he definitely did that. It is possible he killed Kent, but that's hard for me to believe. Anyway, if we're going to save our market, we have to solve it, and we only have today. So keep an open mind." Penny grinned at Rosalind's worried look. "Try not to worry. You be her friend. I'll be the sleuth." Looking for Black Nightshade, she didn't say.

Rosalind, if not totally reassured, seemed to have put it out of her mind when Sibyl appeared at her back door and came out to greet them. By her side a large Australian shepherd dog walked slowly and somewhat awkwardly, as if its joints hurt, wagging its tail slowly back and forth. Sibyl wore a scarf over her curly grey hair and the kind of old-fashioned farm apron that Penny remembered her grandmother used to wear to save her morning dresses as she called them, while she was cooking and doing housework.

Sibyl smiled at them. Penny couldn't remember having seen her smile before.

"Come on in the kitchen. I've just finished making strawberry jam, and I've got a new lemon sponge cake I want you to try. I might take it to market, if you like it."

"If we still have a market," said Penny.

"I also sell at Sanford, but I doubt they'll close us down in Riverdell now that Herman's been arrested. I've never known them to close a market or even a restaurant around here, though they threaten all the time."

Sibyl's kitchen was bright and sunny. Blue and white gingham curtains stirred in the breeze. Twelve new half-pints of bright red strawberry jam were cooling on one counter. Sibyl gestured to the table covered with an oil cloth with a daisy pattern and set with three mugs, cake plates, napkins, and forks. In pride of place was a golden yellow tube cake with pale yellow frosting running down its sides.

"Looks delicious," said Penny, pulling out a chair. "I hope we're not keeping you from something. It's a busy time of year."

"Oh, I have a colored man to help me." Sibyl smiled, and Penny winced inwardly.

"He'll be out working in the strawberries. I will have things to do before lunch, but I was ready for a sit-down. I get up at five and generally take a coffee break about now. Then you wanted to see the orchard and the berry bushes, and I have time to show you."

"It's a beautiful place," said Penny. Sibyl cut them each a generous slice of cake and poured fresh coffee into their cups.

"She's worked so hard since Arnie died," put in Rosalind, taking a bite of cake. "Ooh, this sponge is wonderful, Sibyl. You'll sell this for sure. In fact, I'll buy one. We have a big family dinner tomorrow night. If you've got time to make one. Rex loves anything lemon flavored."

Sibyl smiled. "I made two. You can take the other one with you."

"It is delicious," Penny agreed. She looked around the large kitchen with lots of counter space, two large refrigerators, cupboards on every wall, a new enamel top stove and a triple stainless steel sink. It was a baker and jelly-maker's dream.

Penny was brought back to the drift of the conversation when Rosalind said, "Henry? Yes, he's with us, still recovering from losing his guitar. He's a pretty sad boy right now."

"Have you learned much about him?" asked Sibyl, picking up their plates and taking them to the sink, where she immediately soaped and rinsed them, then set them in the rack.

"No, not much. Maybe Penny knows more. He was dating her daughter Sarah and staying with her, I think."

"Yes," said Penny. "He moved out of Sarah's without saying anything to her. She'd been feeding him for several weeks. I'm surprised you hired him, Rosalind. I've never had the impression that he was a worker." That was putting it mildly. Ah, she and Sibyl were united in one thing: they didn't trust Henry.

"We shall see," said Rosalind defensively. "He's a pleasant young man, but so far he has been too upset to work. We're giving him today. Then we need him to carry his load."

"Of course you do," said Sibyl as if scandalized. "I couldn't have a slacker here. Abbie helps me when she's not on shift at the hospital, and I work dawn to dark. We have to if we want to make the money we need to live and run this farm. Farming's not a life for people who like to sit around."

She looked at Penny, who, of course, being a poet and a writing teacher, did do a fair amount of sitting around. There were even hard-to-explain times she needed to sit and do nothing, let her mind percolate, in order to write a good poem later. It was time to get things back on track. "I can't wait to see your berry bushes. You make most of the fruit you grow into jellies and jams, right?"

"Yes, I do. I make better money from the jellies for the time involved. Let's go have a look unless you want more coffee?" She turned to Rosalind, who shook her head and stood.

Sibyl led them out a side door past a huge herb garden near woods, with the berry bushes and grapevines farther along. A huge grapevine grew over a large framed support of beams and lattice work, about twenty feet by twenty feet. Other, smaller vines were similarly supported nearby. They looked incredibly healthy with bright green leaves, and the tiny grapes were already forming.

"The big one is Scuppernong, and the two on the right are white and black Muscadines, which fertilize the Scuppernong. They all make good jelly, and I can grape juice, too. Here on the left are Concord grapes. They make wonderful jelly, too, and good juice. I keep the Niagara for eating. I don't make wine, but it's a good wine grape."

"Andy Style has Muscadines," added Penny. "I've made jelly a few times. I love the Muscadine flavor."

"Me, too," said Rosalind. "Oh, there are her blueberries. They're already making berries."

"Yes, though they won't be ripe for another three or four weeks. After them, in July, the raspberries will start."

Penny loved raspberries and had always thought they needed a mountain habitat or cooler weather than in central North Carolina. "They do okay here? I'd love to have raspberries."

"I've had good luck with them," said Sibyl. "Once they start, they bear to frost. These are the red Everbearing ones. I cut the canes back after frost. They do best that way. Once established, they go and go."

After they'd walked through the orchard's orderly rows of peach, pear, plum and apple trees, they turned back toward the house, and Penny slowed down, wanting time to look carefully at the herbs. Couldn't she just ask for an herb garden tour? "I see you grow so many herbs. I've grown some, but I have trouble keeping sage. What a lovely, large bush."

"Yes, once it's established, it does well. This one is eleven or twelve years old. It makes a good tea for a cold, too."

"Do you have other medicinal herbs?" Was she being too obvious? Worth the risk though. Sibyl seemed content to point out the various ones.

"This large one at the edge was here when I married Arnie back in 1970. It's an old timer. People used it for fever in the old days. It's spice bush or fever bush." They stopped to admire it, about fifteen feet high with berries forming.

"I'd heard of it," said Penny, "but I've never seen it. Interesting."

"Here's her galax," contributed Rosalind. "I remember once when I was over here with my girls, and Abbie cut her finger, and you put galax leaves on the cut to stop the bleeding."

"Yes, it's useful for cuts and kidney problems. Do you know this one? Woundwort?"

She pointed to a dense ground cover of what Penny had learned about in Wales. "Yes, but we call it Self-Heal. Good for colds and allergies."

"And wounds," added Sibyl. "It's an astringent, as well as a natural antibiotic."

"I've made tea with it, but I've never used it for wounds. How do you apply it?"

Sibyl stopped and picked a leaf. "*Prunella vulgaris* is one of the most useful herbs. I make a strong tea and use that to clean wounds. You could probably make a salve, but I've never bothered to do that."

She twirled the leaf in her fingers and turned toward the side door. "I'll get your cake, Rosalind. Then I'd better get back to work. I need to make more jam now that the strawberries are coming in. I should have them for market, too, this week."

Penny looked back at the herb garden. Her eyes had been searching for Black Nightshade though all she had to go on was the photo in Andy's book. Then she saw jimson weed close to the woods the herb garden backed up to. It definitely wasn't being treated as a weed. There were half a dozen cultivated plants. She walked over to it, and on the other side saw what must be the nightshade. The white flowers looked just like they did in the book.

"Penny, we need to go." Rosalind was calling her from just inside the back door into the kitchen.

"Coming." Her heart was pounding, but she couldn't let on that she'd noticed anything. She wasn't good at hiding her feelings. She'd have to keep pretending how impressed she was with everything, pretend she hadn't noticed any deadly herbs being cultivated. She entered the kitchen through the back door, but she didn't say much for a few minutes, trying to calm herself down while Sibyl put the lemon sponge cake into a bakery box. Rosalind gave her fifteen dollars, saying it was worth more than that to her.

"I envy you your big place," said Penny when she thought she could speak normally. "You've inspired me to try raspberries and sage once more. Do you have any secrets about sage?"

"Not really. It's done well in that spot. I do sometimes move plants if they're not doing well, try them somewhere else. Sage does like lots of hot sun."

"Thanks, and for the cake and everything."

Rosalind gave Sibyl an impulsive hug, but Rosalind hugged everybody. Penny couldn't do that, but she thought she'd acted the part of a fellow farmer, interested in learning from Sibyl and impressed with her farm, fairly well. She hoped so.

Kenneth was grilling cheese sandwiches when she got back to their apartment a little after noon. He had two on the cast iron griddle and a bowl of radishes and carrots on the kitchen table. "Is one of those sandwiches for me?" asked Penny. "I'm starved." This despite the lemon cake she'd had earlier.

"I can make more," he said. "I didn't know when you'd be back. This is an unexpected pleasure." He leered at her and wiggled his eyebrows.

"One is fine for me." She sat down, exhausted suddenly and distracted now that she could think about what she'd seen. She was pretty sure that Sibyl was the poisoner, but her having Black Nightshade in her garden didn't prove it. At this point it was only a hunch, but it fit some way she couldn't quite get hold of. At first Kenneth didn't pick up on her mood, though normally he did instantly.

It was when he carried his griddle over to slide a beautifully browned sandwich, with cheese oozing out between the bread slices, onto her plate that he caught her eye. "Penny, what's wrong?"

"A lot."

He slid a sandwich onto his plate, then put the griddle back on the stove and sat down next to her. "Tell me."

"Rosalind and I went to see Sibyl Kidd this morning. Kenneth, she has an herb garden with some Black Nightshade plants in it."

He looked puzzled. Hadn't Derek told him what the poison was that had killed Kent? Uh oh. She knew about it because Sammie had sneaked a look in Derek's file. "It may have been what poisoned Kent. I learned his symptoms, and Andy let me look up the poisonous nightshade plants in his herbal encyclopedia."

"So?"

"Well, Sibyl was there early that market day, too. She'd been coming late, but she was there when Kent was there. She never came down to the punch table, but I thought it possible."

Kenneth looked relieved. "Penny, Herman must have done it. He was at the punch table. Look at his behavior. The man's violent. Why don't you see it?"

"But there's no evidence he did it, Kenneth." She felt like crying. Why couldn't he see what was so very clear to her, even clearer the more she thought about it. Sibyl was so worried about Abbie's men. She didn't want any slackers, no poor farmers or itinerant musicians. Of course, Kent had status as an ag agent, but suppose she didn't want Kent either for whatever reason? His playing around with women maybe?

Kenneth focused on her, his expression solemn, his words careful. "You have some new evidence that points to Sibyl, love?"

"Not a lot, but what I know now is suggestive. She has a big herb garden with lots of medicinal plants. I saw two that are very poisonous, and I think Kent died because of Black Nightshade poisoning, and she's growing it, and she was there at the right time."

"Penny, love. That's not evidence. Nora grows a lot of herbs, too, and that was another reason Derek was suspicious. Try not to jump to conclusions. It's dangerous. One of these farmers is very dangerous. I think it's Herman, and he's locked up for the moment, but please, love, don't try to solve this one. Leave it to Derek."

"But Kenneth, they'll close the market tomorrow. I can't let that happen without trying to solve this. Please understand. This is very important to me. I thought it was to you, too." She felt tears coming.

He put his arm around her and said quietly, "Penny, you are very important to me. You scare me to death when you go haring off to find a killer. Please, Penny, please, love, be sensible."

She sighed. He didn't get it. What should she do now? What could she do?

Nineteen

May 13, Tuesday afternoon. Fortunately, the phone rang. Penny hadn't figured out what to say to Kenneth. She wasn't getting through. Her normally understanding and supportive husband had closed his mind. She knew from long experience that she wouldn't get anywhere arguing with him right then, but it was hard to stop. She had to convince someone. So the phone call was a blessing, and it was Sammie wanting to talk to her. Thank the goddess.

As he handed her the phone Kenneth said, "We'll talk more later. I have to get back down to the station. Derek has a project for me. Be smart, Penny. Don't go anywhere. I'll emphasize to Derek the urgency you feel, but please, love, stay out of it." He held her eyes. Yes, he was definitely worried.

She didn't want to hear any more. He loved her, and he was scared for her, which was probably why she started crying. She brushed away her tears so he wouldn't see them. He hugged her and left.

"Penny?"

"I'm here."

"You sound terrible. What is it?"

"Everything."

"Tell, girlfriend. You want me to come over?"

"No. Just a minute. Let me lock the door. Kenneth's just left."

"You had a fight?"

"Sort of. Okay, here's what I've learned. Does it make sense to you? Kenneth thinks I'm full of it, and everybody else thinks Herman is guilty. They don't want to consider Sibyl."

"Sibyl? Wow, I never thought of that. Tell, girlfriend."

So she told Sammie her suspicions and what she had observed in Sibyl's herb garden.

"That's got to be it, Penny. You must be right. Derek and the others–Kenneth, too–are just chasing their tails. But how can we flush out Sibyl and not get poisoned our own selves?"

Penny laughed. "You are such good medicine, Sammie."

"'Course I am. You let men's foolishness get to you too easy, girlfriend. They try to be so logical, but they don't make sense, just go 'round in circles, and we have to figure it out for them. Why don't you come over? I'll feed you fried pies, and I got some delicious, fresh roasted beans to make coffee."

"I'd love to, but Kenneth would probably have a fit. He's scared I'll set off a murderer. Can't you bring your pies and your beans over here? I'm alone. Maybe we can figure this out."

"Okay, we won't send Kenneth into panic this time. Put on the water. I'll be there in a flash, and we'll solve this thing once and for all. I talked to Henry, too. Wait, before I come maybe I should catch up with Abbie. She'd know about her mother's herbs and stuff. She was there, too, that day. Do you know what shift she has at the hospital?"

Penny looked at the clock. "It's one-thirty now. I think she gets off at three."

"I have a friend works the same shift in the Emergency Room, a nurse. I'll call up there and get a message to Abbie to meet me at the hospital coffee shop when she gets off. If I learn anything interesting, I'll bring her along. You want to come with me?"

"No, I'll use the time to calm myself down and think it all through carefully. I feel like there's something I should know that I've forgotten about. Maybe it will come to me. Meantime, I need to start a pot of pintos for supper."

"Okay, cook beans. I'll see you four-ish."

It was only three-thirty, and Penny had turned off the pinto beans after adding salt to them when Sammie knocked. Behind her was Abbie, looking tired and distraught. Her blonde hair was pulled back tightly into a bun. Normally, it was hard to believe she was twenty-five, because she looked about sixteen. But today she looked more like fifty, pale and tense. It was warm, at least eighty degrees outside and about that in the apartment, but Abbie was rubbing her arms as if she were cold.

Sammie said little, merely, "We decided to come here. It's more private, and that way you can ask Abbie direct, and she can talk freely. Not easy with all the gossipy types at the hospital."

Abbie smiled briefly, and they settled around the kitchen table. Sammie handed Penny the fried pies in a paper bag and the coffee beans in a brown package marked "Fair Exchange. Grown in Nicaragua."

"I didn't expect you quite so soon, but it will take only a minute to heat the coffee water."

"Put the pies in the microwave for a minute to warm 'em up. Abbie's having a bad day, too."

Penny was glad she had something to do as she filled the teakettle and lit the gas flame under it, then ground the beans and set the pies on a plate in the microwave. How could she share her thoughts about Sibyl as a poisoner with her daughter, who already looked like she carried the world on her shoulders?

Maybe start with that day. Abbie might have new information. Why hadn't they thought to talk to her before? "You must be tired after your shift, Abbie. Have a pie. Coffee in a minute." She poured hot water over the grounds. When their coffee maker broke, she and Kenneth had devised a system for pouring the water onto the basket filled with the grounds and setting the thermos pot under it.

"I'm totally fed up," Abbie said. "All I do is work. We're always short-staffed at the hospital. I love kids, but they were all cranky today. I couldn't wait to get outta there. I'm so glad Sammie turned up. I couldn't face going home. Thanks for the coffee and the pies."

Penny poured more water on the grounds and set the milk pitcher on the table. "That does sound hard, but you seem so at ease with little children. I remember how you helped Mark with them when we did the seed planting. My grandson and the twins next door had a great time."

"It was fun. The twins–Andy's kids, right?—are so tuned in already to seeds and gardening. He said they help out here."

"They do. Even little Seb gets into the act. His father is Leroy, the man I come to market with. He lives in Andy's basement apartment, and Seb visits him a lot."

Sammie glanced at the kitchen clock and said, "Can we check out your impressions of the market that day that Kent died? Are you okay talking about it?"

Abbie shrugged. "It was creepy. I was talking to him a lot that afternoon. Then he goes off and dies." She shuddered. "It gives me the willies. I try to forget all about it, but he was Mama's friend, you know, and she worries at it all the time."

Penny nodded. Sibyl had cause to worry. "You were helping Henry set up his speakers that day, his first day to play. You and Henry were working right across from Leroy and me, and then Nora arrived and parked next to us. She was upset with Kent for being there when she'd told him not to come back to the market."

"I wasn't paying much attention to Nora. She yells a lot. But Kent never does what people ask him to–never did, I mean. Mama and I could have told Nora that. He was his own law and would never listen to a woman. Did you know he proposed to me? He's old enough to be my daddy."

Penny had wondered how serious Kent's flirtation was.

"I wasn't interested. Who needs an old coot like him? He's totally bossy and crude. The more you get to know him, the cruder he gets. If I'd been his wife, I wouldn't have been able to work. He'd have wanted me home having babies and cooking. He'd want sex all the time, and I'd probably have to grow his garden, too. He may have been an ag agent, but he didn't like to work. You know, like Mama and I do and have done since before Daddy died. But Mama didn't want him to marry me either."

Abbie stopped to eat a bite of pie.

"More coffee?" Penny held up the pot and refilled everyone's cups.

"Really good, Sammie," Abbie said. "Mama makes big apple pies, but I'd love your recipe. These little pies are scrumptious."

"I'll give it to you. Your mama seems to care a lot about who your husband will be." Sammie said this as if merely curious in a normal, conversational way, but she glanced at Penny. Abbie's answer could be crucial.

"Oh, Mama wants me to marry a specialist, a famous pediatrician or an oncologist. They're mostly ancient, and they sit around and act rich. I like work at the hospital most of time. It's never boring, and I can get away from Mama. We have some nice doctors on the ward, but they're all married, and anyway, they're totally dull. Mama's afraid I'll end up dirt poor like her and have to kill myself trying to earn a living, as if I wasn't killing myself now. She can't seem to get it that I have a nursing degree, and I like nursing most of the time. Plus, I have yet to meet a doctor or anyone else that I want to marry. I admit it's tempting to marry to get away from Mama. She's the original slave-driver."

Abbie stopped to finish her pie and drink her coffee. Color had returned to her cheeks. She was reviving. "But, you know, I want somebody my age, young and interested in what I'm interested in. Probably Sarah's the same way?" She turned to Penny.

"Sarah hasn't married yet. I'm not sure she knows yet what she wants–not Seb's daddy. She thought she wanted Henry, but the trial run didn't work out too well." She looked to see if Abbie was aware that Henry had abandoned Sarah without a word when he took up with her.

"Oh, Henry. He doesn't know what he wants either, but near as I can figure, he's looking for a woman to support him, pay the rent, tune his guitar." She grinned, and her dimples showed. Then she must have remembered his guitar catastrophe. She looked stricken. "That guitar was the only thing he cared about. He's a mess now."

Then her smile returned. "If I'd buy him a new thousand-dollar guitar, he'd be fine, but he'd love the guitar, not me. I like to hear him play. He's really good, but like with Sarah, I don't think he'll ever get tied down or committed. He wouldn't do his part–you know, work, help with chores, stuff like that. Any woman he marries will do everything for Henry. He's a baby really. If he's unhappy, he leaves and takes up with somebody else, like he left Sarah and came after me."

"Sounds about right," Penny said, "but you're young, there's no rush. Rosalind and I were out visiting your farm today. Beautiful place. I don't see how your mom keeps it all going, with only one hired hand, you and her."

"By working us all to the bone. I'm in no hurry to get married, see, but Mama drives me nuts. I go into work at seven, but I'm up at five with her. I have to do chores before I leave, and when I get home, I do more until nine or ten at night, especially in the spring and summer. It's no fun. So I run away sometimes, like now. If I go home, I'll be picking strawberries for tomorrow's market until dark."

"Which brings us back," said Sammie, looking at the clock again, "to maybe having no market tomorrow if we can't find out who poisoned Kent." It was four-thirty already.

"Mama says we will have a market. Don't the police have Herman in jail?"

"Yes," admitted Penny, "but I don't think he poisoned Kent."

"He is such a creep. He was sure mad at somebody when he burned Henry's guitar and ruined Mark's crops."

"Right. From what he's told me, he was jealous. You knew he liked you?"

Abbie shook her head. "I want no part of him or his sick fantasies. He's nasty, too."

They weren't getting down to cases. Try another tack. "I was surprised your mother had such an extensive herb garden, Abbie. She likes to doctor people, I take it?"

"Oh, yes. Mama wishes she'd had my education and could have been a nurse or doctor. She used herbal remedies on me growing up, said the chemical medicines were too hard on the body system. I never even had an aspirin. She has this and that for colds, headaches, stomach ache, constipation, diarrhea, whatever. She treats a lot of our neighbors, too. Sometimes she puts the medicine in a jelly, like mint or apple."

"What about belladonna? Used for stomach upsets and to calm nerves, I think." Penny looked at Sammie, who closed her eyes.

"Oh, yes. Belladonna. Only tiny amounts, you know. It only takes a few drops to calm the stomach. It can kill you fast if you get too much." Abbie seemed completely unaware of the implications of what she'd said. Penny breathed in slowly, and then let it out. Please let her keep talking. She didn't know she was nailing her mother's coffin shut, but if Sibyl was the killer, they had to stop her.

"What about a medicine to make you sweat? A sudorific, it's called, I think."

"Oh, yes, sometimes people with flu or high fever need to sweat, Mama says, and she makes a syrup, like a cough medicine with *Solanum Nigrum*. It's in the nightshade family, too, like belladonna. It's related to tomatoes and peppers. There are hundreds of nightshades, even tobacco. Mama has all sorts of plants, and you have to get the doses just right, like with pokeweed. It's a good spring tonic to clear out your system, but Mama's known foolish country people who have died from eating poke. Mama's always very careful."

Then Abbie looked at the clock. "Gee, it's going on five. I'd better go home. I'm sure you have things to do." She didn't sound like she wanted to go home.

"Oh, my supper's about ready. I made a big pot of pinto beans right before you came. Don't rush off. I have to make rice and fix a salad, that's all. Kenneth will probably be back about six."

Sammie said, "I hate to tell you, Penny. I forgot earlier. Derek called me when we were on the way over here. He has Kenneth helping him organize a lot of paperwork. They're going to order in pizza. I was supposed to tell you, but I'm free tonight. Why don't you invite Abbie and me to stay for supper, girlfriend? Girls' night out? I could use that, couldn't you, Abbie?"

"Perfect." Penny got up. "I'll start the rice now. Abbie, please stay. You and Sammie could go pick some lettuce, onions, radishes, carrots, and see what else might go in a salad. I have a wicked malt vinegar and garlic dressing for it."

"Should I stay?" Abbie stood, looking lost. "It's really okay with you?"

"You're a grown woman, Abbie." Sammie picked up Penny's vegetable gathering basket from among the boots and shoes under the hooks for coats and jackets. "You decide. We'd love to have you. Girlfriend, if you need anything else, we can run to the store for it."

Abbie looked from one to the other. "Your husbands don't mind?"

"No. Why should they? If they want to work their tails off, let 'em. We'll play while they're so busy. Besides, Penny had an argument with Kenneth, and I'm not too happy right now with Mr. Lieutenant Derek. They're probably scared to come home."

"Hardly," said Penny. "Don't worry, Abbie. We're not corrupting you, but you look like you could use a break. Sammie and I would love the company. We need to freshen our perspective, right, Sammie? Even old married women like us need that from time to time." She grinned at them.

"Especially old married women," said Sammie and opened the screen door. "Come on, Abbie, let's pick us a salad."

Twenty

Tuesday Evening, May 13. It was shortly after six when the three of them sat down to their beans and rice feast with the enormous and beautiful salad that Abbie and Sammie had put together. Penny hadn't had much chance to think about what she'd learned from Abbie. It all pointed to Sibyl, but she could still hear Kenneth saying, "It's not evidence, love."

He had called a few minutes earlier to check on her, and she had assured him she was fine and in good company. It sounded like it. Abbie and Sammie had been giggling as they cut up the vegetables. She didn't tell him what she'd learned. Not yet. Abbie was relaxed now. She obviously needed a break from her mother, though Penny was sure she herself would win no points with Sibyl if she discovered where Abbie was.

"Abbie, have some salad and pass it. You two think you made enough?" The biggest stainless steel mixing bowl she had, not counting her huge bread bowl, was overflowing with several kinds of lettuce and artfully cut radishes and carrot curls. Young onions had been sliced over the top. Both women laughed merrily.

At this point Sarah knocked on the screen and peered in. "You busy, Mom?"

"Come in, Sarah." Penny stood up. Behind her was Mark, carrying Seb. They were moving right along in their new romance.

"You're eating," said Mark, stopping at the door.

"It's okay. We have plenty. Look at this salad."

"Gamma, beans?"

Penny picked up Seb, who had squirmed to get down. She held him while she gestured to two more straight chairs. "Really, pull up a chair. I'll get plates."

"Sit down, Mom. I can get plates. It looks wonderful."

Sarah quickly found plates and silver for the three of them, and Penny put a few beans on Seb's small plate, making sure they were cool enough, and sat down with him on her lap.

"Carrots, lettuce," he said, and she shared some of her helping of salad.

Then she looked at Mark, who was watching them. He gave her a big smile and said, "Sebbie likes beans. So does Mark."

Penny thought of how he'd wished to find a wife good with children. Abbie was, but he seemed to fit with Sarah and Seb so easily as no one else had, and with them both, too. She could honestly say that she'd had very little to do with it. Furthermore, she did approve, though she certainly wasn't going to point that out unless asked.

Sarah leaned near him to whisper something, and he laughed. Nor did Abbie seem to feel bad that Mark had moved on so swiftly. Better yet, Mark was obviously no longer suffering the way he'd been only two days earlier. The young are resilient, she reminded herself.

They didn't talk a lot until everyone had eaten to satiety. Then Seb wanted down to go play with the basket of toys she kept for him and was happily rolling a truck along the edge of the living room rug when talk turned to Mark's garden.

"We'll help you plant it again," insisted Sarah. They all agreed.

"It's too late for most of it," he said, "but if you want to help me plant the summer stuff like okra, corn and beans, I'll welcome the help." Then he looked sad. "But how will I keep Herman out? I couldn't go through that again." He shook his head as if to forget the pain that wasn't far away.

"Herman feels bad," Penny said. "His dad is threatening to disown him over it. I don't think he'll do it again."

"Still, I might be smart to build a fence. I haven't had deer problems yet, or rabbits, but I may have. That would get me down, too."

"We'll help build the fence," said Abbie. Mark looked startled. "You sure you want to, Abbie?"

"I'd like to, Mark. I might get Henry to help, too. He needs to stop feeling sorry for himself. He won't keep Rosalind's job if he sits around moaning all the time."

"If you can get him to do some actual work, you're a better woman than I am," said Sarah. They both laughed.

"If he'll work, Rosalind needs him first," Penny pointed out. "He's eating and sleeping there but not working yet. From what she said, tomorrow is his fish-or-cut-bait day."

"Don't forget, tomorrow's market day," Sammie reminded them, "unless we get closed down."

"Do they still think Herman killed Kent?" asked Mark.

Sammie nodded. "Everyone except Penny and me. They don't have any real evidence against Herman, but they're not looking for anyone else. I'm afraid he's going to get stitched up for it. He made a bad mistake, damaging your veggies and Henry's guitar. Nobody trusts him now. Some would just as soon hang Kent's death on him, too, 'cause he acted so mean."

"He wants to give you money, Mark," added Penny. "He's been saving from his market money for a greenhouse. I'd take it."

"I couldn't," said Mark, "not take another farmer's money, but it will be a while before I'll trust him again."

The phone rang at nearly seven o'clock. Kenneth? It was Andy. "Is Abbie at your house, Penny?"

"Yes."

"Sibyl called. She was worried sick, said Abbie always comes straight from work and isn't home yet. Could you ask her to call her mom?"

"I will," said Penny, "but I think she wanted a break."

"Just tell her, okay? Then you and I have done what we can. I know she works Abbie too hard, makes her want to run off."

"You're right, Andy, and, yes, I will tell her."

They were all laughing when Penny returned to her chair, but they stopped the instant Penny said, "Abbie, your mama called."

The four women and Mark were still talking comfortably at about quarter to eight when someone knocked on the screen door. Sarah jumped up to open it and ushered in Sibyl. They all watched Abbie's face. She looked furious. "Mama, why'd you come over here? I told you'd I'd be home soon."

"It sounded like a party." Sibyl looked at them one by one but frowned at Mark. "I brought you some strawberry shortcake. Are other farmers welcome?"

Sammie was the first to recover from the surprise and stood up. "Please have a chair, Sibyl. We were all about to go home, but the cake looks impossible to pass up. You can sit right here. I'll get another chair."

"I didn't bring cream, but it's a sponge cake. It will soak up the berry juice. It doesn't actually need cream."

"I wonder if Leroy has any cream. I'll call him."

She and Sammie walked into the living room hunting chairs and out of a mutual impulse to confer. "I'm calling Derek on my cell phone, Penny. I have a bad feeling about this," Sammie said quietly.

"I do, too. I don't think Sibyl's very happy with any of us."

"Did you see how she looked at Mark?"

"If looks could kill ..."

"You're on target, Penny. Call Leroy, too, and alert him. I don't know how long Kenneth and Derek will take to get here." While Sammie slipped into the bathroom to call Derek, Penny walked to the phone in the living room and summoned Leroy. He had cream, he said, and would bring Nora, if that was okay.

Hearing that Mark, Sarah and Seb were there, he offered to take Seb for the night, if Sarah wished.

"She may," said Penny. "They're already cutting the cake. Hurry on over." She considered calling Andy. Her legs felt trembly. What had she gotten them into? Here was little Seb playing within a few feet of this angry woman. Sibyl wasn't showing her anger, but Penny could feel it now behind the blank, expressionless face. It had flashed in her eyes briefly when she saw Mark sitting there next to Abbie. Give me wisdom, she prayed. Was it better to leave Seb playing or hold him? He'd soon tune into the cake and run into the kitchen. She'd hold him. If need be, she'd run into the bathroom with him. At least she'd know exactly where he was.

Sarah was getting out plates and forks. Leroy and Nora arrived with the aerosol version of whipped cream as Sibyl finished cutting the cake and Abbie spooning berries onto it.

The small kitchen was crowded. "We could sit in the living room," said Penny. "More places to sit. These are the last two extra chairs." But no one moved.

"Cake, Gamma," exclaimed Seb and leaned from her arms toward the table.

Leroy put a small amount of whipped cream in the bowl that held Seb's small portion. He stuck a spoon in it. "Penny, why don't you finish putting on the cream? I'll take Seb in here to have his cake. That frees a chair."

Perhaps as well, thought Penny. Sammie, right next to where Sibyl was standing, gave Penny a look that said, "Karate as needed," and smiled.

Keep it normal, Penny told herself. Stay with what it seems like. "This is really nice, Sibyl. I love strawberry shortcake."

"The berries are good," said Sibyl. "Enough rain but not too much. Oh, Penny, I brought you some strawberry jam." She turned back to the counter where she'd set the bowl of berries and the cake and with her gnarled hands held up a half-pint of bright red jam.

Her movements were awkward, and Penny could see how rigidly she was holding herself. Ramrod stiff. Was the jam poisoned? "Thanks, Sibyl. That's sweet."

Or murderous?

"You can add it to your cake, if you like. I eat it that way sometimes."

"No, thanks. I'll save it."

"Oh, come on, try it. You saw I'd made some this morning. I made this batch after you left."

"Later, Sibyl. I can't wait to enjoy your cake."

Nora hadn't said much. She picked up her plate heaped with cake, berries, and cream. "I'm game, Sibyl. Put some of that yummy jam on top of my cake. A good dollop."

"No, this is Penny's gift," Sibyl said stubbornly. "I'll give you some another time, later."

"Here, Sibyl, sit right here," said Mark, getting up from beside Abbie. "I'll get one of these other chairs."

"How come Penny's suddenly so special?" persisted Nora. "I thought you loved me, Sibyl. I'm jealous now."

Nora was teasing, but Sibyl's eyes had a flash of panic in them.

Abbie watched her mother sit down, shook her head and suddenly blurted out, "Mama, did you put medicine in Penny's jam?"

Sibyl glared at Abbie. "Of course not. Don't be crazy, Abbie. What's got into you today anyway?" Penny thought, that hit home. "Why would I do that?" Sibyl protested, glancing up, dismay in her voice. "'Course not."

Penny caught Sammie's eye and watched as Sammie inched over to stand behind Sibyl.

Penny's next impulse came out of the blue. She couldn't afterwards imagine why she suddenly picked up the jam. It may have been the tension in the room. She could feel it, and Sammie was onto it. "There's one way to find out. Sibyl, why don't you taste it first? Then we can all have a taste."

Sibyl grabbed the jam jar and hurled it at Mark, who was about to sit down in the straight chair pulled earlier from Penny's desk. He was only five feet away.

He saw it coming and jumped to the side. The jam jar hit the floor with a loud smash. Glass splinters and jam splatters went everywhere. They all turned toward Mark, but Penny and Sammie kept looking at Sibyl, who turned to the counter, grabbed the cake knife and lunged toward Mark. Sammie was right behind her, grabbed her arms and bent her wrist until she dropped the knife, then tripped her and put her flat on the floor on her stomach, just short of the splattered jam and glass smithereens.

Leroy leapt up from the couch with Seb. "Take him in the bathroom, Leroy," Penny said. "Mark, help us!"

So Mark, edging around the jam, got Sibyl's hands forced behind her back, and Penny pulled a roll of nylon cord out of the bottom drawer next to the sink, which Sammie then used to tie her hands and feet.

Sibyl was thrashing around. She yelled, "Nothing's wrong with that jam. I wanted Penny to have it. Let me go. Abbie, help me." But Abbie stared at her and said nothing. Sammie tied the last knot and sat on Sibyl. She got out her cell phone and dialed Derek. "Where are you? Hurry then. I'm sitting on your new suspect."

The others were stunned. Then Abbie was crying. Sarah put her arms around her, but Abbie was more angry than sad. "Mama, you're a witch. Did you kill Kent?"

"Ah," said Nora, "I begin to see the light."

Penny let Leroy out of the bathroom, as Sibyl was well guarded by Mark and Sammie. "Maybe take Seb home with you? I'll send Sarah over in a few minutes. Here, take his cake." So Leroy and Nora left with Seb just as Penny heard a siren. Then she remembered what had been niggling at her. A memory came back of looking down the farmers' market aisle between the vendor tables and seeing Kent turning away from Sibyl's table after telling her, "Thank you." Thank you for what? Jam?

Twenty-One

Tuesday Night, May 13 and Wednesday afternoon, May 14.
Once Derek and Kenneth arrived, Sibyl said nothing. She
epitomized stony silence. Her dignity was wounded, but she took
the handcuffs stoically. She glared at Abbie but said nothing
even to her. Abbie had refused to go with her mother. She left
without saying anything.

Sammie, Mark and Sarah stayed to help Penny and Kenneth
clean up the rest of the jam jar mess and the dishes. Kenneth
wasn't happy, but Penny thought it was more because she'd been
at risk than because he thought she'd nailed the wrong person.
He didn't say much until the others left, Sammie to go face the
music with Derek, though she was grinning, and Sarah and Mark
to go back to Sarah's. They were so pleased with each other that
neither seemed troubled by Mark's narrow escape.

When he'd closed the door, Kenneth said solemnly, "Now
do you see why I want to carry you off to Wales? We don't fight
with poisoned jam at home. We Welsh are peace-loving people."

Penny wiped off the sink and squeezed out the sponge. He
handed her a cup of Ovaltine, and they sat down on their couch.
It was only nine-thirty. A lot had happened fast. "I'm peace-
loving, too, Kenneth. It's why I needed to find our killer and stop
her. Don't you see? Now we can have our market tomorrow."

"You'll have to convince Derek first. I don't think he
believes you about Sibyl."

"Do you?" She looked at him over the edge of her cup. That
usually brought a smile to his lips but not this time.

"I think …" he started and then set his cup down. "You do
seriously want to know what I think, love?"

She quailed inside but regarded him steadily and nodded.

"I think you need to learn karate or whatever it is that Sammie does to catch criminals if you insist on spending time here in the states." He paused, awaiting her reply.

"I'll go with you August first, but I want to help get our market back to normal first. Can you understand? I do want you to be happy, too."

"I begin to see the light," he said.

"You think Sibyl's guilty now? There still isn't what you and Derek would call evidence."

"Penny, everything's pointing to your being right. If you are, Derek will come around. He does. We both always do, or haven't you noticed?"

She relaxed inside, a little bewildered but reassured by his smile.

"Definitely take up karate, love."

"But why do you fight me so when my intuition hits me between the eyes? It hurts, Kenneth."

"Because I'm embarrassed, I guess, that you should see where I am blind. But you have to promise about the karate."

She did.

After lunch on Wednesday Kenneth returned to the Sheriff's Department, and Penny was gathering up what she needed for the Farmers' Market. Thank goodness it was going forward. She was slicing carrots and radishes to take for a snack when someone knocked at the door. She was surprised to find Abbie. Her eyes were red. She'd been crying.

"Come in, Abbie. What's up?"

"I can't stomach doing the market, not with Mama in jail. Could you take our berries?"

"I don't see why not. I'm sure Nora would understand, and then I'll get the money to you. Your mom needs it for a lawyer?"

"She doesn't want a lawyer. She's going to plead not guilty herself, but nobody will believe her." Abbie had stepped inside. She sounded shaky.

Penny gestured to a chair, moved some things and sat down at the kitchen table next to her. "That doesn't sound wise, Abbie. A lawyer might keep her from getting the death penalty, and the state has to provide her a lawyer free if she doesn't hire one."

"You don't understand." Abbie yelled.

"Explain it to me then," said Penny calmly. She glanced at the clock. They liked to load up at two and leave at twenty minutes after. It was quarter of two now. "Leroy and I need to load up soon, but I can give you a glass of mint tea and chat for a few minutes."

Abbie nodded, and Penny got up to get two glasses and the jar of mint tea out of the refrigerator.

Abbie drank hers thirstily. "Everything is terrible. Mama's acting stupid, and I know they'll give her the death penalty. Sometimes I hate her, but I don't want her to die. I can't do the farm by myself with one old black man. He has the nerve to bug me since Mama's not there. He says I need to help Mama more and work harder. I can't. I'm so tired. I can't do any more. I'll have to sell the stupid farm. Everything's too hard. I can't, I can't …"

"What about hiring more help?"

"There's no money. We scrape along. I can't run the farm and hold down my job. I can't even sleep at night anymore. I'm so tired. Henry came over last night. He wants us to get married."

"You know that won't work, right?"

"Yes, but I can't get rid of him. He won't help. He worked one day for Rosalind, and then he left. He says farm work will ruin his fingers for playing."

"Probably not," said Penny. "Peasant farmers for centuries have played guitars, banjos, fiddles. It would be nice if he'd help you. Good for him, too."

"He won't," said Abbie savagely. "Mama says he can't stay there. I don't want him, but I can't make him leave." She was crying now.

"Speaking of leaving, Abbie, I need to get your strawberries and start loading. Leroy's probably already loading."

"Don't leave!"

There was a desperate note in Abbie's voice. She sounded like a child about to throw a tantrum, but fierce, too, as if determined to have what she wanted.

Penny had started to rise but sat back down again. She found herself explaining slowly and carefully, "Abbie, I have a job, the farmers' market, today, and I need to leave now and get packed up for it. I'm sorry. You can come back after the market and get the strawberry money. Why don't you come down with me and help me get the strawberries loaded in Leroy's van?"

"No!" Now Abbie stood up. She grabbed the paring knife Penny had been using to cut up carrots and radishes. "You're not leaving. I don't give a shit about the berries."

"Put the knife down, Abbie."

"No."

"What's wrong? Why do you want to keep me from going to the market?"

"Mama didn't kill Kent. I did. I'm going to kill myself. I'll kill you if you leave. Nothing's going right. Everything's messed up. Why did you have to get Mama arrested? I liked you. I'd rather have you for a mama than her. You don't bug people all the time."

Penny said nothing. Abbie, flushed and tear-stained, was holding the knife tensely, watching Penny's face. Now what?

The phone rang. It would be Leroy, reminding her they needed to load.

"Don't answer it." Abbie looked more desperate. She glared at the ringing phone.

All Penny could think of to do was to keep her talking and hope Leroy came up to investigate, though that might make things worse. Why had Abbie killed Kent? She had seemed to like talking to him, even if she didn't want to marry him. Penny had gotten the killer wrong this time. Maybe she hadn't trusted her intuition enough. She would have to trust it now, play it by ear. She didn't think Abbie had ever held anyone at knife point before.

"What did Kent do that made you hate him?" she tried.

"He messed with me when I was ten years old. Mama used to let him babysit me. He came over almost every week. I never told Mama. She was so grateful to him, and I was too scared of him. Nasty old man. Even when I was grown, he wouldn't go away. I had to kill him to get him to leave me alone."

"I'm sorry, Abbie. That must have been hard when you were so little." Penny's mind was racing. That karate would come in handy about now. Kick the knife out of her hands? But she hadn't had the lessons yet.

"It was hell, if you want to know. He was a terrible man, but he loved grape jelly, and Mama was always spoiling him, so I made up some special for him and told Mama to give it to him. She did that day. He died a fast, horrible death, and I'm glad."

Penny hadn't liked Kent either, but the way Abbie said that made her shiver.

Abbie didn't seem that hostile to her, though clearly she wanted to talk, to explain and justify what she'd done. So she'd let her talk.

The phone began to ring again.

"No!" yelled Abbie. "Don't answer it."

"I wasn't going to," said Penny as calmly as she could, but now she couldn't keep herself from shivering. She wished she knew more about the psychology of desperate people in hostage situations. She was the hostage, but she'd have to be the negotiator, too, and work her way out of this. Abbie was burning her boats. Where did that leave the hostage? She needed to say something or do something, but what? Next Leroy would come up to investigate. That would either make things better or worse. High risk.

Then her mind seemed to relax, and something else took hold. She knew at once that she could trust it and needn't be afraid of Abbie, knife or no knife. Wasn't she still a ten-year-old girl, terrified at what her anger had pushed her to do?

"Of course you hated Kent," she said. "I see that now. I didn't like him either. Nora said he hit on all the women. She was worried about him hanging around you."

"A little late to worry about that, but Nora's nice. I was glad when she was in jail, though, but I was gladder when Herman was. He's creepier than Kent. I was glad when they arrested Mama, too, but I don't know how to live now. Everything's terrible. You didn't help me, Penny. Why didn't you believe Herman did it? Herman is meaner than I am, much meaner than Mama. Why did you have to get Mama hauled off like that? You're sneaky, Penny, you know that? Before I kill myself, I'm going to kill you. I don't want anybody to know what I did. I've told you too much." Her last words wavered. She sounded shaky.

"Don't you think, Abbie," said Penny gently, "that there's been enough killing?"

Suddenly Abbie threw down the knife, put her head down on her arms and began sobbing. Penny walked over, took the knife and slipped it into her jeans pocket. Then she quietly unlocked the door, leaving it ajar, and put her arms around Abbie. "You're brave, Abbie. Thank you for putting down the knife. I'll be sure you're in good hands. You have been having a very hard time." She held her and only glanced up when Leroy pushed open the door. She nodded to him. "Leroy, I'm delayed here. Could you ask Kenneth to help you load up and get Abbie's strawberries? She's feeling bad. If Kenneth could come up here first, I'll explain things to him."

Kenneth arrived five minutes later. As she had hoped, Leroy had picked up her sense of crisis and conveyed it to Kenneth, who brought Derek with him. They entered the room quietly, Leroy waiting in the doorway.

"Abbie is very upset," Penny said.

Abbie lifted her tear-stained face. "Don't put me in jail. Don't tell Mama!" She began to wail.

Penny held her. "Abbie, you need to talk to them and tell them what you've told me." Kenneth moved to one side of Penny and Derek to the other side.

"No!" shrieked Abbie.

"I'll come, too," said Penny.

Abbie was still crying as they handcuffed her and led her down the stairs and put her in the unmarked car. Derek took the knife from Penny, and she and Kenneth sat on each side of Abbie in the back seat. Leroy said he'd take the berries and go on to the market.

After Abbie had been booked, and Penny and Kenneth were ready to leave, Derek beckoned them into his office. "News, Penny, that confirms what we've just learned from Abbie. The strawberry jam had nothing poisonous in it at all. It was perfectly ordinary strawberry jam. Mrs. Kidd's daughter, however, did tell us that the day Kent died, Mrs. Kidd had a gift of grape jelly, his favorite, set aside for Kent Berryman, and Abbie had prepared it. So he must have eaten some on his peanut butter sandwich. I don't know what happened to the jelly jar. Our best guess is that after he started eating the sandwich, it tasted funny, and he threw out the jar and the rest of the sandwich. The woman who found him, one of the janitorial staff, emptied the trash before we could examine it. I guess the grape juice in the punch disguised the jelly being there, too."

"Did Sybil have anything to say?"

"No. She won't say a word even now. She's afraid of Abbie looking bad. She could help lighten Abbie's sentence if she confessed to leaving Mr. Berryman with her so much as a child. Hopefully, she'll come to her senses. It seems to me that she's as guilty as Abbie. I've contacted Kate Razor about being Abbie's lawyer, and Kate has agreed. We'll keep you posted, but Kate's very good, as you know."

"Thank you, Derek."

"But I've told Sammie, and I'll tell you. Stay out of police business, Penny. I don't want to lose either one of you." There were tears in his voice. "Could you do that for me, Penny?"

"I can't promise, Derek, not when people I care about are involved. But I promised Kenneth, Lord help me, and I'll promise you, to learn Karate."

He laughed. "A deal, and I'll call the state ag people to urge them to keep your market open."

When Kenneth dropped her at the market at five, Penny found all the vendors there except Abbie and Sibyl. Leroy had used their space and set up a makeshift table to set out the buckets and buckets of strawberries. There was an air of sadness among the farmers, even though they were relieved to be selling their produce again. Several expressed the hope that Sibyl would soon be back with her baked goods and offered to help her and Abbie in any way they could. They were shocked when Penny told them about Abbie's confession and arrest but relieved that all was now known. They were grateful for the return to normality.

Mark was handling his own loss well, telling people cheerfully he'd be back selling by late June. Penny bought two huge buckets of berries, which she stowed in Leroy's van. Since Mark had nothing to sell, he'd brought Seb and was following him as he wandered the aisles, begging cheese and fruit samples. Penny gave Seb a strawberry for each hand, and he had red juice running off his chin. Mark told her he was buying for "dinner tonight with your beautiful daughter and grandson."

George was quite cut up about Abbie, as was Herman. At first he wouldn't look at anyone, but once he'd found Mark, told him he was sorry and made him take a check for a thousand dollars, he recovered some. His father hadn't kicked him out. Herman also insisted that Mark take some of his peas and cabbage. Most of the customers had no idea that Herman had wreaked vengeance on Mark's vegetables and Henry's guitar.

Once Penny settled at their table, Rosalind came over to report that Henry was back at their farm, begging for work, and she'd re-hired him to give the goat barn a thorough cleaning. She wasn't sure how long he'd hang around, but she'd told him he still owed her the rest of the week for his room and board on the days he hadn't lifted a finger. "He was moaning about his bad luck with women. I told him physical work is often good for us when we're depressed," she said, smiling.

The sun was still warm and not far down in the sky when Sarah arrived from work. First thing, Mark took her over to Sammie's table to pick out a bouquet from the three remaining. She chose the hollyhocks in different shades of pink. They then went to Rosalind and chose some goat cheese. Several other farmers gave them vegetables, having learned of Mark's misfortune. His happiness could not be dimmed, and his eyes were alive with his pleasure in Sarah, holding her bouquet, and with Sebbie, carrying so carefully the paper bag of cheese.

They left before she and Leroy had to pack up. Nora came over to help. "Guess you know, doll, you got one fabulous farmer here to partner with?" she demanded of Penny.

"I know. I wouldn't trade him."

"You're gonna be mad then, doll."

"How so?"

"'Cause I'm gettin' ready to steal him."

"Yes?" Penny looked at Leroy, who was beaming at her. Leroy, who never beamed.

"Does that mean you will marry me?" he asked, looking worried, doubtful, and obviously forgetting that several people were listening.

"Damned right," Nora said. She threw her arms around Leroy and planted a big kiss on his lips.

Meet Author Judy Hogan

Judy Hogan founded Carolina Wren Press (1976-91), and was co-editor of *Hyperion Poetry Journal* from 1970 to 1981. Her first mystery, *Killer Frost* was published by Mainly Murder Press in 2012.

A published poet, she has taught all forms of creative writing since 1974. She joined Sisters in Crime in 2007 and has focused on writing and publishing traditional mystery novels. In 2011 she was a finalist in the St. Martin's Malice Domestic Mystery contest. The twists and turns of her life's path have given her plenty to write about.

She is also a small farmer and lives in Moncure, North Carolina.

Excerpt

Killer Frost
by Judy Hogan

One

Tuesday, February 13, 2001. It was a love that came upon her out of the blue, which she knew she would never understand or be able to explain to anyone else, not even to Oscar and especially not to her husband. As calm and rational as Kenneth had been for the eight years of their marriage, he couldn't or didn't want to understand why she cared so much about Oscar, and she never had told him the whole story. She knew she was lucky to have Kenneth in her life, but her love for Oscar had been like a lightning bolt out of a cloudless sky, one of those connections you accept finally without understanding them.

It began when their dear friend Rick Clegg, Pastor of Ebenezer Baptist in Riverdell and a long-time activist, called them in Wales in early February and told Penny there was an interesting teaching job open for the rest of the 2001 spring semester. His friend from grad school, Oscar Ferrell, was the new Chairman of English at St. Francis, a black college in Raleigh. Oscar had fired a part-time teacher, and he needed someone right away to take her place. Could Penny and Kenneth come back to Riverdell two weeks early so she could teach part-time for him? With her experience teaching composition and creative writing at Orange Community College, this HBCU (Historically Black College or University) would be a piece of cake and pay better, too. He talked her into it, and Kenneth was game, too. They changed their air tickets and in twenty-four hours were on their way to North Carolina.

Once Oscar had seen her résumé and spent half an hour with her, he hired her before she'd handed in her official application. They had arrived in North Carolina on Saturday, and he hired her Monday. Her first classes were on Tuesday.

Oscar was waiting for her in his office at 7:45 a.m., and they walked together down the hall to Classroom 402. "Are you nervous?" he asked.

"A little," she admitted. She set her bag on the floor beside the desk (battered heavy oak but functional), took out her notes, the sign-up sheet, and the seating chart she had prepared. Classes had begun January 10, and it was February 13. She knew she needed to learn their names as fast as possible. She'd had students at the community college try to fool her. "Oh, I was here, Ms. Weaver," when she'd marked them absent. Then some African Americans had experienced white people not being able to tell them apart. She could and would.

Oscar said, "Jane Avery, the teacher I had to fire, was so lethargic as to be inert, plus she was incompetent. Don't assume they've learned anything. Do what you can in the nine weeks left in this semester. Maybe you can get some of them through this Pre-Comp course so they can move into Freshman Composition next term."

"I hope so," Penny said. The room they were in was square, as large as two normal living rooms, and the walls were a discolored cream color. Various styles of student desks, from old wooden ones, scarred with pencil and knife marks, to shiny new molded black plastic with chrome legs, were in no visible order. Maybe the last class had broken into groups? After consulting her, Oscar began arranging them in rows while Penny wrote her name and telephone number on the board.

She had just written down the homework assignment for February 15 when the first student walked in. He had to walk around his muscles. Penny had never seen anyone look so bloated. He wore jeans that had slipped to ride around his hips, revealing his red and white striped boxer shorts. Was he showing off the St. Francis colors? The muscles across his upper arms and chest (were those his pecs?) were huge. He had rolled back his tee shirt, the better to show them off. He walked slowly, awkwardly, not looking at her, and headed for the seat farthest away from her in the back row by the window. Then, once he'd worked himself into a chair, he stared out the window. It was as if she didn't exist. She glanced at Oscar, who turned and walked over to the young man.

"Good morning. I'm Professor Farrell, Chairman of the English Department. May I know your name?" Oscar was polite, down to earth, but his voice commanded attention.

The young muscle man looked at Oscar, who was slight, smiled, then glanced out the window again as if whatever he saw there was far more interesting. Then he turned back. He looked at Penny while he said, "It's Ronny. Ronny Glover. She our new teacher? I heard Miz Avery quit."

"Yes, Ronny, you'll have Ms. Weaver for the rest of the term. Where are you from?"

"Camden, New Jersey."

Oscar nodded. "We'll get started in a few minutes." They all looked toward the door where a young woman had entered. She was heavy-set, soft-looking, with long, straightened hair resting on her shoulders. She didn't look at Penny or Oscar but turned sharply when she reached the next to last row of chairs and walked toward Ronny, choosing the last seat, next to him, in the back row.

"Good morning," Oscar said, turning to the young woman. "May I have your name?"

"Merilee Taylor," she said softly.

While Oscar drew out Merilee, Penny finished writing down the homework assignment. Other students were drifting in. Oscar had said she had twenty-five students in this class—too many for a comp class, but he had only recently gotten the Provost's permission to lower the maximum enrollment to twenty for the following fall semester. He had taken over the English Department the previous August.

Penny glanced at her cheap Casio special. 8:05. There were about twelve students who had taken seats. Where were the others? She began passing around the roll sheet, which asked for campus contact info, and then a seating chart. She explained it to the young woman who had just scooted in and was sitting in the front row next to the door. "This is the seating chart I'll use so I can learn your names more quickly. Look at it upside down. This is the front row here. If you like this seat, write your name here, and then pass it around. I'm Ms. Weaver, by the way, your new teacher."

The young woman nodded, looked Penny over, and without smiling, took the chart and wrote "Lashandra Steele" in the square that represented her seat. Then she looked up at Penny, tossed her dreads, which were carefully braided and bright with colored beads, and smiled. She handed the paper to the girl sitting behind her. Penny smiled back as Oscar walked to the front of the room and said to the whole class, "Good morning."

He got their attention instantly. They quieted, then echoed his greeting. I'll have to remember and use that ritual, Penny thought. It has a calming effect on them, and on me, too. Oscar waited while two more students hurried in at nearly ten after. There were still about ten students missing. "Close the door, please, Terence," Oscar said to the last young man who'd glided in. When he smiled at Oscar and returned to get the door, she saw that most of his teeth had gold caps. His dreads had not been combed recently. They looked matted and shopworn. What was the term? Nappy. He had an air of unconcern, like he couldn't be bothered with what any teacher or person in authority thought. He was insouciant. That was it. Oscar must know him. He was staring at him.

Terence grinned slyly at Penny as he eased his lanky body, well over six feet, into the black plastic chair next to Lashandra.

"Class, as some of you know ..." He gave Terence a hard look. "... I'm Professor Farrell, the Chairman of the English Department here at St. Francis. I'm here today to introduce your new instructor for English 21, Ms. Weaver. She'll be with you until the end of the spring term. Ms. Avery has left us."

Terence raised his hand. "Why?" he asked before Oscar could recognize him.

Oscar gave him a hard stare and didn't answer. "Ms. Weaver has been teaching composition at Orange Community College. She'll be of great help to you in passing this course, which is a non-college credit course. When you pass it, you'll be able to enroll in English 30 next term, the regular Freshman English course, for credit. The placement test you took when you enrolled placed you in English 21. That means you have a lot of basics to master, and if you do your part, I'm confident you'll be able to move quickly to English 30. Any questions?"

Lashandra raised her hand. "Do we still turn in our assignments from when we had Ms. Avery?"

Oscar turned to Penny, who nodded. "Yes," he went on, "and I expect you all to work hard to catch up to where you need to be as entering freshmen." He looked again at Terence, who was whispering to Lashandra. "Now please give Ms. Weaver your full attention." Oscar took a seat in the front row, to the far left of Penny, and smiled at her. She stepped over to stand in front of her desk. "I'm very happy to be here at St. Francis. I live in Shagbark County, in Riverdell, about forty miles from here. I've always heard good things about St. Francis. I'm also a poet. I'll be teaching a Creative Writing seminar this term, too. I've written my email and home telephone number on the board in case you need to reach me. I have no phone on campus."

She glanced at Oscar, who was frowning. "My office hours will be 11:15 to 12:00 on Tuesday and Thursday, after that Creative Writing class, in the Writing Center, which is in room 406 right around the corner. I'll also usually be there after this class until the seminar at 10:00. Because I'm part-time, I don't have an office, and I'll only be on campus Tuesdays and Thursdays from 8:00 to 12:00."

At this point the door opened, and three more students, all boys, came in, looked nervously around, and walked to the back of the room, where they slid down into their seats as if they wished to be invisible and grinned covertly at each other. They were all heavy and muscular but nothing like Ronny. Their muscles didn't look like balloons. Football players?

Oscar glared at them, got up, walked across the room behind Penny, and turned the lock on the door, then stood with his back to it, watching the students, not unlike a cat, ready to pounce if a mouse dared show its whiskers.

He's not sure I'm up to these kids, thought Penny. I'm not sure I'm tough enough either. There had been people who had tried and failed to manipulate her over the years. Not only landlords and her ex-husband, but all her children had given it a try when they were not much younger than these freshmen. She would have her challenges, but she was maybe more comfortable in the black community than Oscar realized. The kids clearly would try to work her, this Terence, for one. So she would have to demonstrate her authority as their teacher. She didn't look forward to it. She told herself it was like all the other hard things she had done in her life. Why was it she was always taking on hard, if not impossible, things?

She looked at the students, some whispering to their neighbors, others waiting patiently for her to continue, Terence staring at his desk. He had no book bag, no pencil or paper. Lashandra, next to him, was watching him when he wasn't looking, then glancing at Penny.

When they realized she was waiting for them, the students stopped whispering. "I've told you a little about me. Now I'd like you each to tell me a little about you. Take two or three minutes and tell me your name, your major, where you're from, and how you feel about being here at St. Francis. I understand that this is your first year, and for some your first semester."

The first three or four students gave quiet, unexceptional answers. But when Oscar slipped out the door, everything changed. It was the turn of a girl sitting in the back row. "My name is Sheila Green. I'm a Drama major from Petersburg." She paused, glanced around. "I hate St. Francis so far. The dorms have roaches, the bathrooms are nasty, the food makes me puke."

Penny saw the smirks on the faces of the girls around her. The football boys, as she would come to think of them, laughed but stopped when Penny looked at them.

Sheila had more to say. She looked very happy as she said, "I have to go to the restroom. May I be excused now?"

Then Lashandra, who had already introduced herself, raised her hand.

"Yes?"

"Can we leave now? The class ends at 9:00, and Miz Avery always let us go early."

Penny glanced at her watch. It was 8:30. "No, Lashandra. This class ends at 9:15."

"No, it don't." Lashandra had a mulish look.

"Miz Avery allus left us time to get us our breakfast. She never kept us till 9," chimed in Sheila.

Penny reacted blindly before she took time to think. "Sheila and Lashandra, I'm not Ms. Avery. We have only seventy-five minutes together twice a week. I will dismiss class at 9:15. You can use the restroom at 9:15. Now, who's next?"

CPSIA information can be obtained at www.ICGtesting.com
Printed in the USA
LVOW08s1450080913

351501LV00001B/47/P

9 780989 580403